For Doug Jones, who is always my hero

For Emily Ciciotte, who is beyond heroic in all things

For John Palreiro, who is missed

CARRIE JONES

girl, HERO

flux™

Woodbury, Minnesota

First Edition
First Printing, 2008

Book design by Steffani Sawyer
Cover design by Ellen Dahl

Flux, an imprint of Llewellyn Publications

Library of Congress Cataloging-in-Publication Data
Jones, Carrie.
  Girl, hero / Carrie Jones.—1st ed.
    p. cm.
  Summary: High school freshman Lily pours her heart out in letters to her hero, dead movie star John Wayne, in which she tells him about the death of her beloved stepfather, her mother's abusive boyfriends, her fears that her father is gay, getting the lead in the high school play, and her burgeoning romance with a classmate who reminds her of Mr. Wayne.
  ISBN 978-0-7387-1051-8
  1. Wayne, John, 1907–1979—Juvenile fiction. [1. Wayne, John, 1907–1979—Fiction. 2. Family problems—Fiction. 3. Letters—Fiction. 4. Self-reliance—Fiction. 5. Interpersonal relations—Fiction. 6. High schools—Fiction. 7. Schools—Fiction.] I. Title.
  PZ7.J6817Gi 2008
  [Fic]—dc22   2008008185

Flux
Llewellyn Publications
A Division of Llewellyn Worldwide, Ltd.
2143 Wooddale Drive, Dept. 978-0-7387-1051-8
Woodbury, MN 55125-2989, U.S.A.
www.fluxnow.com

Printed in the United States of America

Dear Mr. Wayne,

My mother's got a man coming to see her. She's all excited, running around, getting ready, making me clean up the whole house. She thinks this man might be the one, you know, the big enchilada, her soul's mate, her life's light, and stuff. She's always thinking that.

She's had men before, since my stepfather died. But this guy's going to stay with us in our house, for a while. Not too long, she tells me. Just until he's back on his feet. This one's moving back east from Oregon and needs a place to sleep while he looks for work.

I think, *that's what hotels are for*, but she's so happy, humming all the time, singing Celine Dion songs, that I don't say anything that I'm thinking in my head.

She's made up the guest bedroom. I don't think he'll stay there. I don't know who she thinks she's fooling. Not me.

He's a tall man, Mr. Wayne, like you. She knew him

a long time ago, back when she was married to my father. On the phone his voice sounds Western, or Texan, like he has traces of sand and grit stuck in it that float out with his words when he talks. He sounds like he's been in the desert a long, damn while and hasn't had any water to drink and has a mighty thirst.

He doesn't sound like he's from Maine, but she says he was born and raised here.

I didn't know that people could move and have their accents change, that all their baby years and teenage years of talking could just get erased.

My mother blows air out her nose when I say this to her, and she taps her fingernails on the kitchen counter, crosses her legs and gets out a cigarette.

"People adapt, Liliana," she says, and the whole sentence is just one long exasperated sigh.

It's kind of cool in a way, the adapting thing. I mean, depending on how bad high school goes, I might want to erase all of it and pretend I'm someone else when I go to college—if I get into college.

My mom thinks this man will be like you: a hero kind of man with a clean face and soul. She thinks that about every man she sees. But they never are. There's only one you.

Dear Mr. Wayne,

So I don't have to think about this man coming, I mosey over to the old Alamo Theater and catch a movie. Good ole American escapism at its best. Right?

Nicole, my best friend, is meeting me. I amble in and pretend like it doesn't bother me at all that I'm alone and everyone is looking at me wondering why. Do I have the worst BO ever? Have I offed a teacher somewhere and just been sprung from juvie? Has my boyfriend dumped me? No. No. And no. I'm just waiting on a friend and wishing I was secure enough that I didn't have to worry about things like this.

I find a seat near the front and settle in. It's got duct tape on the chair arm to hold it together, and the red upholstery is ripped up some good. We don't have a lot of theaters in Merrimack, Maine. There's just Hoyts, where they play two new movies, almost always the latest slasher flick for the teenage boys and some new romantic comedy for the bored moms. Then there's the Alamo. That's where they play what my stepdad used to call the "oldies but goodies." We used to come here a lot before he died.

Pulling out my notebook, I put my feet against the chair backs in front of me because I'm too short to sling my legs over in a cool way. Once I'm settled in for a spell, I start writing.

I pause every now and then to take good deep breaths of old movie theater air. There's nothing better than the way a movie theater smells before one of your shows. The air is cold and aching. There are traces of popcorn and beer that's been there before. It smells like wanting, like waiting.

I smile real slow because soon you'll be filling up that screen, a giant man with a mission, a gun on his hip and a swagger in his smile.

Nicole comes in and yells my name. I wave. She yells it again. I wave bigger and she starts down the slanted aisle, looking tipsy in her heels. She's wearing a miniskirt, which is stupid, because her type of guys (jock guys) never come into the Alamo. It's all arty-nerd types and me. So, there's no one here for her to get all flirty with.

"You're so short. I didn't see you." She flops into the seat. "What'cha writing?"

"Nothing."

I slam my notebook shut and sit up straight.

She pulls her skirt over her lap with a quick snap and says all accusing, "You're writing to John Wayne again."

I shrug. Sometimes there's no point in denying things, you just have to cowboy up.

She sighs a fake, overblown, exasperated, mother-type sigh. "No one even knows who John Wayne is, you know. Like you could be writing fan letters to someone really cool, really hot, but no…John Wayne. Cowboy, gun-toting man."

She tries to impersonate you and falls way short, sounding more like a cartoon character than a Western star: "How-dy pard-ner. How-dy ma-am."

I put my notebook in my backpack and close my eyes. Nicole doesn't take the hint and keeps yammering on. I swear she is the reincarnation of some dead French queen's poodle, all yippy. I still love her, though. We soldiered through eighth-grade camping trips together up at Baxter State Park. She let me cry when Stuart Silsby totally humiliated me at a CCD dance in seventh grade. She let me hang out at her house twelve nights in a row after my stepfather died. You can forgive someone for being a poodle when they guard your back like that.

"I mean," Nicole says and starts yanking out popcorn pieces and stuffing them in her mouth, "he's not even around anymore. You know that, don't you? You know that he's not even alive."

"Yeah," I say and shake my head when she offers me some popcorn. "I know that."

"He's dead."

I sit up straight as I can and try to get her to stop talking by staring her down. "I know."

5

"You are writing to a dead movie star." She accentuates every syllable. A piece of popcorn flies out of her mouth and into the empty aisle of seats in front of us. We start laughing.

"I mean, really, Lily. We're about to be freshmen. Do you want everybody to think you're a freak?"

I don't say anything and examine the watermarks on the ceiling. Sometimes I think friends are a necessary evil, say like McDonald's burgers. You need to have them, you want to have them, but sometimes they make your stomach ache.

Before I can think of a good line, from the back of the movie theater a boy's voice yells, "Liliana!"

Nicole's mouth opens, because, let's face it: it's not all that often boys yell for me. Fearing a shower of soda or a popcorn pummelling, I turn around real slow. It's Paolo Mattias, this popular boy in our grade that I've never talked to much. He's the kind of boy I'd expect to see at Hoyts Cinemas with his arm around a girl's shoulders and his tongue down her throat, not alone at the Alamo.

He does not throw popcorn. He does not spit soda. He smiles. I freeze, gun finger twitching, even though I don't have a gun.

"Wave to him!" Nicole commands in a loud whisper-voice.

I give a halfhearted wave.

"Tell him to come down!" Nicole insists, poking me in the ribs.

I look at the five or so other people scattered around

the seats, mostly old people like Mrs. Samuel, who is a big John Wayne fan too and works in the fish section of Hannaford's. I feel bad for yelling, but I do. "You want to come down?"

He bangs up out of his chair, a rifle bullet blasting off, and strides down the aisle. He's got popcorn too. He folds his long body into the seat next to me and smiles at me. Then he smiles at Nicole. He smells like that fake butter-oil they put on popcorn and Old Spice deodorant, which is a weird combination.

"Cool," he says and nods.

I nod back. Nicole starts to giggle again. She hikes her miniskirt up an inch to reveal more thigh. I mouth the word "Ho."

She wiggles her eyebrows and I turn away to take a side look at Paolo Mattias. He's got a piece of popcorn on his shirt. I flick it off in a super-bold move, and then blow it by blushing.

"I saw you riding your bike," he says. "You ride it a lot?"

Nicole leans forward. "She rides it all the time. Whenever she's upset, she rides her bike. The only place she doesn't ride it to is school."

I punch her in the arm. She giggles. Paolo just smiles and goes, "That's cool. You must have strong legs."

Nicole giggles more. I sneak a peek at my legs.

The ancient projector makes this hiss noise and starts. That cool old-time music begins, and there's your name in big gold letters filling up the screen.

"You like John Wayne?" Paolo asks, slumping and

slinging his own damn legs over the chair backs because he's tall enough. He's got his arm on the rest and we're almost touching.

"Yeah," I say. "You?"

"He's great," he says. "So cowboy hero, you know?"

"I know!" I start to say, "He's so fantastic, so solid and so—"

Nicole groans, leans over me and pulls the trigger. "Lily writes him letters."

Paolo stares at her. I imagine everyone has heard that gunshot.

My skin burns. Everything in me plummets; all my internal organs are on the floor of the Alamo. There's my heart flopping next to my liver, which is sliding past a piece of Hubba Bubba bubble gum. Paolo Mattias lifts his eyebrows at Nicole and then says to me, "He's dead."

"Yeah, I know . . ." I don't know what to say. My hand flutters up and makes circles where words should be. Paolo Mattias shakes his head and laughs. He touches my shoulder with his hand and all my organs hop back up into place.

"You are some strange girl," he says and I can't tell if it's an insult or a compliment. The lights go down, thanks to the gods of the Alamo projection room. I breathe in, because no matter what's just happened, the waiting is over.

North to Alaska begins for real. The guitar music plays, and there you are bigger than life on the screen. John Wayne. For almost two hours I don't think about my mother's man, or Nicole's stupid miniskirt, or Paolo Mattias knowing about the letters. For almost two hours all I see is you, Mr. John Wayne, the DUKE, righting wrongs and riding into the sunset. For almost two hours, Paolo Mattias and Nicole fade into the background like extras no one can remember because they aren't the stars. No, that's not true. Paolo Mattias stays right there; a smell and an idea that's trying to make itself known.

Paolo laughs so hard he almost snarfs soda out his nose during the bar fight, when the bartender's hat flips up every time he's hit.

"You have a real snooty look, missy," you tell the whore in the dance hall. "And I don't like dames that have snooty looks."

Paolo laughs, looks at me and points. He whispers, "You have a real snooty look, missy."

I blush. I feel like that bad guy in the bar fight, the one who's slumped to the floor with an upside-down cuckoo clock on his head. I don't have a clue about what's going on, but I've got a goofy smile on my face and I think I like it.

Dear Mr. Wayne,

My mother's new man sent his stuff ahead of him.

The UPS man lugged six big boxes to our front door, the one we never use because you have to walk right past the septic-tank hole, and we don't have enough money to get the septic tank pumped right now and it needs it, you know, it smells bad.

On the phone he told my mother, "You go ahead and open them. Make sure they didn't break anything."

"I don't know," she said.

"Why not?" he asked.

"It wouldn't feel right?"

"I give you my permission, baby," he said. "I can't wait to see your beautiful shining face again."

Blah. Blah. Blah.

I hung up the phone so I didn't have to hear anymore. That man sure is going to be some disappointed when he gets here. She should have sent him a picture of what she looks like now, because it's been fourteen years and a baby since she's seen him last and she looks none the better for it.

I mean, when I was a little-little kid I thought she was beautiful the way little kids do, but, well ... she really isn't; not in the traditional sense of the word. No offense to her. The beauty is on the inside, right?

She told him that she'd open the packages but she hasn't. The boxes just sit there, all piled up on each other, in the middle of the kitchen floor. They look like a mountain. They say to me: *He's coming. He's coming.*

Sometimes when my mother isn't here I kick at them with my foot and say, *I know. I know.*

Days go by, Mr. Wayne, and she still hasn't opened them. She just sweeps around them, puts the mail on the flat top of one of them and sorts the bills.

"I'll do it when I have time," she says.

She says that about paying the bills and opening the boxes. But she never gets around to either. With the bills, she always waits until it's too late.

Dear Mr. Wayne,

I hope you are well. I'm trying to rustle up something positive about my day, but it's some hard. I wonder, did you have a good first day of high school? Were they mean to you? You still had the name Marion then, right? That's a burden right there, Mr. Wayne, so lord knows why I'm complaining.

My father drove over from his house in Hancock today to bring me to my first day of high school. He said it was too special to go on the bus with all the other "ordinary" freshmen. He picked me up in his little beige car. I hate his little beige car. Everybody drives trucks in Maine, except the tourists who drive Jags and Beamers and the moms who drive Subarus. No dads drive little beige cars. My dad, as you know, has to be different.

He put his hand on my arm when he drove, like when I was a little kid and he was always afraid the seat belt wasn't good enough to keep me from flying through the windshield. I hate that too. I feel so trapped in there, just like the way high school is going to be. You can't go out without asking or you'll be one of the bad kids breaking the rules.

You don't seem like the kind of man who always plays by the rules, Mr. Wayne. You seem like the kind of man who knows that sometimes the rules just stink.

My father is not like that.

When I'm in his car, my father doesn't even let me cross my legs because he's afraid my shoe might scrape up against the dashboard and make it dirty. Dirt shows up on beige-everything.

When he dropped me off, he squeezed my knee and said, "I'm so proud of my little girl. You're all grown up."

I didn't look at him because his blue eyes were in danger of going liquid, but I fiddled with the front zipper on my backpack and said, "Uh-huh."

Then he started to cry. Really, a man crying! Can you believe it? And the worst thing is that he does it *all the time*. You wouldn't have done that. You would've been proud of your daughter, right? Told her to mosey on in there. So that's what I did. I kissed him and got out of the car real fast before anyone cool saw. Fathers aren't supposed to do that crying thing. Mothers are. Sometimes.

But I guess he thought he needed to fill in, like my mother was too busy with her new man coming to do the right things like take me to high school on the first day, and cry because I'm getting old and more than halfway to leaving.

Now, listen to this, when I hopped out of my dad's car, Paolo Mattias saw me and I tried to look the other way so he wouldn't notice me, but he said, "Is that your dad?"

"Uh-huh," I said and did my stupid bottom-lip wiggle thing that makes me look like a complete idiot. Nicole once said it looks like my lip is an inchworm trying to wiggle off my face.

Paolo Mattias is a pretty cool boy. After that whole movie thing where Nicole the jerk-off blew the whistle on me about the letters, the fact that he was talking to me was so astounding I forgot to be scared. It's amazing I managed to even say "uh-huh." So, I can forgive myself the lip wiggle.

In the distance, I thought I heard a low whistle, like a bank robber gang member sending a signal to his boss in the distance. *We've got her cornered, come on in.*

"Yeah, that's my dad," I said to try to be a little articulate.

Paolo Mattias stared at my lips, nodded, and said, "It's cool that he dropped you off. I always have to take the bus. You know, even on the first day and everything."

"Oh," I said, real stupid. No movie line. You're supposed to say movie lines to boys like Paolo Mattias and men like you, Mr. Wayne.

I'm so bad at movie lines. They flap inside my mouth like a dying fish, moving around but never escaping out to sea.

Paolo looked at me, up and down, and I tried not to

meet his eyes because if I did I'm sure my lip would have wiggled again. He was all spiffed up for the first day of school and his jeans had creases in the middle of his legs like maybe his mother ironed them for him or something. He didn't have the clothes of a cowboy, not with those creases, but he was standing like one, feet a little too far apart, ready to pull out the gun nestled on his hip. His sneakers had grass stains on them, though. I stared at them.

It was so quiet, despite everyone else getting off their busses and being dropped off. It was so quiet just between the two of us, that I swear if Maine had a tumbleweed I would have heard it blowing. We don't have those lonely tumbleweeds though. Paolo pulled his gun first.

"Is he really gay?" he blurted.

I gulped and Paolo's sneakers took a step back.

"Who?" My lip wiggled.

"Your father."

Someone slapped Paolo's shoulder. He gave them a wave and then turned back to me.

"My father," I said, my voice squeaking like I was a boy going through puberty, "is a truck driver."

I stared him down. He blushed. So did I.

"It's not a big deal. It's just what people are saying."

My hands went to my hips. "What people?"

"It's not a big deal, Lily. Nobody cares." His hand went up and rushed through his hair. He shifted his weight. His sneakers moved.

"If nobody cares, why are you asking me about it?"

His breath rushed out. He tried to smile, and quoted you at me: "You have a real snooty look, missy."

But I didn't bite. I couldn't bite. Instead, I just walked away from him into the dingy school cafeteria that smelled like old pickles and cheeseburgers. I found a seat with a bunch of kids I knew from eighth grade and waited for the day to begin, so we could start classes and I could hide my head behind the desk.

I started chanting things under my breath, just one little sentence really.

Truck drivers can't be gay. Truck drivers can't be gay.

They're like cowboys. Cowboys can't be gay either, right?

I was still chanting when the morning bell rang. I turned around to head to English class and I witnessed Mary Bilodeau trip over the extended foot of Travis Poppins, Nicole's brother's best friend and all-around evil hombre.

That stopped my chanting.

Mary Bilodeau's brown paper lunch bag flopped on the floor and her tuna sandwich, apple, pickle and Cheez-Its fell out on the cracked linoleum. People started stepping on the Cheez-Its, crushing them and making a really big mess. Mary Bilodeau just stood still, looking down at her lunch. She started scrunching up her face like she was going to cry, and her hands shook. I couldn't watch. So I pushed my way through the crowd and yelled, "Hold it!"

just like you did in *Stagecoach*. Well, that's what I wanted to do anyway.

You don't know her, but Mary Bilodeau is a big geek. She's smart enough and everything, but she's doughy like half-risen bread. You think you could stick your finger in her and watch the dent form where you'd poked. Once you take your finger away, the dough moves in just a bit more and holds. She's the girl no one wants to sit with; she smells a little like chicken soup that has too much garlic in it. She stammers. She cries if she gets called on even though she knows the answer. The only person she's really friends with is Katie Henderson.

But I made my way over to her anyways, through the throngs of walking mall-clothes, and knelt down and started picking things up. If this were me, I'd run away and hide, or else maybe if I were feeling a little more brave, more like you, I'd have pointed my finger at Travis Poppins and said, *You and me. A word.*

Poor Mary. It's bad enough having a brown bag for lunch on the first day of high school when everybody knows if you're a girl you're supposed to just get a bagel or French fries in the a la carte line, but to be tripped and then to drop everything.

I avoided feet and plucked her sandwich up off the floor. It was wrapped in plastic, so it was still edible, and her apple could be washed off. I grabbed the apple as someone's Nike tapped it and it started to roll.

"Here," I said and handed her the sandwich and apple. She took them, but her eyes didn't look at mine; instead, they watched the orange Cheez-Its being scrunched by all the feet heading to first-period classes. They were all broken to pieces, and it didn't look right like that, so shattered. I know they get that way between your teeth when you chew, but that's in your mouth, not on the tile floor where sneakers that may have stepped in dog poop or vomit or something are now stepping. Their orangeness just stood out and seemed to scream out how messed up everything was. How nothing was right and pure, just processed, packaged, dyed and filled with chemicals. Now I sound like one of those macrobiotic freaks. Which I'm not. I eat salami. But only if I can brush my teeth afterwards, just in case someone randomly decides to kiss me. You can't kiss anyone with salami breath.

"Thanks," Mary mumbled. She clutched her sandwich, her ripped bag and her apple to her chest and turned her dewy eyes on me and I didn't like how they looked, like she worshipped me or something.

"Not a big deal," I said as she shuffled off, hurrying so she wouldn't be late.

"You're such a hero," Travis Poppins snided out at me.

"And you," I said, still crouched on the ground, "are such an ass it's hard to believe you can talk through your mouth instead of your butt."

"Oh, brilliant one..." He fake-laughed and hopped off like he'd won.

I mumbled the next words. "He is so bosh."

"Bosh?" There was Paolo, cowboy-strong legs a little apart.

"It's cowboy slang," I muttered. "It means nonsense."

He reached out his hand to help me up. I took it. His fingers touching mine made me feel more solid somehow. I smiled and took my hand away. "Thanks."

"He's an idiot."

"Yeah," I said. "I know. A lot of us are idiots."

"Like me?"

"Yeah," I said, thinking about what he'd said about my dad. "No ... I mean ..."

I smacked my forehead with my hand. He grabbed it by the wrist. "You're going to hurt yourself."

"I meant that I'm an idiot."

"Yeah, right." He shook his head, smiled, and ambled away.

Dear Mr. Wayne,

We opened the boxes today.

Mike O'Donnell's boxes.

Let me tell you what happened.

My mom came home from work, slipped off her shoes and started yanking down her panty hose. "His boxes are still here."

"Uh-huh," I said, wondering what she thought might happen during the day, like they might tip onto their edges and flop out the door or something, moving all clumsy like a walruses on land trying to get back to the water, the place they belonged. I wish.

She inspected her panty hose, all loose and crinkled elephant skin in her hands. There was a big run in them. She balled them up and tossed them in the trash.

"I suppose we should open them," she said, taking off her coat and hanging it in the closet by the door. I never hang my coat there. Once, when I was a little kid, I had my snowsuit in there and mice came and made a nest in the hood. When I put the hood up over my head, dog food and pumpkin seed and mouse stuff all fell out into my hair. I didn't scream or anything because I'm brave, but you can bet I didn't forget it. Plus, it smells in that closet, like wet basement and mothballs. I always drape my coat across one of the chairs at the kitchen table.

"Help me carry the boxes to the table," she said.

We hefted them up into our arms and heaved them over to the table. My mom grabbed the scissors out of the junk drawer and opened them. She stabbed one blade into the box where it was taped down and said, "I don't feel right doing this."

"I don't either."

"He said to open it for him."

"You sure?"

"Of course I'm sure. He wanted to make sure nothing was broken."

"Couldn't he check that himself when he comes?"

She shrugged and stabbed the knife through the masking tape and pulled apart the lid of the first box. Inside, there were picture albums and photos of him and his kids. My mom picked things up, shifted through them and said, "Nothing looks broken."

The moment she opened the box, a strange musky smell began to permeate the kitchen. I sniffed. It smelled like a man. We haven't smelled that smell here for a long, hard while.

When my mother started opening the other boxes, I took out the photo album. Inside weren't photos, but newspaper clippings, tons of them, all about a bar fight and someone dying.

One Man Dead in Fight at Rusty Grill
Police Looking for Member of Devil's Canyon
Victim Loved by All
Father of 8-Year-Old Girl
Family Heartbroken
Knife in Back Ends Promising Future

And on and on.

Numb and probably with my mouth hanging open, I read them all. My mom, who was sorting through photographs of Mike O'Donnell's family, finally noticed and said, "What are you looking at?"

I shut the photo album and put it back in the box. "Nothing."

"Don't feel guilty." She took the album out and opened it. "He told us we should look through his things."

"I don't feel guilty."

She flipped through the pages and her face got all sad. "Oh, he told me about this."

"He did?"

My mom sat down and so did I, scooting my chair closer to her. "He was there. This man was his best friend."

"The man who died?"

"Mmm-hhhm."

"He was there?"

"Yep, sitting right next to him." She shut the book, put it back in a box, the wrong box, and stood up again. "Help me put these boxes in the guest room."

"It's like he's moving in," I said as I carried the box into the guest room, which was painted brown like dark stained wood. It was my room when I was a baby. I can't imagine how my development was stunted being in a dark brown room those formative years. I don't want to think about it. When my sister got hitched and moved out, I got her room, which is blue.

My mother flattened out the bedspread, which was also brown and had rusty orange in it; all these hexagons connected together. "Just until he gets on his feet."

"How long is that going to take?" I asked.

"Not long," she said, but I could tell she was lying, and that the hope making her eyes sparkle had nothing to do with him leaving soon.

In the movies, bad men turn to good with the love of a decent woman, and good men turn bad due to a need for revenge or because they are denied the love of a decent woman. Real life works different, I think, but I don't really know, do I? You'd probably say I'm just a damn kid, wet behind the ears. I don't know much about anything except this ache inside me, right between my lungs, whenever I think of love and need and sex.

It freaks me right out to think that my mother might be feeling that way, too.

Dear Mr. Wayne,

Before you were a movie star, did you have to do home-work? I should get a biography about you so that I can know these things, but I'm afraid to. What if I open up the book and start reading and find out you aren't who I think you are? I want people to be who they're supposed to be, but nobody ever seems to want to. I'll give it to you firsthand, Mr. Wayne: nobody in this world seems to be who they are. And my guess is that most people don't even know who they are supposed to be. Which sucks.

I'm not supposed to use that word. My mother acts like it's worse than the f-word or something. You would probably say the same thing.

My homework was easy: just some geometry prob-lems and some reading for English. I covered all my text-books—cut up some grocery bags from Sully's Superette with my mom's nail scissors because I couldn't find the real scissors. All the edges were jagged because it's hard to cut with nail scissors, but I folded the corners under anyways so no one can really tell.

I doubt high school teachers inspect the book covers. They just want to make sure the books are protected from rain and stuff.

After the books were covered, I wrote some quotes on some, and song lyrics on others. Clean book covers are lame. If I were in love with someone, I would write: *Lily loves* _____.

You can fill in the blank.

And if I were a really big greenhorn, I would encircle that with a heart and write: *True Love Always*. And then I'd draw five-petaled daisies and scribble his name all over the place in big loopy letters and I would write my name with his last name, my name with my last name hyphenated next to his, or I'd just write his name with "Mrs." in front of it.

I haven't drawn a heart in a long time.

I hate when my mom gets mail like that, mail that is addressed to Mrs. James Gonzalves. Like she doesn't have a first name, like her whole identity is Mrs. To make it worse, she isn't Mrs. James Gonzalves anymore because my stepfather is dead.

When I was done with writing inspiring things on my book covers, I thought about cleaning. But I didn't want to.

I don't know why I have to clean for this guy from Oregon who isn't even coming for another week. He's not my guest. Instead of wiping down the heaters, I called Nicole to talk about school.

Nicole talks, and when she talks? She talks a lot. Like one of those TV talk show people or those radio guys who do the announcing for the Red Sox games. Sometimes it's a little annoying when she doesn't let me say anything. Sometimes it's so bad that I keep trying to interrupt and interrupt and she doesn't even notice. I've said whole sentences while she's talked, without her hearing. My mom says that if I use a louder voice people will hear me better and pay attention. I have to have authority and confidence in my voice, my mother says, but then I just imagine sounding like my father and I can't do it.

I can't believe Paolo Mattias thought he was gay.

What's the point of having authority and confidence in your voice if you break down crying in a dinky beige car outside of high school?

"Tell me about the red pants guy," Nicole said. Nicole always lets me talk when I have information that she doesn't. The red pants guy was in the cafeteria buying Certs from the vending machine at the same time she was. Nicole is "not in love" with him.

"Mr. Fire Engine Pants?"

"They do look like fireman pants."

"Uh-huh. Like fire hydrants—"

"No they don't. They're a calm pair of red pants, a nice shade."

"Like something a dog pees on," I finished.

"Let's call him Mr. Fire Engine Pants until I find out

his name," Nicole said. I could hear her chewing. She told me she's eating Chef Boyardee Beefaroni. She already had three bowls of Corn Flakes. She can eat anything and stay ridiculously skinny. She was probably chomping on a Certs in between ravioli bites. She's addicted to Certs.

"Isn't that too long? Mister Fire Engine Pants."

"Okay, it does take too long. Let's call him the Fire Man."

"That's good," I said. "It makes me think of emergencies."

"Like the emergency of love. I'm in love. Hear the sirens of my heart? Whooo. Whoo. He is *so* cute, isn't he?"

"Uh-huh," I said. "That siren of love stuff is too corny."

"Love is not corny."

"Sure. Did you get a topic for your New England History paper?" I asked her this while she was quiet and thinking of the Fire Man. Mr. Johnson has given us our topics for our quote-unquote term paper for New England History. It's supposed to be fifteen pages long and is due right after Thanksgiving weekend.

"Oh. My. God." Nicole paused to slurp whatever she was drinking. She drinks everything with a straw, even milk, and I could hear that she was at the bottom of the glass. I knew that pretty soon she'd excuse herself for a minute to go refill the glass. "Oh my God, you will never believe what that idiot assigned me. It's the worst topic in the universe. It's horrible. And fifteen pages. I don't know how I'll ever write fifteen pages on anything, let alone on what he gave me."

"I bet you could write fifteen pages on the masculine attributes of Fire Man," I said.

"Masculine attributes? You sound like a *Cosmopolitan* article."

"Not *Seventeen*?" I said.

"No, they aren't intelligent enough to use the word attributes. They'd think we wouldn't understand it. I hate *Seventeen*."

"Me too," I said. "So, what's your topic?"

"Some old logging company on the Union River. Jordan Brothers Logging or something like that. I wrote it down. Isn't it awful?"

"Uh-huh." I waited for Nicole to ask me what my topic is.

"I can't believe he gave me that. Fifteen pages on loggers. Do you think anyone will ever like me? I can't go all the way through high school without anyone liking me. I'd go out with anyone, even Travis Poppins."

"That's disgusting. He's your brother's best friend. That's like incest or something."

"No, it isn't. It's just a last resort thing."

"You'd rather go out with a jerk than go out with nobody?"

"Yeah." She munched on something and circled back. "I can't believe I have to write about a logging company."

"Mine's on Hannah Dustin," I said, since I'd realized Nicole wasn't going to ask.

"Who's that?"

"She's this old, odd-stick colonial woman who got—"

"Odd stick? What the hell is odd stick? Are you talking cowboy again?"

"No. It just means eccentric."

"Eccentric?"

"Weird, okay? Whatever. She got kidnapped by Indians and then killed them all." Hannah Dustin is my ancestor, but I don't tell Nicole that.

"No way."

"Uh-huh. She scalped them."

"No freaking way! You already know that?"

"Yeah, we learned about her in seventh grade," I lied. "Don't you remember?"

"No," Nicole said. "I probably wasn't paying attention."

And when she said this I felt all mudsill for lying, because I could tell (because I know her so well and because she's my best friend) that Nicole just remembered she's supposed to be smart this year.

"I should go," she said. "I have to do homework."

When we hung up, I looked at the clock and saw I only had ten minutes before my mom came home from the Sheraton, where she's the secretary to the personnel manager. I hadn't cleaned anything.

"Crap," I said and went to the cabinet beneath the kitchen sink where my mom keeps all the cleaning stuff. I grabbed some Windex and a cloth. I don't think Windex glass cleaner is what you're supposed to use to clean radiators, but I couldn't remember what my mom used. I don't think she'd ever done it before. It's all for this stupid man from Oregon.

I pray every night that he's cool, like you, Mr. Wayne. Sometimes I worry that he's the type of man who wears pocket protectors in case his pens leak. Sometimes I worry about those newspaper headlines. I told Nicole about those at school. She wiggled her fingers and said, "FREEE-AAKKK-YYYY."

Then she changed the subject, and talked about whether we'd be cooler if we highlighted our hair.

I didn't tell her what Paolo Mattias said about my dad. I haven't told anyone about that, other than you.

Dear Mr. Wayne,

Let me tell you, Sunday mornings are the worst. You'd think they'd be great. My homework is done, and you'd think I'd have a whole day to do nothing except maybe ride my bike or gab with Nicole on the phone or watch your movies.

This is not the case.

My one day of freedom, Saturday, is over and I'm forced to wait, all morning, for my father to call. Sundays are our days together. When I wait, I watch your movies. I have thirty-six of them, which isn't good enough to be a real collector, but I'm halfway there.

Most of the time my dad calls around ten, right in the middle of a movie. That's what he does this time. I'm full into *Hatari!* and ring, there goes the phone. My mother makes me answer it.

"Liliana?" he says.

"Hi Dad."

"How about I come pick you up around eleven thirty?"

"Okay."

"Anything special you want to do today?"

"No," I say, and I think, *not with you*. This is an awful thing to think, I know, but I can't seem to help it. Sometimes when I think that way, I feel so bad that I imagine I'm on this sinking Navy boat and the men are running frantic, the waves leaping up over the hull, and there I am standing there yelling, "Hold on, men! Hold on!" But there's no point. There's nothing to hold onto because we are sinking, sinking fast.

"Well, let's see," my dad says, and he pauses all namby-pamby. I go and open the silverware drawer. In the background, I can hear Grammy talking to him. She's telling him to take me to a movie or the mall.

"Do something girls like," she yells.

He doesn't listen. "Why don't we go to an engine show up in Blue Hill?"

"Okay."

Grammy moans so loudly I can hear it through the phone lines. I look at my reflection in the handle of a knife. I'm warped, all nose and zeppelin-shaped eyes.

We hang up the phone and my mom comes in, real chipper, like she's a sitcom mom, only in sitcoms parents are never divorced and if they are, the stepfather doesn't die. And the reason the sitcom mom is chipper isn't because the dad called and she knows they'll get a check this week. You weren't ever on *The Brady Bunch*, were you? It's an ancient sitcom they run on cable. I hate *The Brady Bunch* even though it's all retro campy. Which means, according to Nicole, that it's now cool. The first time I ever saw you was on the oldies channel, and you were on a Carol Burnett show, guest starring. You looked strong and so tall. Six four is big for a man, Mr. Wayne, which I'm sure you know. I'm only five feet. That's not good even for a girl. My mom's even shorter.

"What are the plans for today?" she asks as I balance the knife on the palm of my hand. It tips over and clangs onto the kitchen floor that my father put in when he still lived here.

"An engine show," I groan, and go into the living room to flop on the couch.

"Oh. Well, maybe it'll be fun."

I raise my eyebrows at her.

"You never know."

I turn away and stare at the back of the sofa. There's no point in watching the rest of the movie. I know it by heart anyways. I listen to the gunfire, your words comforting slow out of your mouth, and examine the threads on the sofa that are woven together all yellow and gold and white. I wonder how my father and mother could have agreed on this couch. They bought it together. It's older than I am. Now my body is as long as the couch when I lie on it. I remember when I didn't even take up one cushion. I'm getting old. Too old to go to engine shows with my father. Too old to have to do anything with my father on Sundays.

My dad belongs to this group for divorced people called Parents Without Partners. They do all these group activities with their kids. This was okay when I was little, but now I feel like the biggest dork mini golfing and bowling with these traumatized six-year-olds while their divorced parents all make goo-goo eyes at each other and set up dates. None of the men talk to my dad at these things. They all wear nice corduroy pants that don't expose their blue underwear, unlike my father. None of them chew toothpicks like him and they all look at me like I'm poor, which I am, sort of, but I don't need to be looked at that way.

At least the engine show isn't a Parents Without Partners expedition.

An engine show.

I will have to pretend to care.

I hate that.

"I don't want to go," I say to my mother, arching my back and stretching down the length of the couch.

"Don't whine, Liliana. You look like a cat, stretching like that." She sits on the armrest of the couch and puts her hand on my forehead. She starts smoothing back my hair. It feels nice.

After a minute she adds, "I know you don't, honey. But he's your father."

I sit up. "You always say that. Like it's the excuse for everything."

"Well, he is."

I clomp into my room and close the door. I won't come out until he cruises up the driveway and honks the horn for me the way a date does in movies; a date that's already met the parents and is way too cool to come inside. My father is definitely not too cool to come inside. He's the kind of man whose pants fall down and you can see his bottom. When you tell him this, he blushes and pulls them up. This is called having a working man's smile or the plumber's drip. It happens all the time, and still he doesn't buy pants that fit. What does that say about a person? What does that say about me? My genetic legacy? A scalper (via the lovely Hannah Dustin genes) and a working man's smile. Jesus. I bet your daughters never had to go to an engine show, Mr. Wayne. I saw that picture of one of them—what, was she maybe four years old and in *Cosmopolitan* wearing $800,000 worth of diamonds for some Cartier's ad? She was beautiful, Mr. Wayne. She must have loved you.

✦

When I get in the car, my father pats me on the knee and leaves his hand there waiting for me to lean over and kiss him on the cheek. I do. One good thing about my father is that he smells nice, the way fathers are supposed to, of minty aftershave and hair stuff, sometimes with a little cut-grass scent underneath. My stepfather smelled like that too, with Old Spice deodorant thrown in.

My father turns the car around at the top of the hill and heads down the driveway. It's easy for him to turn the car around. He's used to tractor trailers, eighteen-wheelers and all that. It must be strange for him to drive something so small.

"How was your week?" he asks me.

"Good."

"First day of school go okay?"

"Mmhmm."

"Things going well?"

"Yep," I say, because I am a woman of few words.

We start down 101 towards Blue Hill and the engine show. I wonder if he'll remember to get me lunch. There aren't many places to eat on the way to Blue Hill. Maybe they'll have popcorn or something at the show. They do sometimes, popcorn in the boxes like they have at the movies and Coke in those little red cups that have wax on them. The wax always comes off on my lips when I'm drinking, and it makes me think I'm drinking candles.

"So, how's your mother?" he asks, biting the edge of his fingernail while we drive past the OK Corral Redemption Center.

"Good."

He always asks how my mother is. For a second I feel bad for him. His big blue eyes stare out the car window at the traffic. He pats my knee.

"She's excited about Mike O'Donnell coming to visit," I say, staring out the window as we drive past an Exxon gas station. I bet they have food in there, Doritos or something toxic like that. Twinkies maybe? I'm so hungry I'd eat anything.

"Mike O'Donnell?"

"Uh-huh."

"Mike O'Donnell from town?"

"Yep. You guys used to know him and his wife or something." I pick at my fingernails because it's something to do. We drive by a horse farm. Horses stand waiting for something to happen. I want to jump on and ride off into the sunset, but it's only noon.

"How's Jean? Is she coming too?" my father asks, smiling and all excited now. He's a social butterfly. He loves all the old friends from his married past. Most of them are still his friends, too. They all gave up on my mother. They don't mind the toothpicks and the falling-down pants, it seems. They prefer it to my mom, the adulteress, who left my dad for my stepdad who died on her.

"Goes around comes around," they say when I go visit them with my dad. They think I can't hear. So stupid. It's too bad that there aren't more people of few words, you know?

"Don't need 'em," my mom always says, swatting her hand through the air like she's swatting flies. She talks real big for a woman that's all alone.

My dad isn't like that. He talks small. My mom doesn't need friends. He does. She drives fast. He drives too slow, usually at least ten miles under the speed limit. I count the cars as they pass us on the left as soon as the spotted highway lines appear. Five pass. It's a good amount of time to let thoughts sink in. You don't want to go at things too fast, right?

"Saddle up," I whisper to my dad.

"What?"

"I think they're divorced or something," I say after a second. "The Mike O'Donnell guy and his wife."

"Oh, I think I heard about that. That's too bad." He turns onto Route 3. He keeps both hands on the wheel when he turns. He's a careful man, not a confident one. "When's he coming?"

"Next week."

"I'd like to see him."

I sigh. "I'll tell Mom."

"Good. Good. You do that."

"She says to remind you that you owe us a check from last week and this week."

"Oh. Okay. Did I forget last week?"

"I forgot to remind you when I got out of the car." I stare at the big knuckles on his hands. "I should've told you when you dropped me off at school."

"You shouldn't have to remind me. It's not right. Me giving you a check."

"You could mail it."

He shakes his head. "It's like I'm renting you. It can't be good for you, me giving you that check."

We pull into the parking lot of the Blue Hill Grange. The sign outside says: *Engine Show. Here Sunday Noon.* There are already tons of rusted-out Ford trucks, Dodge SUVs and Chevy vans. All the cars here are American. A trivial fact that I note and then don't know what to do with. Another trivial fact here is that everyone wears grandpa clothes like we're stuck in the 1980s, these old jeans and big belt buckles and plaid shirts or T-shirts with truck company names on them. I shake my head.

As my father parks next to a baby blue van that looks like it's been involved in a good twenty-seven kidnappings, he says, "I'd never remember to mail it."

I look at him, confused.

"The check," he says. "It would drive your mother crazy."

I nod, unlock my car door so that I can get out. I don't like talking about these money things.

The cuff of his blue pants lifts up a bit. It shows me his ankle and calf. Light blue nylon covers them. No, not nylon, cotton. Cotton tights stretched so tight that the black leg hair matted against the weave is visible.

My father is wearing tights.

★

Engines big and little shine their metal inside the grange hall. They sit on card tables and men, mostly old men like my father, walk around them and talk about things like carburetors and engine years. They touch the moving engines the way a woman touches a baby, reverently. Their hands stay away from the inner spokes of the spinning wheels; their heads nod up and down with the levers. The engines are lined up in rows and all the men do is walk up and down slowly, staring at the engines, touching. I usually count the colors to keep myself awake, place bets on whether there'll be more green or red engines at this show.

Sometimes I imagine a gunfight. Maybe a crazy, played-out man comes in with wild eyes. The engine show community has slighted him and the man with the souped-up John Deere engine stole his wife away after singing her some country Tim McGraw song at a late-night karaoke. He's got nothing to lose, this man. He's got a bomb strapped to his shirt and his eyes are cold steel and everyone is terrified. The men with the plaid shirts dive for cover. One man with an American Legion hat lunges for him, but the terrorist whacks him down with a karate chop to the neck. He crumples.

I wait. I think. The crazy man gives threats.

"Everyone down!" he yells. "Or we all die together!"

I do not go down on the floor. I will not give him that. Instead, I squat behind a big generator. I peek out and when he's not looking I lunge, grab his legs and he falls. With two hands, I rip the bomb off his chest and throw it through the window. It was velcroed on or something.

The bomb explodes outside. A bit of ceiling falls on us and another window shatters but no one is hurt, except me. I've got a gash across my cheek and it bleeds.

Everyone is silent. A tumbleweed blows down the center aisle at the grange and then suddenly everyone starts cheering.

My father, who is suddenly tall, wearing normal socks and a cowboy hat, stares and then lifts me from under my shoulders saying, "That's my girl. That's my girl."

All the old men pet me on the shoulder and think of when they were heroes, too. Someone buys me a pizza from up the street and my picture is in the paper. At school, everyone loves me, even stupid Paolo "Is Your Father Gay?" Mattias. The principal lets me wear a six-shooter on my hip to school to help ensure its safety.

I draw my pretend gun and turn my index finger into a pretend barrel.

"Pow," I whisper to the engine show people. "I'll save you. Pow. Pow. Pow."

But there is no crazy man, just happy old guys rubbing their hands together, jawing away, looking at moving parts.

Dear Mr. Wayne,

On the way home I cock my gun, spew it out, and I say to my dad, "I'm not looking forward to this Mike O'Donnell guy coming."

"Why not?"

I shrug. My stomach growls real loud. My father's eyes go big.

"I forgot to feed you!"

"It's okay," I say and cross my legs.

"That's no good. Oh, how can I do that?" He smacks his forehead with the palm of his hand. It makes a horrible sound, like a gunshot.

We're at my driveway. I put my hand on my dad's arm and play the heroine role, sweet, understanding. For extra oomph, I shake out my hair, because that's what they would do in a movie. "It's okay. I'm not hungry."

He shakes his head. "What kind of father am I? I can't even remember to feed you."

I kiss his cheek. "I'll see you next Sunday, Dad."

"Okay," he says, hands clenching the steering wheel. "Okay."

★

"How was it?" my mom asks all bright and cheery.

I shrug and open the fridge. "Okay."

"Did he give you my check?"

"No." I grab an apple, slam the fridge door, and she groans and swears beneath her breath. I can't take this. "I'm going for a quick bike ride."

"Fine." She's already turned away, picking up the phone. "Be back in time for dinner."

★

My rear brakes squeak whenever I press the grip. It sounds like cats scared behind a tavern somewhere. For a second while I'm pumping up the hill towards Bangor, I imagine you driving by in a big old truck. It's red, an antique Ford, I think. You lean out and wave to me. I get inside. You pick up my bike and haul it into the back like it weighs nothing.

"How was your day?" you ask.

"Okay."

You push a brown bag towards me. There's a Veggie Delite from Subway inside it. "My favorite."

You wink and just keep driving.

You drop me off at the track. Paolo Mattias is rushing around it, long legs smashing records like he did in eighth grade. Paolo sees you drive away.

"That your dad?" he asks.

"Yeah," I say.

"Wow." His eyes light up and you can just tell that he's thinking how amazing it would be to have a dad like you, like John Wayne, a hero kind of dad. "Cool."

Mr. Wayne, just tell me something. Why does being alive have to hurt so much? You must know. I've seen that look in your face on the TV screen when they replay your movies. I've seen your face, Mr. Wayne, and I can tell that you know something about pain. You watch the sunset. You watch the movie men, the Italian Indians. I know you know something about it. So tell me, Mr. Wayne. Why does being alive have to hurt so much?

Dear Mr. Wayne,

Since my father forgot to feed me after the engine show, I race to the kitchen as soon I'm back from biking. The apple didn't do it. I'm hoping that my mom's made beef stew for tonight. I love beef stew, especially the carrots and the potatoes all coated with gravy stuff. But there isn't a Crock-Pot on the counter. I can't smell anything cooking. A package of stew meat sits on the counter, unopened. Food poisoning waiting to happen.

"Mom!" I yell. "I'm home. What's for dinner?"

There's no answer. Maybe she's been kidnapped, I think, but, c'mon, really. Who would kidnap my mother? Still, I throw myself down and shimmy across the linoleum of the kitchen floor. Inching forward, I listen for the bad guys... Saddle up.

"Mom?" I take a chance, call again.

"I'm in here." Her voice comes from our living room.

"Are you alone?"

"What?"

I can tell by her tone she's alone, so I stand up and head for her. She's sitting in the tall yellow chair with the roses on it looking out the picture window. Her face is splotchy and three quiet tears are dropping down her cheeks. First, I think that someone, maybe my Nana, has died. But she isn't sobbing. She would be sobbing if someone died. When my stepfather died, she sobbed and sobbed and clutched me and moaned that our world was over and we'd never survive without him.

All I wanted to do was run away, then. I know this is awful and I'm a little ashamed to admit it, but it's true. It's true. My face mashed into her shirt, and it was too soft and close. Her hands clung to my back and she shook and shook. I kept wanting to push her away and run to this special place I have in the woods where all these ferns grow and the light streams down in big golden rays, slanting through the trees. I wanted that more than anything, the peace there.

I'm sure that's how you've felt a few times, like when your second wife turned out to be a prostitute and a drunk and she waved that gun in your face when you came home. I bet you wanted to just go by the ocean somewhere or the desert, and have a drink or two, alone. But you didn't, did you? You stood there like a man and you faced up to your troubles, that's what you did.

That's what I did too.

My mother isn't sobbing now. There's just those three tears. I hope that maybe it's just that Mike O'Donnell isn't coming. I cross my fingers. I think about the newspaper headlines. *One Man Dead In Fight.* Maybe he's been arrested. I want to bounce around like a G-rated goofball and say, "Oh happy day! Oh happy day!"

I don't. Instead, I switch back into the role of your daughter in that movie where you fight the oil fires. I'm strong and good and kind.

"What's wrong?" I ask and touch her shoulder. It trembles.

"I don't want to tell you."

"Oh," I say. "Okay. You don't have to."

I know what that's like, not wanting to tell someone what's wrong, because if you tell them it isn't a relief. It just makes it more real, or maybe if you tell them they'll pity you, and when you add someone's pity onto your own sadness it's like all the strings inside of you become untuned, stretched too tight, and you can feel them ready to snap apart if anyone says anything, or if you even move.

Even though I know that, I swallow. I swallow big and hard, and all the grit from those oil fires feels like it's stuck there.

I'm not sure if that's true, but it sounds good.

My mom hiccups. I notice that her eyes stare right ahead. I wonder why she hasn't looked at me. Maybe she's in a coma. Or shock. What do I do if she's in shock? I try to remember what we learned in health class in eighth grade.

"Are you cold?" I ask. "Maybe you should lie down on the floor. I'll get a pillow for under your head."

I imagine new headlines. *Quick-Thinking Girl Saves Mother From Shock.*

Her hand lifts from the armrest and flutters at me like I'm a bug she's brushing away, which is an absolutely evil thing to do no matter how upset she is. I turn.

"No, Liliana." The fluttering hand grabs my forearm, and it's surprisingly strong. "I'm not cold. I'm sorry. It's just ... your sister ..."

"What about her?"

"She's ... oh. I don't know. It's probably nothing."

My mother stares into my eyes. It looks like little red snakes are stretching all around her eyeballs. She's been crying more than three tears. She must have been crying hard before I came home. I never should have left. I should have stayed here and protected her.

"What happened?" I fix her with my gaze. It's the same gaze you would use to get horses to listen to you. I call it the trainer gaze.

My mother always submits to it. "She came over and she had this bruise. A very large bruise. All on the left side of her chin."

"A bruise?"

The clock chimes on the wall. I stare at it, trying to figure out what the damn numbers mean.

"Brian hit her?"

My mother lifts her hand like it weighs a hundred tons. "She says her jaw was locked and Brian had to hit it to unlock it. Her jaw does that."

"What a lie."

"We don't know that."

"He is such a freaking jerk." I scoop up an unlit cigarette that's been dropped on the floor. Outside, there are crows chasing a hawk above the big pine tree at the end of the yard.

"Liliana!" She holds out her hand for the cigarette. "Ladies don't use that sort of language. I have never said that word in my entire life."

"What's your point, Mom? It makes you holy or something? Her husband is beating on her and you're all pissed off about me using the f-word. Yeah, right on the scale of things, that's the big crime, huh? Jesus. It wasn't even the real f-word. I said 'freaking.'"

I toss the cigarette at her and walk from my mother's chair across the living room to the door of the family room that used to be a garage. It's cozy, with big barn beams on the ceiling, bricks on the wall and a Franklin stove. I don't go in there though. Instead, I just do stupid little manic laps around the yellow living room, the color of a bruise that's almost healed.

"Jesus Christ," I say.

My sister is fifteen years older than I am. She married Brian when I was three.

"She said her jaw was locked. She wouldn't lie," my mom says. She stands up and puts hands on my shoulders to make me stare into her face. I'm taller than she is. I grew two inches last year. She is so short. "She wouldn't lie to me."

"Mom. Everyone. Always. Lies."

She drops her hands. Her face crumples, but I ignore

it and start towards the family room to get the laptop. I have a report to do. I'll have to go through the living room to get back to my bedroom. I don't want to do this report stuff at the kitchen table. Not right now. My mother checks the top of the piano for dust, brushing her fingers really slowly along the dark wood and inspecting.

"Maybe you should call Dad if you're so worried," I say.

She looks at me like I'm crazy, which I probably am.

"Your father? Like he'd have any idea what to do."

"Do you?" I ask.

"No."

"Oh. So it's up to me." I take a step down into the family room, imagine going over to my sister's house and putting a knife to Brian's throat. I say out loud, "Looked to me like somebody was getting a dirty deal. Just thought I'd cut in."

My mom snuffs in with her nose. "Is that a John Wayne quote?"

I shrug. "It's from *Haunted Gold.*"

Her voice rises. "What does that have to do with anything?"

"He'd know what to do," I say, sitting on the edge of the sofa, because it's true you would know what to do. The laptop is heavy on my lap. I stare at it.

"There are no heroes," she says, sitting up straight and pointing at me with the white pen she does her crossword puzzles with. "Got that? No men are heroes. Get my lighter for me?"

"John Wayne is a hero." I grab the lighter off the

kitchen counter and hand it to her. She looks so old all of a sudden. There are lines by her lips and her lipstick is smudged.

"John Wayne was a movie star. That's all." She lights up a cigarette and rolls her eyes. "The world has gone on fine without him. Why don't you go do your homework?"

The phone rings and she brightens up; literally leaps up from the chair she was too tired to move from before. "Maybe it's Mike."

She grabs it and I can tell by the way her voice softens that it is. No heroes, huh?

In the kitchen, I grab a bread knife and tuck it inside my pants pocket. I grab a steak knife too, and put it under my pillow, just in case.

Dear Mr. Wayne,

The man in my report, Hannah Dustin's husband, saved his children. Fleeing from a party of scalping Native Americans, he ushered seven of his children in front of him. He stood rear, shooting at the Native Americans who were intelligently hiding behind the trees and bushes. They shot back, but he had better aim. He did this shooting and running, shooting and running, for over a mile, pushing most of his hysterical family to safety, hurrying them on, giving them strength. He brought them to a house and guarded it. The Indians that were following him eventually left.

I can't find the name of the nation anywhere. I'll have to go the library to look in the encyclopedias there. I've already tried the Internet and came up with nothing.

Lord, were they angry though, running through the town, ready to kill anyone. I can understand that. It's what happens when you get pushed too far, and I expect those

Native Americans got pushed a lot. I can't believe Hannah Dustin is supposed to be a hero. Her husband is another story. That's a father.

If they made it into a movie, that would be your role. I can see you standing there, standing tall, shooting, aiming, protecting your children. You would know what to do.

Dear Mr. Wayne,

When my mother's gone to sleep, I creep into the kitchen. I grab the Tupperware cheese container out of the fridge and cut off a piece with a bread knife. It's not too easy to cut all the way through, and it comes off jagged. Next, I go over to the breadbox my father made before I was born. It was a birthday present for my mother one year. She thinks that's funny. He made her a breadbox for her birthday. I split the cheese up into little pieces and smoosh it between the bread. The way the yellow cheese breaks up the smooth brownness of the bread makes me think of my sister, Jessica. I don't know why. I don't know the why about anything. Sometimes you just have to let the gaps in your thinking come and not explore the connections, like why cheese in bread reminds you of your bruised sister.

Sitting on the stool by the phone, I eat all the bread and then I dial Jessica's number. Her husband answers.

"Hello? Hello?

His voice is low and thick with beer. I like how people's voices tell you what their soul is like. It makes life a little easier, I guess, but we get distracted by how they look and what they do, so we forget the clues of the voice.

I muffle my voice, try to make it like low and twangy, a John Wayne tough-guy voice. "Touch her again, you die."

I don't hang up the receiver. Instead, I disconnect the line. I reconnect it, call my father's number, and hope that my grandmother doesn't answer.

He picks up the phone and his voice is groggy from sleep. He goes to bed every night at nine.

"Hello?" he says. "Hello? Who is it?"

I hang up on him, too, just disconnect the line and then I feel so guilty it's all I can do not to call back. Instead, I go back to bed and try to think of ways to save the day, save my sister, but I fall asleep before I can even think of one. Some hero.

Dear Mr. Wayne,

I heard a story about when you were a kid in the California desert. You and your dog, Duke, had a paper route and there was this awful boy who called you girlie because your name was Marion. He beat you up. Those must have been some dire circumstances there. I have to tell you, I was shocked, Mr. Wayne, because I thought that you were always popular, a hero kind of man, not a get-smacked-around-and-called-girlie kind of man.

That didn't last long, though, did it?

Firefighters taught you how to use your fists, but you still avoided that bully for as long as you could. I respect you for that. I respect you for using your fists as a last resort. There aren't many men like that nowadays, but I think there are a lot of women, a lot of women who wouldn't know how to make a fist if their life depended on it.

It's also good to think that there's hope, you know, for

us people on the fringes. If a boy named Marion can grow up to be the Duke, well, anything's possible isn't it?

I would tell Nicole that story to make her feel better, but she's not a big fan, Mr. Wayne. She prefers those boy-band singers. The ones with the skinny hips and shoulders to match. The ones with those high voices. I don't think they should even count as men. No offense.

The reason I should tell her this story of yours is that Nicole thinks we have to be popular, and right now. This girl's got her finger on the trigger and it's twitching 'cause she's ready to shoot.

Nicole is determined that our popularity is not going to be a lost cause, like in *The Cowboys* when you had to take five hundred head of steer through bad country and all you had for cowhands were little boys. That was a good movie and a lost cause.

You die in that one. That should never have happened. You refused to back down to the bad guy, refused to turn around, and he shot you in the back, again and again, while all those little boys watched.

I hated that.

I think Nicole's popularity quest is probably a lost cause for me if Paolo Mattias has told everyone that he thinks my father is gay. It's hard to be popular when your dad wears ladies' panty hose, you know what I mean? I don't know if he's gay or not. I've never seen him with a boyfriend or anything, and he doesn't talk about guys being hot. I mean, he's a truck driver, right? Truck drivers can't be gay. Hairdressers are gay. Art directors are gay.

Right? Plus, maybe he's a straight cross-dresser not a gay cross-dresser, or something. Those exist.

Oh, God. Why does it matter?

If Paolo Mattias has gone blabbing like a weak-kneed hostage facing twenty-four banditos with guns, well, I just don't have a hope of being cool. Being cool is not the point when you're short like me, and your mom's got a man coming to see her and your sister's got a man hitting her and you've got no man at all.

I've still joined Students for Social Justice, Amnesty International, and the Modern Foreign Language Club, not because I want to be popular, but because I want to. I tell Nicole this at lunch. Students for Social Justice meets after school on Mondays, so I won't be able to talk to her on the phone today.

"What?" Nicole says. She spreads the cream cheese on her bagels in circles. It has to be perfect or else she won't eat. It all must be even, no lumps, no bumps, no thin spots. The spreading takes her forever, and I've usually finished my bagel by the time she starts hers. Still, it's nice to look at, like a bagel from a commercial, with little ridges in the cream cheese from the plastic knife the cafeteria worker gives her when she goes through the line.

"What?" Nicole says again, because I haven't answered. "You're not serious."

"Why not?" I say, sniffing the air. It smells like a pool in here, like bleach. They must have disinfected the whole cafeteria over the weekend. I sniff my bagel. It smells like plastic.

"Those are not popular-people clubs."

"And what are?" I ask. I pick up the metallic wrapper the cream cheese came in and put it on my paper plate. I yawn and stretch. I did not get enough sleep.

"Track. Or cheerleading," Nicole says. "You yawn like a cat. It's weird."

"I'm not doing any of those, except maybe theater," I say, pulling my legs out from behind the bench that's connected to the cafeteria table. I want to throw out my lunch stuff in the metal garbage can at the end of the table, just a few feet away. I keep talking while I'm walking. "I could never be a cheerleader. I'm not perky enough."

"Your boobs are."

"Jesus!"

Nicole laughs. "You can run."

"Not fast."

"Yeah, you can."

I throw my stuff away and sit down again. Running fast scares me. I can do it. I can do a mile in six minutes and twenty seconds. They timed us in eighth-grade gym, but to do it I have to pretend that something is chasing me, something scary and awful, and this feeling sucks into me as I run, this feeling of no escape. Everyone laughed at how fast I was, because I'm so short. "I'm not joining track."

I'm not. Riding a bike is so much better. With the wind in my hair I can pretend I'm flying a bomber in World War II, saving the world, or I'm riding a horse across the range, rescuing my family from bandits, or I'm in the streets of Massachusetts warning everyone that the British are coming. Running is not like that. Running is fear. Biking is power.

Nicole chews her bagel, thinking. "Do you want to be popular?"

"Sure."

I guess I do. I mean, I don't know. I'm not sure if I care, at least not the way Nicole does. In no-man's-land there's no such thing as popular, is there? Out in the desert, it's just you and the cactus and sun-bleached bones. I imagine jumping on a horse and walking the cattle across the prairie. I gaze across the cafeteria like it's my path through the fields. Who are the people to watch? Who are the cattle thieves? Who are the heroes? A football player by a table near the soda machines throws a Coke can at his friend like it's a beer in a saloon. The friend catches it in his hand. Bang. Smile.

Mary Bilodeau walks by with her bag lunch. She waves at me and smiles. I give her a little wave back. Nicole snorts out her disgust.

"You don't want to be a big loser all your life?" Nicole asks me. When I don't answer, she says. "Hello, Lily. This is earth."

"No, of course not," I say and try to pay attention. I spread my thumb and first finger on my forehead. "Do I have a scarlet *L* on my forehead?"

Nicole laughs like I knew she would and says, "No, but you might if you don't join track and keep smiling back at Mary Bilodeau."

"Is this according to your brother?" I'm angry now. I

pull change out of my pocket to see if I have enough for a Coke. That Coke machine waves at me like a giant red oasis in the middle of the Nevada desert. I've got a sore thirst. "He's not in track, is he?"

Hannah Dustin's daughters had five brothers. I don't have one. I can't imagine being Nicole and having someone there all the time leaving jock straps everywhere, shaving and burping and tormenting my old Barbie dolls, maybe shooting at crows with a BB gun.

"Yes," Nicole says. She fidgets with her hair, pulling strands of it over her ear. "I'm joining."

"No offense," I say and look over at where Nicole's brother is sitting with Travis Poppins at a table of eleventh grade jerks. They shoot quarters across the table at each other, two of their fingers on each hand forming pretend hockey goals. "But your brother isn't exactly the most popular boy in the whole world."

"It's by choice," Nicole says, flipping her hair back over her shoulder. "He's above that."

"Oh, right. And I'm not," I say, and Nicole opens her mouth to answer but I get up to get a Coke. I have enough money. In fact, I have a nickel extra. I murmur, "Saddle up."

When I walk by Christopher, Nicole's brother, who I do not want to walk by, Travis nudges him and he says in this stupid cowpoke voice, "Hi, Liliana."

"Hi."

"You popular yet?" Travis Poppins asks. I'm so close to him I can count the pimples on his nose: seven.

"More than you," I shoot back. Bang.

It's like you said in *Rio Bravo*, Mr. Wayne: I don't like a lot of things. I don't like it when a stupid boy makes fun of me. I don't like it when people know what I want. I don't like it that Nicole told her brother we're trying to be popular and that he told his friend. Some things people do should just be kept to their fool selves.

I make it to the Coke machine and punch the button to get the Coke. When I walk back to the table, I take the long way around. I see the boy who had the red pants, Mr. Fire Man. He smiles at me. I smile back. Next to him is Paolo Mattias. He smiles at me too and says, "Hi."

My heart stops, but I give him a slow nod the way you would, Mr. Wayne. I am cool. I am not a cowpoke. But I'm squeezing my Coke can and with each squeeze, I'm thinking, "Yes. Yes. Yes. Yes."

And my feet are having a hard time not doing some happy little Irish jig on the ugly over-waxed linoleum floor.

Must be cool. Must be cool.

When I sit down Nicole asks, "You mad at me?"

"No," I say, smiling big because I'm not any more. But I don't tell her about her beloved crush, Fire Man, with his hair that looks like a gaggle of pigeons nested in it, two tables down from us, breathing the same air we do, maybe. Since we've never seen him before, he must be from Hancock or Trenton or Aurora, one of those feeder towns that come to our high school because they aren't big enough to have their own.

And I don't tell Nicole about how I felt inside when Paolo Mattias said hello.

Maybe, if my father *is* gay, he wouldn't care? Maybe this boy has more going for him then I've given him credit for. You've got to let a man show his worth, right, Mr. Wayne? You've got to give him room to do the right thing.

Josiah Murphy, a junior football player, starts hooting and jumps up on the table to do a little pelvic salute to the fluorescent lights. He dances in a circle and stomps while the other guys all holler out, "Get a babe. Get a babe."

They try to pull Caitelyn Crowley up on the maroon tabletop with him, but she shrieks and runs away, which is good because now I don't have to save her.

But the football players don't give up.

"Get a fag. Get a fag," they start chanting and Josiah points to Daniel Labelle, who everyone has known would be gay since he turned up at first-grade show-and-tell in Mrs. Kinsley's class with a Barbie and Ken doll set, and he'd made them matching white disco outfits all by himself. Ken's outfit had more tassels on it than Barbie's.

Anyway, Daniel doesn't want to be saved.

Daniel shrugs and waves and yells, "Hi girls" to the boys. But before he gets yanked up on the table, the lunch monitor comes and Josiah jumps back down and laughs. His friends each give him a buck and high fives.

Yeah, like Paolo Mattias wouldn't care, Mr. Wayne? Sometimes I think I'm more deluded than a fat member of the Donner party.

Saddle up.

After the Students for Social Justice meeting, I get a ride home with Sasha Sandeman's sister, who is a senior. Olivia wears Indian-print shirts and batik skirts and sandals. She drives a Volkswagen bug, lavender, which is probably the coolest car ever. She calls it the Love Mobile.

Yes, I know, it is not exactly a John Wayne car. I can't imagine you even getting your legs inside of it, but I'm short and it seems perfect to me. I am a girl.

All the way to my house, we talk about Darfur, Iraq, China, and theater stuff. Their mom's the director at the Palace Theater. Sasha's one of those really peppy people; she's pretty popular, actually, in a hippie-cute kind of way. She has black hair and freckles. My mother says she's perky. Not her breasts. Her personality. We weren't really close when we went to middle school, but we always said hi and everything. She's in a couple of my classes now.

When I climb out of the car, Olivia says, "Are you going to go to the Amnesty International meeting on Wednesday?"

"Yeah," I say, leaning over Sasha to talk to Olivia.

"You have nice breath," Sasha says and smiles. I don't know what to say. Sasha's always blurting things like that, tiny compliments, like you have eyes the color of peonies, or you have the best socks. It's part of her Spreading Kindness Campaign.

"Want a ride home from that too?" Olivia asks me.

"That would be great."

"Cool," Sasha says. "We could just give you rides every

day so you don't have to do the bus thing, which is way too bourgeois for you.

"Cool." I shut the door and they turn their car around at the top of the driveway. *Cool*, I think. *Cool*.

They honk the horn and I wave. The car has a cute horn, just a little tooty beep. I want a car like that. Back in middle school, Sasha and I had the same homeroom in seventh grade and we used to salute the world when we were supposed to pledge allegiance to the flag. We'd put our hands on our shoulders and mumble that we pledged allegiance to the world, to all countries and people, for peace and justice. No one ever noticed. I should start doing that again. I wonder why we weren't close in eighth grade. Different classes, I guess. It's crazy how what classes you have determines your whole life when you're in middle school. And it's all so arbitrary, just some principal randomly picking names and potentially ruining your whole year, if not your whole life.

But I don't care about this now because I'm in high school, and you can pick classes and clubs yourself, sort of. Well, you can as long as Nicole's not barking over your shoulder like some feral dog about being popular and how Students for Social Justice is lame and just for wannabe hippies.

I am almost skipping when I skedaddle up the walk to the back porch. The trees in the yard look like they're getting ready to turn colors, to turn brilliant. Maybe I will be like those leaves. Maybe I'm about to change from ordinary green to something exuberant. One of the granite slabs of the walk isn't level and I stumble a little and almost fall, like some giddy five-year-old. Imagine if I skinned my knee. It serves me right for being happy. I think of my sister's face and my father's blue tights. I think of my mother's man coming.

All the happy fizzles out.

Inside, I put my backpack on the kitchen table and think about calling Nicole. Fire Man was in the Social Justice club and I know his real name: Tyler Reed. He seems pretty nice too. Not Nicole's type. She usually goes for sturdy jocks, football types not the leaner soccer players, guys whose arms fill out the tops of their shirt sleeves and make them seem like they're going to rip.

The phone rings and I jump, my fists up and ready to fight. Then I feel stupid, because I'm ready to haul a little nasty on a telephone. I pick it up. It's probably Nicole.

"Liliana?"

It's my grandmother. My father's mother.

"Hi, Grammy."

Grammy is eighty-seven. She lives with my dad.

"I want you to be nice to your father, Liliana."

"Uh-huh." I look around. I turn to look out the window. There are no bandits out there, skulking behind the trees with their rifles ready. Darn.

"He loves you."

"Uh-huh."

"He's a good man."

"Yep," I say and twirl the phone cord between my fingers, think about getting a knife and cutting the line.

"He loves you."

"I love you, Grammy."

"Oh," she says and this stops her for a minute. "Next time you see your father, have him bring you to the house. I'll make you a pie."

"Okay."

"Remember, he's a good man."

"I know, Grammy."

"Good. He sometimes tries to call you and he gets the numbers mixed up and quits trying."

"Okay." I yank my fingernails out of my mouth because I've been biting them.

"And sometimes, I know, he forgets to feed you."

"Yep." I twirl the phone cord around my index finger and pull it tight so that it makes marks, little grooves to remember it by.

"Men are like that. It means nothing. It means nothing about love."

And she hangs up. I look at the phone in my hand. There's nothing on the other end. She's always like that, just hanging up. She thinks that if she says goodbye that someone will die, whoever she's talking to, she thinks. Because if there is a God, which she doubts but then thinks is possible when she looks at the beauty of nature, God would make sure it was she who wouldn't die, because God knows she wants to, and needs to; she's just an ugly burden to us all.

Actually, Grammy isn't ugly at all. She's old, and her skin is like tissue paper that's been crumpled up after Christmas and then flattened out to use the next year, easily ripped and full of wrinkles, but her eyes are violet and beautiful. She reads two books a day and can quote almost anyone, Milton, Nietzsche, Goethe, political scientists I've never heard of, you name it. My father says it's hard to be the dumb son of a bright woman, but that it's harder for his mother, who has no one to talk to now that she won't leave the house because she thinks she's too ugly and old for the world to see.

Grammy is always calling and saying things like this. Or else she just calls and cries into the phone, telling me she's too old to live, she wants to die. No one should have to live this long. I like it better when she gets on me about my father. She says she's Moravian. We all have depression in our genes. It's the melancholy of the Czech region, of mountains blocking the sun and invaders ready to run down into villages, striking down anyone in their way and changing their country's name.

After I hang up with Grammy, I look for a snack. On the refrigerator, a note waits. I've attached it here, Mr. Wayne, so that you can analyze my mother's handwriting if you want to. Although I'm sure you have better things to do.

Liliana,

Please polish all the glasses if you have a chance. I

want them to look nice when Mike comes. I love you. I'd tell you to do your homework, but I know you will. Please thaw some meatballs for supper.

Love, Mom

Polish glasses? How do you polish glasses?

Dear Mr. Wayne,

I have been working on my report.

Hannah Dustin was born Hannah Webster Emerson. She named her first daughter Hannah too. That seems pretty egotistical to me. Imagine if my mother had named me Rita. God, my whole life I'd be condemned by my mother's name. Jessica had it bad enough. No one is named Jessica anymore. Although maybe I shouldn't be blaming the mothers; maybe it wasn't Hannah's choice. Maybe it was her husband's idea.

I could see it being your idea, if you were her husband. You would see the baby, pick her up in just one of your big hands, and smile. The camera would close-frame your face and the baby's. The baby would coo or grab your finger with her tiny digits.

"Beautiful just like her mother," you'd announce. "We'll name her Hannah."

She couldn't argue with that.

But how do they know which Hannah her father called for when he ran out of the house with his children? Did he yell all his children's names as he ran? When he yelled "Hannah!" did the first Hannah, the mother, know that it wasn't for her he was yelling? She was too sick from childbirth to run. She would slow them all down. Sacrifice them all. Did she tell him, "Go. Go quickly without me. Leave me here to be slaughtered. Save yourself. Save our children. Go." And did they kiss a long kiss, even in front of all those children, knowing it was their last? Or did he say, "Come, Hannah" and she stayed in bed because she didn't know which Hannah he meant?

Dear Mr. Wayne,

When I was a really little kid, I used to think that I wasn't human somehow. Maybe I was a changeling baby like they talk about in Ireland. You know the whole thing. Fairies sneak into the hospital and switch babies, snatching the human baby beneath their wings and leaving in its place a fairy baby. Or maybe while she was sleeping, my mother was artificially inseminated by a UFO alien and I was the result: half human and half alien.

That's how I feel now, trying out for *South Pacific*: half alien. Like I don't belong on this planet and everyone is about to discover what I really am: a freak.

I can't believe this is supposed to make me popular. Although I guess it worked for you, Mr. Wayne. Although you were a big football star first. Right? But before that, before all that, you were just Marion, a boy with a paper route who had a dog named Duke.

Nicole is not trying out.

She glared at me in English class. "Are you kidding?"

"Why not?" I asked her. "You'd be good."

She rolled her eyes and leaned over across the aisle, and spoke to me like I was a mentally deficient five-year-old. "If I didn't get a part, I would be an automatic loser. That would completely derail the popularity train."

I stared at her. Stuart Silsby, who sits in front of me, turned around and gave me disgusted eyes and sang really loud, "Love, Love, My Poo."

"Oh, mature..."

He laughed. "Liliana eat a banana."

"Brilliant. Stuart is capable of rhyming," I said, shaking my head.

He switched to a manly man voice. "I'm capable of a lot of things, baby."

I shuddered, and when he turned around Nicole said, "He so likes you."

I eyed him.

He turned his head so we could make eye contact, and mouthed "eat a banana" again.

"Bananas have too many calories," I told him.

"Like you need to worry about that," he snapped back. He patted his stomach. "Me, on the other hand..."

Nicole hiked up her skirt to show more thigh. Stuart noticed and rolled his eyes. I tried not to laugh but it was hard. Nicole glared at me, like it's all my fault. I leaned towards her.

"Try out with me," I begged her.

"No way."

Scene over.

No matter how wimpy she is, I wish she were here trying out with me, because then I could laugh at all the nasty things she'd say about everyone. Sasha is not nasty. Sasha is supportive, which just makes me more nervous because that makes it all seem life-or-death important.

We sit in the back of the auditorium, which is sea green and smells like basement, wet and moldy. On the other side of Sasha, Stuart Silsby jitters his leg. He's tiny, maybe only four feet eleven inches tall. He's probably the only boy I know who hasn't grown yet. Back in second grade when we had our class pictures taken, he was the boy mothers always pointed to and asked who he was and commented on. He wore a tie and a button-down shirt for the picture and smiled like a flashbulb. He's still like that, all showy and confident and full of cornball jokes, but no one thinks he's hot stuff anymore because he's so short.

We're in ninth grade now, Mr. Wayne, and I do feel like a baby, all nervous and anxious with my palms sweating despite the kisses Sasha plants on the top of my head. She'll be a good mother

I try to think about how you would be here, just confident, ambling into the theater, standing tall. But Sasha keeps kissing the top of my head for good luck, distracting me.

"This is what my mother does," she says in a big drama-important voice.

I nod my head. "Uh-huh."

"No, seriously. She does it for luck. It calms you down. There's this super-important chakra there."

"You don't need luck."

"Of course I do!'

"You get every lead."

"That was in middle school. We're in the big leagues now."

"Then I should be stage manager and not try out."

"Liliana Faltin!"

"What?"

"You are not stage manager material anymore. Plus, you've never tried out." She shakes her head at me. "Do you remember when I taught you how to cheat at poker in the greenroom?"

I nod.

"Distract the boys with your eyes, blink at them, put your hand on their arm," she'd say. "They can't handle that. Then you slip an ace into your lap or you take a couple extra."

Man, she was good. She'd be one of those women in the saloons, drinking with the boys and taking them for all they're worth, you know. They'd write in the movie trailer: *And Sasha Sandeman plays Belle Monday, the scarlet woman with a heart of gold. And a purse full of gold, too…*

What would I be?

Woman # 4 in crowd, cringing.

We watch people audition. First we do the mono-logues, then we all come back one at a time at night and sing. Sasha comments on people while we wait our turn, and her criticisms seem nice almost.

"Oh, no presence. How sad, but nice articulation," she whispers behind her hands.

Or about Alyssa Cutler, of all people: "Good diction. No volume."

I'm antsy and going crazy and feel like I'm all holed up in jail, guarding some prisoner, and I know that at any second the outlaws are going to come, rifles blazing, and try to break their buddy out. There's nothing I can do but wait for the action to happen, and my nerves are shot to hell, like I need a stiff shot of tequila or something.

Then it happens. They call my name, and with me they call Stuart Silsby.

Sasha stands up with me, grabs my hands in hers and whispers, "I had a baby brother who got his head stuck in the crib and died. My mom heard him crying and everything and couldn't get his head out of the bars in time."

I stare at her. Her big brown eyes are almost crying. There's so much pain in there.

She nods real slow and kisses me on my chakra, then pushes me away.

"He died," she says. "Go."

I trot up the steps and my shaking hand takes a script from Mrs. Gallagher, the director. I stand across from Stuart and I feel almost dead inside, just numb and full of ache. I say all my lines and I say them loud enough, but I forget to act. All I can think about is Sasha's baby brother's head stuck between the bars of his crib and his mother trying to save him. I read the lines, but my lips tremble because I'm thinking of Mrs. Sandeman's face when she knows there's no hope. I say the lines and I am Nellie, the nurse in *South Pacific*, and I'm telling Emile—Stuart—that I can't stay with him. We can't get married. I have to go. I think of babies. I think of my sister's bruised face. It's all too sad. I cry, long streams of tears escape my eyes and slip down my cheeks. Stuart stares at me like I'm the biggest loser in the world. I can't believe Sasha's baby brother died.

When we're done, Mrs. Gallagher goes, "Good. Good."

She claps her hands together like we're dogs and she's trying to get us to come. I put my face in my hands. I cannot believe I cried. Some cowboy. I look up, determined to get the hell off the stage. At the back of the auditorium, Sasha bounces up and down like a cheerleader. This is something she would never be. She says it's too degrading. I agree, I think, but I'd like to be able to do all those splits and back handsprings. Sasha gives me the thumbs-up sign and starts winking like crazy. She looks so happy. Why is she so happy? Her little brother is dead. I run down the aisle back to her.

"You did it!" she whisper-screams into my ear. "You were awesome. I knew it! I knew it!"

She elbows Stuart Silsby in the gut as he gives her this look like she's cream gravy, trying to get him to agree, but he's completely clueless.

"I know I was," he says, tilting his chin up in the air and sticking it out like some sort of nerdy version of Superman.

He puts his hands on his hips, just like the Man of Steel and everything.

Sasha pouts and shakes her head before she starts smiling all over again. "Not you, silly. Lily. She was so good. She cried. Did you see her cry?"

I gape at Sasha and say real slow, "You thought I done good?"

The way I say it sounds like you, but Sasha doesn't notice.

"I'm just so happy!" she bubbles and tries to elbow Stuart again, but he's moved away.

Mrs. Gallagher is clapping her hands for quiet, because she's done taking notes on Stuart and me and is ready to call up two more to the stage, so I lower my voice and lean into Sasha asking, "Sasha. How can you be so happy when your baby brother...when he...when he's...you know...dead?"

"Of course he's not dead, you silly goof." She gives me a huge smile and a giant hug. "It was a trick. My way of helping you get into the scene. Don't you see?"

Before I get to ask her what the hell she's talking about, she hops up to the stage because her name has been called. She gets a happy, comic scene to try out. Mrs. Gallagher alternates happy scenes with sad. Stuart and I watch her and forget to blink, she's so good. We laugh at her. So does everyone else. Sasha Sandeman.

"One day she's going to be a star," Stuart whispers to me as we watch her lanky body do an impromptu one-handed back handspring as she holds a script in one hand and says her lines.

"I know," I say, because it has to be true. And it takes me a minute to realize that I'm talking to Stuart Silsby again; the boy I'm supposed to still be hating from seventh grade. I guess it's all because of Sasha and all her visualize world peace/love each other stuff. What good am I at trying to end wars in Africa or freeing Tibet if I, myself, can't even stop hating Stuart Silsby?

"You were good up there," I whisper to him, still watching Sasha.

"Thank you," he says, lifting up the collar of his shirt. "I know."

I look at him with my eyebrows up kissing my hairline, a look that's meant to say, *you're an obnoxious jerk*.

He smiles, a car salesman smile, and says, "You were good too."

✦

Everyone else goes home. I pretend like I have a ride and hide out by the soccer field under the bleachers. I whisper-sing my song over and over again for hours. I practice it and practice it. My dad used to sing this song all the time when I was little, way back before my parents even got divorced. It's about being corny like Kansas in August and loving this wonderful guy. I can still remember him twirling me around the living room, giggling.

That was a long time ago.

I'm the first one up. Nobody else is even in the hallway waiting yet, because we signed up for time slots.

"Go ahead," says the woman who's in charge of music. "Come in and let me hear you. Liliana, right?"

"Right."

"Good job earlier. Let's hear if you can sing."

I pull myself up onto the stage, ignoring the stairs. I open my mouth and the notes come out, playing into the darkness, loud and true as gunshots. They drill their way into everything.

"Good," she says when I'm done. "Good. Send the next one in."

I open the auditorium door. Sasha gives me five and rushes in.

"I'm here! I'm here!" she says. The door shuts behind her. I wait for her. She'll give me a ride home.

At home, there's another note on the refrigerator:

He's coming tonight. Please vacuum. And dust. And heat up the spaghetti I left in the fridge. Don't forget to wash the dishes. Please. And throw away this note, too. We'll be in around nine.

Love, Mom

Warmed-up spaghetti. Oh boy, that sounds good. Not. No

mention of doing my homework either. She must really be excited. I go to the hall closet and pull out the vacuum. When I plug it in, sparks of electricity fly from the outlet and I get shocked by the bursts of white and blue. I close my eyes and see the red of my lids. All the colors of the flag.

"Damn it."

I look around like there's someone there who saw the whole thing, but I'm alone. I close my eyes and hear wild horses stampeding towards the house. They're getting closer, closer... they'll trample me. I have to think of a diversion. I hold up the vacuum and point it at the picture window. "Back! Back!"

Sometimes I am so weird I can't handle myself.

I thump the vacuum back on the floor, pull the plug back out and look at the rug in the living room. In the family room. Fine. Hall. Fine. Guest room. Fine except for a piece of maroon blanket lint, which I pick up with my fingers and put in the pocket of my pants because I'm too lazy to put it in the trash. My room and my mother's room are okay too, I guess, but he won't be going in there so it doesn't matter, right? Yep. Right. Let's say that sometimes my mom is a flannel-mouthed liar where men are concerned.

As I get the dustrag and polish, the phone rings. I jump.

"Liliana?"

It's my sister.

"You going to be there awhile?" she asks.

"Uh-huh," I say.

"I'm coming over."

"Okay."

"I'll be there in ten minutes," she says and hangs up.

I hang up too. I put the dustrag and polish down on the kitchen table. I have ten minutes to do my homework before she comes. I can always dust while she's here and maybe she'll help. Panic settles in near my heart like I've got indigestion, and I don't know if it's about my homework or if it's about my sister and whether or not she'll have another bruise, or if she knows that I called her husband and threatened him. But I disguised my voice. Nobody could tell, right?

I haul out my vocabulary sheet and the dictionary and start pumping out definitions. I've just finished my geometry when she comes in. There are no new bruises, which is a damn good thing, or one ugly fellow might have lost an appendage, and it isn't one you write with or walk on, if you catch my meaning.

"I'm worried about Mom," Jessica says and she pulls her hand through her hair and some of the strands break off. She used to have beautiful chestnut hair, hippie hair, long and straight and as thick as algae, but she's cut it off and had Brian's cousin perm it a few times, so now it's almost orange like she's a 1980s woman; it's kind of the color of rust, and split-ended and so brittle that it cracks when you touch it. She doesn't have bangs either because Brian hates bangs. And she doesn't wear makeup because only tramps wear makeup. All that macho stuff.

"Liliana," she repeats, turning on the faucet to get herself some water, "I said I was worried about Mom."

"Mom's worried about you," I say and then bite my lip. Saddle up.

She drinks the water in gulps and puts the glass on the counter. "I don't want to talk about that now."

"How come?" I pick up the rag and squirt some fizzy polish stuff on the kitchen table. I work the foam around in circles, making it as shiny as a mahogany bar on the set of one of your movies.

She glares at me, outlaw eyes. "I just don't. *I'm* worried about *Mom*."

"How come?" I ask again, same words, different question.

"Because of that man coming." Her voice breaks a little, making her seem more damsel-in-distress than outlaw. Her hands are red and flaky. She gets eczema when she's stressed.

I look away from her hands and focus on my own, stalling for time. "Mike O'Donnell?"

"Uh-huh."

She refills her glass and gulps the water down the same way dad does, and her throat is so skinny I can see her Adam's apple bob up and down when she swallows, like a man.

"You've met him before, haven't you?" I ask. I try not to look at her old jaw bruise, but it's there like a neon sign, flashing at me.

"Yeah, when I was a kid."

"You remember him?"

"No. Not really. He was tall. Weird blue eyes."

"So why are you worried?"

"I just don't think she knows what she's getting herself into."

"Oh."

"I mean he's staying here with you. He has family. Why isn't he staying with them?"

"Maybe some people don't like staying with their families," I say, thinking of how awful it was to stay with her and Brian when I was little, with him yelling at everything all the time.

She grabs another rag from beneath the sink and I pass her the polish. We walk into the living room to do the end tables and coffee table and she says, "I think he wants Mom's money."

"What money?"

"That's just it. There is no money, but he probably thinks she has some."

"Why?"

"That's what these men are like. And she has the house. She could sell it."

"Jessica." I take the polish back and squirt the end table. "You don't really think that."

She nods. "Brian does."

I move the lamp from the table and mutter, "Brian doesn't know everything."

This is for sure, because he doesn't even know how to be a man. No man who hits his wife does. Right?

Jessica's face tightens up, and she looks like she's about to run away like a buffalo who's just seen a hunting party on the horizon, so I add, "I think he just has a crush on her."

"I hope so," she says and rubs along the sides of the coffee table, sticking the rag in the crack where the leaf drops, moving it slow and hard to get out all the dirt.

"I tried out for a play today," I say because this seems safe, like something that won't make her run. "A musical."

"Good. Good." Wet drops of sweat, tiny but visible, show up at the edges of her hair and she rubs. "I'm pregnant. But don't tell Mom. I don't want her to know yet. I'm not far along."

"Oh." My voice comes out weak, like a whisper, because it can't get louder than my heart, which has started thumping in my chest louder and more serious than a herd of spooked steers.

I stare at her stomach. It looks flat. How could there be a baby in there?

"Don't you want to congratulate me?"

I think of Sasha's little brother and his head stuck in the bars of the crib, even if that wasn't really true. What if that happens to Jessica's baby?

"I'm sorry." I leave the living room, go into the kitchen and drop the rag into the sink. It splashes me; suds cling to my hands and shirt like tears.

She comes thundering after me. "What do you mean you're sorry?"

"It's just..."

How do I tell her, my sister, who has wanted a baby her entire life, that I'm afraid of what will happen? That this baby means she will never leave Brian. That it will become Brian.

She whips me around by my shoulder and I look up at her face. It's red. It's almost crying.

"What. Do. You. Mean?" she asks again, each word a bullet that makes my courage recoil with the backlash.

I do not saddle up.

I reach around and hug my sister. I can feel her spine. "I mean congratulations. I'm sorry I can't hug you right. My hands are wet."

I move away and smile at her. She smiles back. She looks happy with her mouth and worried with her eyes, but the water does not spill onto her cheeks.

"You'll make a great mother," I say.

"You think so?"

"Yeah."

Dear Mr. Wayne,

Because my sister is the type to worry, and it isn't good for her, I don't tell her some things.

My mom says that if my sister keeps fretting about everything like Mike O'Donnell or the way Brian scowls at me, or the eczema problems, she will give herself at the very least an ulcer, or maybe even cancer. My mother says there is a definite link between cancer and stress.

People who are pregnant aren't supposed to worry, either. It can hurt the baby.

So I don't tell my sister about what I'm worrying about, which isn't whether or not this Mike guy has a crush on my mother. It's about whether he's really a bad hombre who killed a man in a bar. The little stress lines appear between my eyebrows because of those boxes he sent and the headlines.

I don't tell her that I worry her baby will die like Sasha

Sandeman pretended her baby brother did, or that I'm afraid that Dad is gay. I don't tell her I'm worried that the letters and emails I write to congressmen just get thrown away while people die and rot in their jail cells without even a tin cup to clang on the bars like in *Rio Grande*.

I don't tell her I'm worried that I'll never be good enough for anything, or that her husband will beat her and then beat her baby.

I don't tell her anything. I don't tell anyone. Just you.

Dear Mr. Wayne,

When my stepfather died, he did it when we were having lobsters and steamed clams at my Aunt Shirleen's. She's really rich, the kind of rich that wears big diamonds and has whirlpools instead of bathtubs. When my stepfather died my mother cried for a long time, and held me all night, sighing, "What am I going to do now? What will we do? Who will love us?"

All that sort of stuff. All I remember about it are those sentences she kept repeating and being smashed against her chest as we slept in a twin bed downstairs at Aunt Shirleen's. All I remember was being suffocated against my mother's breasts as she cried and wondering how babies who are breast-fed can stand it, being that close, so close that every breath you take in through your nose smells completely of your mother, obliterating everything else.

That's how I feel now, suffocating, everything smelling

of one thing: Mike O'Donnell's arrival. My sister has gone off to see her stupid husband with the meaty hands, and I've eaten my leftover spaghetti. I've called Nicole and talked until her mother made her get off the phone. I would call Sasha, but she doesn't like talking on the phone unless it's necessary. She prefers to talk in person so she can see what the person does while they talk, see what movements they make, where their eyes go, whether they look blank or startled. She says people can lie on the phone too easily. I think she just likes studying people so that she can use it in her acting.

When my stepfather died, it was the first time my mother was without a man there to tell her what to do, which bills to pay first; without a man to hold her and snore her to sleep each night. She started dating my stepfather before she divorced my father. She once bragged to me that she's never been without a boyfriend for over a week. It's been three hard years since my stepdad died, and that's a long time to be single for a woman whose previous record was a week. She's had dates, of course, and some men lasted a month, but it wasn't the same thing. I think about this and how my mother must feel as lonely as I do right now, sitting in the living room, all my homework done, the encyclopedia open to the entry about Hannah Dustin. There's nothing on television and it's too late to call anyone because it's a school night. I've already watched one of your movies tonight: *She Wore a Yellow Ribbon*. My mom says I only get one movie a night on school nights.

Mr. Wayne, please don't ever show this letter to my

mother because she'd kill me. Although, you're dead, so of course you can't show her the letter. What am I talking about? God, Nicole is right. I am a freak.

My dad sent the child support check yesterday. My mom ripped it open with the edge of her nail, just sliding it through the paper, the same way she opens Christmas presents. She smiled and sighed and then her face turned all hard. "That man is so dumb, how could I have ever married him?"

My lips tightened and my eyes narrowed, the way yours do when you see a cattle thief making his way into the saloon, and I said, "He's not dumb."

"He switched around the numbers and he spelled 'hundred' wrong. Plus, how late is this check?" She arched her eyebrows at me, turned her back and put the check in her wallet. "What would you call it then?"

"Forgetful," I said.

She turned back around and pulled me to her, wrapping me up in one of those big hugs of hers, and said, "That's all fine and good, except when he forgets about my baby."

Since she couldn't see me, I rolled my eyes.

Did you ever not get a part? Were you always the star?

It is ten o'clock and still my mother and Mike O'Donnell aren't here. It's so dark outside. My cat, Fandango, hops up on my lap and with my fingers I separate the colors of her fur; orange, black, white, gray. We sit on the mushy chair in the living room, looking out the picture window at the car headlights that drive down Jenkins Road, waiting for one of them to turn into the driveway, for my mother and this man she likes to come home, but none do and pretty soon I fall asleep just like Fandango. My head slumps forward, so that when I wake up my neck will ache and have a crick.

"Honey, wake up, Mike's here."

Someone touches my shoulder, and my head jerks up and my eyes open, but everything is blurry like my eyes are still asleep and can't remember how to focus even though my brain is alert and ready for action. I can make out the shape of my mother's head in front of me and I smell her breath, boozy. I don't know what kind of alcohol it is, but it stinks like when Sam Quinn brought that bottle of vermouth to Blackwoods Campground at Acadia National Park on our eighth grade trip. I don't think it's vermouth. The only things I've ever seen my mother drink are Black Russians, and only then on Christmas and New Year's.

There's this tall, tall man beside her and I say, "Mr. Wayne?"

She laughs, and all her smelly booze breath smashes into my face and makes me cough.

Back when I was in third grade, my stepdad converted my sister's old bedroom, which was a garage before that, into a family room. He put big barn beams on the ceiling and painted the shingles on one wall red, and then he put in a Franklin stove and a bar that runs across the south wall. The bar has all kinds of bottles behind it. Thirty or so. Maybe thirty, and my mom never touches them. She's just not much of a drinker, so I especially can't imagine her guzzling vermouth.

"Say hello to Mike," she says, pulling her head away from mine. I gulp to get fresh air. "Mike, this is Liliana."

"Pleased to meet you, little lady," he says and sticks out his hand for me to shake. I grab it and it is cold and dry, like holding Italian bread that's been cooked too long, flaky.

"Hi," I say and roll my head away.

I can't believe I thought he was you when he came in. I had just been dreaming that we were out roping steers on the range and there were these convicts who were about to shoot you dead, right through the heart, but I flung myself off my stallion and grabbed your waist, pulling you down just in time. Then I had my rifle, aimed and cocked, ready, and you pulled me behind a rock and said, "Thank you, little lady."

Then they came home. I wish I could go back to my dream. I like dreams.

"A real beauty just like her mother," this Mike O'Donnell man says, eyeing me. I curl my lip.

"She's still half asleep," my mom whispers, and smiles like I'm a cute little dog.

"She should get to bed," he says, "not sleep here on a chair."

"I was waiting for you," I say and look at Mike O'Donnell's face, now that my eyes are focusing. I have to look up high.

This man she brings home is tall, Mr. Wayne, way more than a foot taller than my mom, which means he's about six three, almost as tall as you.

I rub my neck, which aches from sleeping wrong, and continue. "I'm glad you got in safe."

"We stopped at the Back Room. That's why we're a little late and we saw lots of people there, which held us up of course and they didn't have the fastest service tonight," my mom says, kissing me on the head as I get out of the chair. She explains too much. She always does if she's had anything to drink. Her talk gets all yappy and chatty like one of those little dogs, the kind that wear rhinestone collars and tiny sweaters and love to bite. I'm glad she doesn't drink much. I guess she can be the diminutive doggy now.

I shrug. "I need to go to bed."

"Good idea," Mike O'Donnell says, his voice all mosey. "Get your beauty sleep so one day you can be as pretty as your mom here."

"Uh-huh," I say while my mom blushes.

She actually says, "Oh, Mike."

She puts her hand on his arm, all flirty, just like Nicole does when she likes someone. Nicole says body language can tell you a lot, like if you sit next to a guy and your legs touch and it feels hot where your legs touch, that means he's attracted to you. I try not to think about my mother's leg touching Mike O'Donnell's.

Mike O'Donnell actually bends down to kiss me too, touches his lips to my hair. I turn my head down to look at the floor so he doesn't get my cheek. His booze breath reeks, but it has this gum smell over it, like he's trying to pretend it doesn't smell, like his breath is cinnaminty clean and he's not totally roostered. His eyes are the bluest I've ever seen, bluer than my father's, and they have a yellow tint to them like the booze has got him full as a tick and the gin is trying to find a way to leak out. His eyes look like my mother's eyes when she cries. He wears a suit. Why would he wear a suit? He wore a suit on a plane, like some businessman. Or is it for the date he had with my mother? No one wears a suit to the Back Room.

I am too tired to think about it. In my room, I shut the door and put my nightgown on.

Tonight I will not brush my teeth. I flop into bed and reach over to set my alarm. It is 2:19 a.m. My mother's never been home this late. What time did she say they'd get here? Nine? Ten? I am too exhausted to remember.

I stare at the ceiling for a long time. I close my eyes. I hear them giggling in the living room. I hear his voice forget to be quiet once in a while and boom out sentences or phrases while my mother says sweetly, "Hush. Mike, please. Liliana's sleeping."

But I'm not sleeping. I'm closing my eyes and listening to my mother giggle, waiting for them to go to sleep. He will be sleeping right next to my room. I hear footsteps, hushed guffaws, a few all-out donkey-snort laughs, the kind you make when you laugh while you're eating and snarf out all your food, and then I hear one door close. I wait for the other. Nothing. Figures.

Snuggling onto my side, I push my head into my pillow, a fluffy pillow. I hate flat pillows, can't stand sleeping on them at Nicole's house. Has Mike O'Donnell brought his own pillow? Does he have a preference?

I'm about to sleep. I feel that wasteland quality come over me, like I'm being shrouded or walking in a heavy fog or have taken cold medicine, but I jerk awake. I hear something. Not a giggle. Not a sentence or a phrase. A moan.

A moan.

A ghost?

No, it's a human moan. His moan. Deep and low. Not my mother's. And in my mother's room, behind my closet, her bed squeaks. One squeak. Another. Another. A moan. My mother's moan now. *Oh my God.*

Dear Mr. Wayne,

You know, it isn't like I think my mother is a virgin or anything. I'm not that stupid. Not like Katie Henderson who thought that her mother got pregnant by sitting on the toilet after her father went pee. She believed that until eighth grade when we finally had health class and a unit on reproduction. I, however, know my mother has had sex. I am here, right? And she had sex with my stepfather too. Of course she did. But, this guy? I don't like this guy. I don't even know him, just his name and his height and his breath.

   She did this once before. Right after my stepfather died. His brother had come up from California for the reunion that was at his sister Shirleen's house. His brother stayed in our brown guest bedroom, too. He actually slept in there. But, a week after my dad died, after the funeral and everything, we went up to Lake Winnipesaukee to spend one last weekend on the boat before we sold it.

My mom said we had to sell it after my stepfather died. She couldn't drive it. I could. I could even get it into the slip without bumping anything, smooth like a car moves into a parking space. She didn't care. She didn't trust me to do things, Mr. Wayne. Didn't think I had the constitution to handle anything like a boat or a bad man or a death. Thought I was just a goddamn little kid, that's all. Just a kid.

The night of Uncle Mark, I went to bed like at nine or so, in the back berth. My mom was supposed to sleep in the bow and Uncle Mark in the middle where the table converted into a bed, but they didn't do that. They had all this tequila and talked about my dad and came back in drunker than a Labrador retriever who's found a keg of beer instead of his water bowl. They were loud, too. They woke me up because they were so loud. My mother is never loud. She is a quiet woman, a woman of soft sounds.

I moved my face from the pillow and saw them kissing, really kissing, the long romantic kind I'd only seen before on *The Hills* reruns, laying in the bow bed, tumbling around and rolling over kind of kissing, and neither of them had a shirt on.

I was a little kid then, Mr. Wayne, eleven or something, and I didn't think much before I did things, kind of like a baby shoves dirt in its mouth and doesn't think of the consequences, all the grit that will stick between his teeth and scrape across his gums, kind of like that. So like an absolute imbecile, when I saw them searching for each others' tonsils I stood up and yelled at my mother, "How could you? How could you? I hate you!"

My mother sat up. My mother's mouth gaped open. Uncle Mark smiled real slow like he thought everything was a damn good joke. She struggled to put her bra back on.

"I hate you!"

It was all I knew to yell. All I could think. That and "Daddy," which is what I called my stepfather. He didn't mind that I called him that. He just was a Daddy, not a Stepfather or James.

"Daddy!" I yelled it like a stupid fool. I yelled it even though I knew he was dead. I saw him dead. I yelled it because I needed someone to help me. I yelled it because I didn't know what else to do.

But guess what? He wasn't there in the dark boat. He was in the ground in a coffin with the teddy bear I gave him and a video of *Stagecoach*, one of your movies that he loved.

I just kept screaming like movie Indians running into battle on mustangs, hoofs pounding, eyes pained, throats quivering with rage and pain and blood.

My mother's breast wasn't adjusted right in her bra and all her white skin just glowed there in the darkness. White like dead skin, it was. White like a man in a coffin.

"How could you?" I yelled. Everything inside of me was cold, just a big black coldness, so sharp it hurt. "I hate you!"

She shoved her shirt on and tried to hold me, but I wouldn't let her, wouldn't let her near, just flung my arms all around in these crazy motions, pushing and windmilling and flailing.

"I'm sorry," she cried, trying to get to me. "I'm sorry."

I scurried away.

Uncle Mark, the mean ol' rip, he didn't even put a shirt on, or say anything, just went out of the boat and took a walk like an extra that's not needed any more.

His footsteps sounded heavy on the wooden dock.

"Keep walking," I thought. "Keep walking.

I wanted him to never come back. I wanted him to walk away forever, but not into a sunset, nothing that romantic. He had made taco salad that night and kept smiling so that even my mother ate it. She never ate spicy food. She said it gave her indigestion. She'd pop a hundred Rolaids after she ate stuffing, and that's not even spicy.

I stopped flailing after she stopped hugging me, stopped shouting too.

She stood there, leaning on the bathroom door, whimpering like a baby, "I'm sorry, honey. I'm sorry. I'm so, so sorry."

I let her cry and apologize, but when she tried again to hug me, to get her arms around me and pull me close, I pushed her away. I was done with being suffocated, done with being hugged.

"Leave me alone," I said and lay back down on the plushy berth in the back of the boat.

★

It's hard to get over a thing like that, I guess. She lay down beside me, so I scooted to the very bottom of the bed beneath the captain's seat where you can't sit up because it's so low. Before my stepdad died, I pretended it was a coffin and I was a vampire waiting to be freed and explore the night. After my stepfather died, I didn't like imagining coffins any more. So I imagined it was a stagecoach like in those movies we watched. It was a stagecoach rocking with the horses' strides heading far away to gold-rush land or something.

I just stayed there below her feet, staring at the fiberglass ceiling six inches away from my face. I listened to her cry the whole night. I didn't let her hold me like when my stepdad died, didn't come up from the small safe place below her feet. This was different.

Inside me there was just this big aching canyon where my heart should be and her sorrys fell in there, into the darkness. Just fell and fell.

In the morning we pretended like nothing happened. She made pancakes on the little stove in the boat. I ate them. Uncle Mark, my stepfather's brother, ate them. They were good.

Dear Mr. Wayne,

How's that saying go, Mr. Wayne? Another day, another dollar?

Only Americans would say that. It's never... another day, another hug? Or, I don't know... another day, another adventure? Nope. Another day, another dollar.

✦

My alarm goes off at 5:45 a.m. and Fandango looks at me. We both yawn. Her pointy teeth frame her tiny tongue.

As I put my feet on the carpet I remember that the cast list for *South Pacific* will be up on the auditorium doors as soon as the first bell sounds.

I don't want to look on the door. I am terrified of looking on that door because I know if I get a lame part or no part, then Sasha and the rest of the world will know that

I'm really a loser. Worse, *I'll* know that I'm really a loser. And it will be doubly awful because Sasha will get a wonderful part and I'll have to have my happiness for her be fuller than my sadness for me. And to make it triply worse I'll have to find out at the beginning of the day and live with knowing all day at school, and I probably won't be able to pay attention at all in any of my classes and forget to take notes, or else take notes so badly that I'll have to ask someone for their notes like you do when you're absent.

It stinks.

No, no it sucks.

Then I remember what sucks even worse.

We have a guest who makes my mother moan the moans. I shudder and put the pillow over my head like some sort of sissified cowboy who's afraid of the damn day.

A real man would have waited a while, wouldn't he? Like you, Mr. Wayne? You wouldn't take advantage. Of course, you'd stay in an actual hotel like normal people do. And you wouldn't be worried about a cast list, because you always get the part.

If Mike O'Donnell weren't here I'd stay home sick. Do a few fake sneezes, run to the fridge before my mother gets up, mix some relish and ketchup and crumble up some Saltine bits and throw them in the toilet to make it look like I've thrown up, put a little on my tongue too, so that I have authentic diseased-person breath.

But Mike O'Donnell is here so I can't stay home sick.

I paddle down the hallway to the bathroom to take my shower. My mother's door is closed. So is the door to the guest bedroom. I guess they are keeping up appearances, I wonder for whose sake.

My mind keeps playing back the photo album, the one with all the newspaper articles in it. The headlines flash in front of my eyes: *Man Killed. Man Stabbed. Town Mourns. Police Have No Suspects. Man Killed.*

Sometimes I get so scared, Mr. Wayne. Sometimes I am so far from being the cowboy with the hat and the horse and my gun drawn and ready. Sometimes I'm so far away from anything I want to be and it's like that sunset you're always riding to but you never quite reach.

I don't see him this morning. He is sleeping in.

"Jet lag," my mother says, smiling like they've invented a fat-free ice cream that doesn't taste like yogurt or Nutra-Sweet.

"Uh-huh." I grab half an English muffin out of the toaster.

"Did you like Mike?" she asks.

I manage to say, "Sure."

She glares at me. She wants to know. She puts my apple juice in front of me on the table, stands there waiting for an answer. I try not to imagine her naked. I try not to imagine anything.

"I didn't really get to see much of him."

Not like you, I think.

She nods.

I start to tell her about the cast list but she holds up her hand and says, "Do you think Mike likes decaf or regular coffee?"

"Gee, Mom, probably decaf," I say but she doesn't hear that I'm sarcastic, just takes out the decaf and I leave the kitchen to pick out clothes that will make me look good when I cry because I didn't get a part.

Real men don't drink decaf, do they?

Real men don't do a lot of things, like bonking your mother the first night they're here.

Just when I'm ready for Sasha and Olivia to pick me up there's a knock on the kitchen door and my sister bursts in, and my mom rushes over to hug her. I lean against the counter and watch.

"So?" my sister says when they break apart.

My mom giggles like she's six years old. "So what?"

"How did it go? Where is he?" my sister asks, her voice much louder, craning her neck to get a good look around the kitchen like the giant man from Oregon could be hiding in the breadbasket or something.

"He's asleep," my mom says, blushing. She wiggles her eyebrows at my sister.

"Oh, really . . ." My sister says, wiggling her eyebrows too. What is with the eyebrow wiggling? Can they not think of something else to do? And when did my sister suddenly get all pro–new man?

They laugh like this forever, and then when I can't take it any more I ask, "Brian know you're here?"

The kitchen goes cold and silent, like someone's left the freezer door open for days. The look I get from my mother could turn me into an ice cube.

My sister pours herself some coffee. "I just stopped here on my way to work. He doesn't need to know."

She turns around. I see her eyes. She looks into mine. She looks away first. Caught her. My mom slams her mug on the counter. "You ready for school?"

"Yep."

"Tell me about him, Mom. Is he still cute?" my sister's voice is all fake cheery, going back to the original topic. My mom's new man.

Before my mom can say anything, I break in. "He's got newspaper clippings. They're all about a murder in a bar."

My sister whirls around and some coffee sloshes out of the mug onto her wrist. She shuts her eyes from the pain. I grab the mug, turn on the faucet and place her wrist under the water.

"It's nothing," she says, even though her skin's a hot lobster red.

"Yeah, right," I say. "You're good at pretending things are nothing."

Before my sister can say anything my mom starts gushing. "Oh, Jessica. Are you okay? Is it blistering? Oh no."

My mother pushes me out of the way and takes over. I go look in the fridge, but it's about as appealing as a sand bath. I stick with my muffin and don't listen while my mom and Jessica giggle about Mike from Oregon.

"Have a good day at school," my mom says when Olivia and Sasha finally honk outside the door. "And ask your friends not to honk. I don't want them to wake Mike up. He might be a late sleeper."

"Uh-huh," I say again. I gulp my juice, throw my backpack over my shoulder and take a bite of my muffin, zipping out the door while trying not to look at my mother and my sister and their silly smiles.

✳

When I get into the car, the Sandemans give me a good look-over.

Olivia raises her large eyebrows at me. "Something's happened."

I shake my head.

"No. No. Something has happened. I can tell by your aura. Little black spots everywhere," Olivia insists.

"She's just nervous," Sasha says, jumping up and down in her seat. She's all excited. "Aren't you? It's okay. I'm nervous too. Is that it? Are you just nervous? Isn't being nervous so amazingly amazing?"

Olivia puts the Bug in gear and says, "I don't think that's it."

I try to hide in back. It's no good for people to know things about you. It's no good to wear your pain like prom makeup—out there for everyone to see.

When we're going down the driveway, I imagine the house exploding behind me. Maybe there's dynamite hidden in the cellar. My mom lights up a cigarette. An ash falls. Ka-boom. Roll credits.

"Do you guys ever watch John Wayne movies?" I ask as we turn onto the road.

"John Wayne?" Sasha says. "He's so macho, so old-timer. So white man."

She starts doing this really good impersonation, which is strange because she's so little like me. Suddenly it's like she takes up all the space in the car. Her voice comes out slow. "You've got it wrong, Lily. I didn't kill that hombre, I swear I didn't and by God I'm a gonna prove it to ya."

I stare at her, open-mouthed. More than anything I wish I could do that; wish I could sound just like that.

Sasha and I run to the auditorium after the first bell rings. Our arms are linked and she tugs me along, a step or two ahead of me. She tugs because she knows how scared I am.

"Failure isn't everything," she chirps. "Plus, I've got this good feeling."

"What good feeling?" I ask as we race by the art department and start up the stairs, scurrying past everyone else who still look half asleep, carrying their books, trudging along to class.

"That you didn't fail," Sasha says. She makes her eyes wide and emphatic.

We slow down once we're up the stairs so no one sees

quite how anxious we are. At least this is why I slow down, and Sasha lessens her pace, too.

"Act casual," she says.

Casual.

Our arms are still linked and we just see the crowd around the auditorium door when this guy in an ancient Metallica T-shirt that's as black as the tops of the pimples on his face mutters to us, "Lezzies."

Sasha and I look at each other and she laughs. "Are you a lesbian?"

"Not that I've noticed," I say.

She nods. "Me neither, although I might be bi."

"Really?" I ask, forgetting about the play for a moment, a real moment. Then I realize she's kidding.

"Well, sexuality isn't an either/or thing," she says, squeezing my arm. "Like no one is just gay or just straight. It's all shades of gray, you know?"

I shrug.

"Like I think you're cute," Sasha says, smiling at me. "All cuddly and tiny and sort of Spanish-sexy even though you aren't Spanish. Are you? I can tell that you're attractive, but I don't want to kiss you or anything."

"Darn," I say in this mock-exasperated way and she starts laughing so loud she sounds like braying donkeys, and people look at us. I'm glad I've pulled that off. I can't imagine what Sasha would do if she knew I worried about people thinking I was gay. She'd think I wasn't open-minded enough, I'm sure, and repressed and therefore part of the problem of gay oppression. Then she and Olivia would counsel me on all our car rides home.

We've gotten closer to the list and I can tell that the people around the door are mumbling, some of them are smiling, some of them look angry and I wonder why. If I don't get a part I won't be angry, just sad.

One big blonde girl with all this blue mascara on gets close to us and mutters, "Two freshmen!"

She walks away, her tall-girl heels clacking at the floor like they're trying to break through to the calculus room on the next floor down.

Then, believe it or not, Fire Engine Pants boy, aka Mr. Tyler Reed, comes up and says, "Sasha! Congratulations!"

She leans back, tipping her torso backwards, all flirty, and I think that for all her continuum-bisexual-spectrum talk she is so straight it's disgusting. "Congratulations?"

"Haven't you seen yet?" he asks. He's cute this boy, brown-haired, with green eyes tinted blue like God made up this special shade just for him and he knows it.

"No!" she says and lets go of my arm.

He laughs. "Come on!"

He takes Sasha's hand and pulls her through the crowd. I'm left standing at the edge of the crowd too scared to push my way in, thinking about maybe going to study hall and not looking at all, because there is probably no point. I wonder if I should wait for Sasha.

"Lily!" she yells, jumping up so that her short head appears for a minute above the crowd.

"Liliana!"

She has jumped up again.

"Come up here!" she says and I come, mumbling apologies for my elbows as I push through.

When she can reach me, Sasha grabs my arm with her hand and I see the pretty dangly charm bracelet she has, silver and amethyst. It's beautiful. The hand that's below this bracelet pulls me to her and to the auditorium doors. She hugs me and I wait a second before I remember that it's polite to hug her back, to show her that I am happy she is happy. I can feel all the warmth of her and this sweet musky smell like incense, or scented candles. I breathe in. I knew she would get a part and I'm so glad for her, so glad that we're friends. But I also ache...I ache like I haven't seen water in days and it's been a long, hard cattle drive. I ache because I am still me, Liliana, also known as Lily, a nothing girl. Not a hero. Not a cowboy. Not even an actress in a stupid high school musical.

It's hard for a pilgrim to go alone in this world, you know, Mr. Wayne? Sometimes you need someone to ride shotgun.

"I knew you'd get a part," I tell her and smile as two girls in matching sweaters look for their names on the list, sigh and walk away.

Then Sasha starts bouncing up and down and saying, "We did it! We did it! You were so good. I knew you would!"

"Did what?" I ask into Sasha's black fruity-smelling hair.

"Look!"

I pull away from Sasha and look at the door. There are two white sheets with names on them. One sheet is the cast. One sheet is crew. Tiny writing. I look down the list for my name and find it. I'm on the list. I look across to see what part I am. Probably Nurse #3.

I'm Nellie Forbush.

"Isn't it great?" Sasha asks.

"Who's Nellie Forbush?" I ask. I can't remember anymore.

Sasha laughs at me. So does Mr. Tyler Reed. So does Stuart Silsby, who is standing on his tippy-toes trying to memorize all the names of who got what parts. He mumbles them under his breath.

"Just the lead," he says, rolling his eyes.

Sasha makes big eyes at me. Tyler Reed laughs and punches me in the arm and then makes googly eyes at Sasha, and Stuart repeats it again in a sing-song, duh voice: "Just the lead."

"The lead?" I whisper.

Sasha nods her head.

"Me?"

"Sasha's the comic lead. You're the romantic lead," Tyler explains. He hits me on the arm again. If I wasn't so stunned I would belt him back, maybe in the chin. I'm going to bruise. Paolo Mattias is standing in the back of the crowd. He looks at me. His lips don't move. He doesn't smile. He doesn't frown. He looks away. He leaves. Jerk. He probably saw me hug Sasha and thinks I'm gay too now. Like father, like daughter.

"For girls," Sasha says. "Tyler here is one of the male leads. So is Stuart."

"Really?" I say, my voice breaking like a boy going through puberty. "Really?"

I start jumping up and down, hugging her.

Sasha just laughs, and jumps up and down with me. "Liliana! We're the freaking stars."

The warning bell rings and we all take off for classes. Stuart trails behind me, detailing his part in his super-nasal hyper voice. "And I get to wear coconut shells like a bra and sing this song. It's a complete humor part, which should expand my range, you know, since I'm so used to playing the straight male lead. Like in *Annie Get Your Gun*. Remember that?"

I remember when they did *Annie Get Your Gun* in eighth grade at middle school, Mr. Wayne. I was too wimpy to try out for that in eighth grade. But now I'm in high school. Now, I can recreate myself. I can be the type of girl who is the lead. I can be the type of girl who can be a cowboy and a liberal Democrat. Someday, Mr. Wayne, I'm going to have to take you to task on all that Republican conservative right-wing stuff you pulled. But not now. Not now. Because today I am the lead!

I make it into study hall just in time but I don't remember my feet taking me through the halls. I want to hug every-one. I smile at Mary Bilodeau and don't worry about being a loser by association. I smile at Alyssa Cutler and don't worry about her being too popular to smile at. I smile, smile, smile and make it into my study hall seat. Mr. Farley gives detention to anyone entering after the final bell and I scurry in the door just as it rings, plop down in my desk and shove my backpack underneath.

"Almost late, Miss," he says to me. He doesn't know my name. He doesn't know anyone's except Ron Baldwin's, and he only knows his because he's always getting into trouble because he passes people notes in study hall that say: *Want some wed?*

He means weed. He can't spell. Or maybe it's some secret code so he won't get caught.

I nod at Mr. Farley and everyone looks at me. I don't say that I'm sorry for being late, but the nod seems to be enough to keep Mr. Farley from losing his cool the way he did when he saw Ron Baldwin passing a cigarette to a friend a couple of aisles over. You would have thought it was Oxy-Contin the way Mr. Farley went on about illicit substances and pollutants and contaminants and delinquency, huffing and steaming and sending him to the principal's office. Ron got suspended. He's still gone. So I put my feet in his empty seat, pull out my notebook and write.

In my head I hear a million feet dancing...square dancing. There's a celebration just for me, Liliana Faltin. The desks of study hall are pushed back to the sides of the room and Mr. Farley's the caller. He's got on lederhosen and a cowboy hat for some reason.

"Do-si-do and around we go," he calls. "Bow to your partner. Bow to the corner."

I start giggling to myself. I can't help it. I just can't help it. I shake my head and try not to laugh too loud.

I forget all about my mother's man, my sister, my Uncle Mark.

Mr. Wayne, I cannot believe I got that part. I can *not* believe I got any part. Did you ever feel that way? Did you ever doubt yourself, or did you know what you were meant to be ever since you saw yourself as an extra in that old John Ford western? When you saw your body, bigger than life on that movie screen, when you saw yourself twenty feet tall, did you say: Yep, partner, that's where I'm meant to be.

In my pocket is a note from Nicole. She gave it to me before I checked the cast list.

Liliana,

I am writing this after my mom made me hang up the phone with you. She can be such a bitch. But anyways, I wanted to tell you that even if you don't get a part in that play, it's okay. I mean it's not that big a deal. It isn't about you or anything and stuff. Not you personally and your worth as a human being. Yada. Yada. Yada.

It's like when we didn't make the soccer team in seventh grade. We survived. Right? And anyways I'll still be your friend. Even if no one else will.

Just kidding.

Have you found out Fire Man's name yet? Please, please, please find out. Next Friday there's a football game and I bet he'll be there. Everyone goes.

Oh my God! I forgot to tell you. Do not ever eat a banana in front of a boy. It's supposed to make them all horny because it's so phallic, like you're eating a penis or something. According to Cosmo it drives them crazy. And when I asked Christopher about it he just shrugged and said, "Lay off, Twerp Case," which means that it does. I think ice cream does too. They see you licking it or biting it and they imagine it's like a blow job. Gross. Or maybe not so gross, I guess it depends who.

Oh, I'm bad aren't I?

So, anyways, we should go to the football game because I bet Fire Man will be there and maybe I can stand near him and suck on a hot dog or something. Just Kidding!

Don't be sad if you don't get a part and I hope that guy who is coming to your house isn't a dweeb.

Luv (not love), Nicole

Dear Mr. Wayne,

What's important, Mr. Wayne, is not Nicole thinking that I'm such an idiot I'd be a massive failure. What's important is that I got a part in the play. No, I got a *lead* in a play. Maybe I'm not such a loser after all. I'm going to have to read the play. Or rent the video or something before rehearsals start. It's a war musical, so it shouldn't be that bad, right? I wish it were a western or the musical remake of *She Wore a Yellow Ribbon* or at least *Annie Get Your Gun*. Something with a little firepower in it.

I think my stepdad would be proud. I think he would hug me and smile and say he never doubted me for a moment. He was like that. He smelled good, like Old Spice, and he had an anchor tattoo all faded on his forearm. He got it in the navy while he was in Vietnam. He said it was his one big mistake, that tattoo.

We all have one big mistake, but it must be hard to

be reminded of it all the time. What if I make a mistake in the play and everyone sees and everyone laughs? What if my skirt gets tucked into my underwear and they're the light blue lacy ones, or worse the ones that look like my Grammy should be wearing them, or if I fall on my face or I faint?

I will be forever a loser.

As I take out a pen to write back to Nicole, I remember that I'm not just a lead. I'm a romantic lead. I wonder if that means I'll have to kiss someone. Who? God, I hope he's cute. I hope he has nice breath. I hope he's a good kisser. I get to kiss someone.

Please, don't let him be Stuart Silsby.

But even better than that is that I'm in a play with Sasha, which means I'll spend more time with her and make sure she wants to stay being my friend. Instead of writing the note to Nicole, I think of Sasha and before I know it a piece of paper shoots across the floor and hits my sneakers. Ka-pow. I jump like a skittish foal right before the big noontime shoot out. The note has my name on it, written in red pen. I reach down and pick it up. I glance in the direction the note came from and there is Paolo Mattias, leaning backwards so that I can see him. He gives a little nod. I smile back, I think. Then I remember what he asked about my dad being gay. That makes me not want to look at the note at all, because what if it's some sort of evil hate note: *Lily, I know your dad probably likes guys. So I will murder him.*

God, that's stupid. I stare at the folded-up paper for

a second and then give in. If it's an evil your-dad's-a-fag note I'll just slowly stand up, walk over and punch Paolo Mattias in his handsome-boy face. Just a nice right hook should do a good amount of damage to his nose and ruin his chances at Prom King when we're seniors. Then I'll just amble back to my desk, open my notebook and try not to think about blood.

I try not to unfold the note too quickly or look like I'm scared.

Liliana,

Congratulations on the play. I'll see you at rehearsal.

—Paolo.

That's all. I flip it over to look at the other side. There's nothing there, nothing about my dad, nothing at all. I let out a big, slow breath. Why do I expect everything to be bad all the time? Maybe, just maybe, I've figured this Paolo guy wrong. I chew on the end of my pen, make little bite marks in the white plastic. I write *thanks* on the other side of the paper and try to think of something else to say, but all I can some up with is: *Are you in it too? What's your character?*

And then I decide that sounds too dorky: *What's your character?* Like I'm a psychologist or something trying to discern whether he "deviates from the norm." Olivia says we all deviate from the norm, that there is no norm. She wants to be a psychologist and work with incarcerated sex offenders. She says they are the toughest to heal, and she likes challenges.

I know there's no way; that they can't be healed. I don't tell her that, though. Then she'd want to know how I knew, and some things I just can't tell.

I fold up the piece of paper that has Paolo's note and my stupid response on it and stuff it in my pocket. I'll show it to Nicole later so that she can analyze his writing. I take out a new clean sheet of paper, wasteful and bad for the environment but I won't tell Sasha, and write:

Thanks. Why will I see you there?

I fold it up and put the note on the floor and kick it to the girl next to me. She pushes it past her right shoe and then gives it a good shove with her left so that it skitters across the linoleum floor and plops right against Paolo's white Nike sneaker. He reaches down and grabs it. It's always hazardous passing notes this way. You never know when someone might not want to play along, and snatch it up and read it themselves even if their name isn't on it. People can be like that. The creeps.

Pretty soon the note comes thudding back to me. Beneath my two sentences he has written:

I'm in it too. Looking forward to it!

I smile, wonder at what the exclamation point means, and then decide to forget it and just reread the Flannery O'Connor story we were assigned for English. It will help me not think about things, like whether or not I'll suck at being Nellie, and whether or not that cute Tyler Reed boy is in love with Sasha and if I should tell Nicole, and whether or not Mike O'Donnell will be there when I get home, and whether or not my sister will tell my mother that she's about to be a grandma.

After study hall Paolo rushes up next to me and smiles.

"Hi," I say.

"Hi."

We walk through the door together and bump sides. Something in me goes all electric-sockety.

Paolo says, "Sorry."

"It's okay."

He bumps me again on purpose, teasing. "Sorry."

I bump him back.

"Oops!" I fake apologize and make my eyes all big the whole time, thinking, *I am flirting*. I am flirting with Paolo.

We keep walking and he bumps me one more time, which is just rich. "So, you're a lead."

"Yeah. Are you?"

Paolo laughs. "I'm just Sailor #5 or something."

"You'll be a great sailor #5," I say.

"Thanks."

"Really."

"I'm cool with it. I've never even been in a play before. So, you know, it'll be an experience." He blushes again when he looks at me. His cheeks are a little stubbly. I want to touch them and see if they feel like sandpaper.

Instead I say, "I was surprised you tried out."

"Because?"

"Because I kind of think of you as a jock. I know that's wrong."

"People think running is all I do."

"Yeah, sort of. That's wrong obviously."

He just laughs and shakes his head, which makes me feel like a total idiot. We bump by some people. Paolo says in a lower voice, "So, um, I saw you talking to Sasha and Stuart."

"Yeah. They got leads too."

"I know. I was wondering..."

I shoulder up for it because I'm so ready to hear him ask it. Even though my stomach is falling out of my body and the world is woozy, I am so ready to hear him ask me about Sasha. Of course, he must like Sasha. That's probably why he tried out for the play and everything.

I miss what he says.

"What?"

He moves his books to his other arm and leans in closer to me so I'll hear him. "I was wondering if you and Stuart had something going on?"

122

"Something going on?" I choke and laugh and choke at the same time.

Paolo snaps back to standing all rigid tall. "What?"

"It's just so funny. Back in seventh grade, he asked me to this CCD dance."

"In the basement of St. Elizabeth Seton?"

"Yeah."

"Those always sucked," Paolo said. "My mom would chaperone."

"Yeah," I say. "This one was my worst. Stuart and I danced a couple of times."

"And?"

And he even got hard, down there and everything, which was embarrassing, and I kept trying to move away from him when we were dancing so that no one would see, but he kept moving closer and brushing it up against me. I do not tell Paolo this.

Instead, I tell Paolo, "So, after a while I said I was tired and I sat on one of the metal folding chairs by the bathroom. He sat down next to me and said, in that real dramatic way of his, moving his chair so it was right across from me and everything. And he goes, 'Liliana, let's face it neither of us are winners in the looks department, but we're smart and funny and I think we should make do with each other, because I can't see us getting anything better.'"

Paolo stops walking. "No, he didn't."

"He really said that. My first date." My heart thumps heavy and hard just thinking about it. "I should not be telling you this."

"He's an idiot."

I cover my eyes with my hand. "I can't believe I'm telling you this."

"No. I'm glad you told me. But he's obviously an idiot."

I wave his words away. "It's not a big deal. The point is that Stuart and I are definitely not a thing. We will never be a thing. Ever."

We're standing outside New England History class. Nicole's inside at her desk, mouth wide open, staring at us.

"I should go in," I say. "You're going to be late."

The bell rings.

Paolo laughs. "Yep."

He grabs my arm with his free hand just as I'm turning. "Lily. Stuart is an idiot."

"Yeah." I shrug. I stare at Paolo's fingers that are so thick and different from my fingers. He's touching my arm. My arm! "I know."

He swallows. He squeezes my arm just a tiny bit and lets go. "You are definitely a quote-unquote winner in the looks department."

He smiles a tiny smile and my mouth drops open. He laughs, touches my chin so I know it's happened. I clamp my mouth closed. Oh my God. I am so played out. He pivots away and he's gone, moving between people like he was never there.

Once I get to my classroom I slam into my seat while Nicole stares at me.

Truth is, I can still remember the sound my metal chair made when it scraped across the floor at that stupid dance. It was a sound like a scream. I ran into the bathroom and hit the stall with my hand. Bang. Bang. Bang. It was cold. Then a mother came in, Stuart's mother actually, and asked if everything was okay.

"Yes," I'd said, cradling my throbbing hand, trying not to smell the pee/mold smell of the bathroom, trying not to cry. "Just practicing my boxing."

Then I smiled a good movie star smile. You'd have been proud.

I'd never lied in a Catholic church before. Although it *was* technically just the bathroom. Nicole says I'm much better looking now than I was in seventh grade. I know I'm a lot skinnier, not as skinny as Nicole or Sasha because I have breasts, but I don't have any of that baby fat crap any more. I hate how they call it baby fat. When you're in seventh grade, you are not a baby.

Wow. Did Paolo really say I was a "winner in the looks department"? Because that is so cheeseball and so, so, good.

✶

Sometimes I like to imagine I'm out in the prairie and there's no one but me. I scan the long grass. I look for the eagles soaring overhead. It's quiet. It smells like sage and tumbleweed, but then this new smell wafts in from the west. It's the smell of fear. I pull out my gun. Nothing is ever as it seems. Right, Mr. Wayne? Inside a whole lot of people is an awful ball of hurt that just gets bigger every time they swallow. It just wedges inside a little bit more. No matter how much ice cream you get during a day, no matter how many parts you win, you know that at the end of the day, you're gonna have to go back home and there's gonna be a tough hombre waiting there for you. That's why you always ride with your pistol at your side.

Saddle up.

✦

In New England History class, Mary Bilodeau actually turns around and says to me, "I heard you got the lead. You're so cool."

I smile at her. What else can I do?

She stares at me for a while. The way Nicole stares at Tyler Reed, aka Fire Man.

I mumble, "Thank you."

She keeps staring. Next to me, Katie Igsalis starts to giggle. Carly Bernhardt looks at me and smiles like she knows how it feels. Mary followed Carly everywhere. When Carly asked to go to the bathroom, Mary would ask to go a minute afterwards and sneak into the stall next to her and listen to her pee. Carly said she would have told her off if she didn't feel so bad for her. How can you tell off someone like Mary?

You just can't. There's a code a person's got to live by, and telling off the needy breaks that code.

"Mary," I say as nicely as I can. "Mr. Johnson's coming. You better turn around before he gives you detention."

She looks panicked.

She smiles at me real quick and says, "We're wearing the same shirt."

I look. We are. Only mine fits and hers is real big, like she's trying to cover up all her troubles in it.

"We're twins," Mary says.

Because there is nothing else I can do, I nod.

Katie Igsalis giggles again and Mr. Johnson comes in.

Mary sits forward again, but I can still smell her: chicken soup with way too much garlic, cheap jasmine soap and perfume from China.

I try to see how long I can go without breathing. It isn't long enough, and every time I gulp a breath I gulp in Mary.

At lunch Nicole grabs me by the shoulders and says, "What are we going to do?"

"About what?"

"About the musical," she says, shaking her head like I'm a supreme idiot.

"I got the part," I tell her and glance away. Travis Poppins and her brother are at the next table trying to burp the alphabet. They are on *H*.

"I know! Now, what are we going to do?" Nicole drops her arms and slams herself down on the bench at the cafeteria table.

I shake my head.

"Lily! Can you belch the alphabet?" Travis Poppins shouts at me.

I look at him. "No, but you make me want to vomit the alphabet."

He rolls his eyes and starts over from *A*.

I put down my books and sling my legs over the bench and watch Nicole. I kick at the air, since my feet don't touch the ground. She's laughing. Then she turns back to me. "This is a really big deal. This is identity-crisis big-time stuff. You are going to be a theater geek forever."

This just annoys me.

"I will not."

She nods. "Forever."

I check my pocket for a dollar. It's time to get away and get a bagel. "Sometimes you don't know what you're talking about."

She stares at me as I stand up. She doesn't have to look up far because I'm so short.

"Right," she says. "I'm the one who doesn't know what I'm talking about."

I walk away.

She stomps after me and grabs my shoulder, whirling me around. "I'm warning you because you're my best friend, Lily. You have to quit. Like, right now. Do you want to be a loser forever? Do want to be a theater freak? What is it, exactly, that you want to be?"

Travis Poppins has stopped belching to watch the scene. Jerk.

I stare at Nicole's thin lips, her perfect hair that she spends an hour on every morning and I tell her, my best friend, the truth. "I just want to be me."

★

But that's not the whole truth, Mr. Wayne. Not really. The whole truth is that I don't want to be a victim. The whole truth is that I want to be a hero.

Dear Mr. Wayne,

Today I'm not happy to come home. I'm scared, real scared. And even the happy buzz that made me smile all day because I'm the romantic lead in some musical? It isn't there any more. Now that Mary and I are twins, I need new clothes, but we don't have the money to get me any. What I'll have to do is go through my wardrobe, create a style somehow. Anything. Plus, I can hide in my bedroom, since my mother's new boyfriend/lover, Mike O'Donnell, is waiting in the house, I think. Unless he went out. There is that possibility. If he's gone, everything will be right fine and I'll be able to put off being scared for a while.

Sometimes men scare me. Not you. Not my stepdad and not my other dad, but other men.

Sometimes I like men way too much.

I make no sense.

I stare at the house and don't move after Olivia and Sasha have dropped me off.

What do you do when you come home to your house and there might be a stranger-guest inside? Do you knock before you unlock the door and go in? I sit on the stone wall for a minute and write. I procrastinate; try to work up some nerve. That's what I do.

Maybe I should case the joint, I think. See if there are any strange footprints outside, any sign of suspicious dealings.

I creep around the perimeter looking for busted glass panes on doors, open windows. I peek inside the living room. He's not in there. I'm too short to peek in the bathroom window, not that I'd want to. I give up and I just open the door like I always do, only I check first to see if it's locked. It isn't. Inside, past the light blue countertop in the kitchen, I see his head. He stands up and turns to greet me.

"Liliana," he says, smiling but it doesn't reach his eyes. It's just a movement of lips. "I'm glad you're home."

I give him my own fake smile and try not to imagine him naked in my mother's bed. It doesn't work. I get a vision of pale, sagging skin, age marks, wrinkles, muscles heaving. Blinking madly, I put my backpack on the counter like usual.

On the kitchen table is a glass of Coke and the newspaper. He gestures at the paper, spread out across the tabletop. "The pickings aren't good."

He's been looking at the help-wanteds. There are a couple of ads circled. One is for a sales representative at the local paper. The other one is written in smaller type so I can't read it.

"That's too bad," I say, backing myself into the counter, hugging my arms around my middle. The counter seems closer than normal and the edge juts into my thigh. It doesn't seem like it's in the right place. Nothing seems in the right place. I don't feel like I'm home with this stranger here.

He shakes his head. "Don't you worry your little head about it. Something will come up. Luck of the Irish."

"Good," I say. He sounds Texan not Irish. How can he sound Texan, all twangy with that little lady stuff, if he's from Maine and he just came from Oregon? It doesn't make sense. It's like he's trying to sound like John Wayne or something.

He stares at me too hard. I go and open the fridge. It looks naked, just some bologna and orange juice and Cracker Barrel sharp cheddar cheese. "Did you drink all the Coke?"

"Yep. I'll get you some more at the store."

I nod, but I need my caffeine fix now. "Can I have a sip of yours?"

"Mine?" he coughs. "Don't think it's a good idea. I'm coming down with a cold."

He smiles at me, puts his big hands on my shoulders. My shoulders go all stiff. He directs me towards the table. "You sit down. You sit right here. I've got something for you."

He pushes the paper out of the way with a quick jerky fold and says, "Stay right there. I'll be right back."

When he's gone, I look at his Coke, put my fingers around the bottom, not the edge where the cold germs would be. Lifting it up I smell the liquid. The shade of the Coke is lighter than normal, like he's mixed it with water for some reason, and it doesn't just have a sugary smell; there's another smell underneath it. A smell I can't quite recognize. Maybe he's been spitting in it a lot. Or maybe it's rum. It is. Wow. What is up with that?

I put the glass back down.

He scampers back, all excited like he's five years old or something. It's kind of cute, he's so excited and I almost forget about the noises he and my mother made last night and all the things it made me remember. He carries a brown bag, a shopping store bag in his hands.

"Now, I didn't get to wrap it," he says. "Men aren't much good at wrapping. But I hope you like it all the same. Just little things to remind you of me. And to say thanks for letting me stay here a while."

I wonder how long a while is and I say, "You didn't need to get me anything."

"I wanted to," he says and stares at me in that hard uncomfortable way. "Geez, you look just like your mother."

I hope that they didn't turn the light on last night.

"Uh-huh."

I take the bag that he's set in front of me. "Should I just reach in?"

"Go ahead."

He pulls the chair so that it's really close to me. I'm beginning to get the idea that this is the kind of person he is, a person who always is in your space, close, physical, and it's a little intimidating because he's already so tall and big and his gestures are huge; he's sweeping his arms all around all the time. I look at his feet, twice the size of mine. He isn't wearing any shoes and his socks are white cotton, but stained orange around the toes like he wore them with good leather shoes and got his feet wet and then the leather colored his socks. My father always wears baby blue socks. He wears everything that color because my mother once told him that baby blue made his eyes look striking. I don't know how your socks can bring out the color of your eyes, but that's how he is.

But Mike O'Donnell's socks aren't what I should be thinking about right now. I have a present in front of me and he's all excited about it, like a little boy, and it is kind of sweet, even if it's weird because he's so old and he doesn't know me at all.

I promise myself that I'll pretend I like it even if I don't, even if it's something hideous like meatballs, or soap made from animal fat, or brilliant blue eye shadow.

I've got to put my hand into the bag and I don't want to. What if there's a rattlesnake in there or a scorpion. Something deadly. I think of those newspaper headlines again. *Man Dead In Bar Fight*. I change it: *Girl Dead From Snake Bite*.

"Wimp," I mutter.

Reaching into the bag, I pull out something soft. Rattlesnakes are not soft. I see that it is gray. Are rattlesnakes gray? I have no clue. But even an idiot like me can tell it's no venom-filled vermin. A gray sweatshirt with a logo of a duck on it and a big *O*. Oh my God.

"It's the Oregon mascot," he says.

"Wow. It's really cute," I lie. "Thank you."

I lean over and kiss his cheek like I do on my birthday, giving each relative the required kiss after the opening of their gift. His eyes light up.

"That's not all. There's something else in there."

"Oh."

I sit back down, which isn't hard because I didn't stand all the way up to kiss him, just unbent my knees a little bit and scooted forward. I reach inside the bag again and pull out a smallish square box. I don't have to push my fingernail between the edges the way I do with presents from my mother, because he hasn't taped the sides shut the way she does. I like that. I lift the lid up, move away some tissue and pull out a green rock.

"It's a wishing rock," he says. "From Ireland."

"Neat."

"It's to remind you of your roots."

I glance up from the small heavy rock, which sits smooth against the palm skin of my hand. "My roots?"

He nods.

"I'm not Irish."

"Everyone is Irish," he says really adamantly, so forcefully, really, that I wouldn't have been surprised if he'd pounded his fist on the table. I jump back a little like some scared cat.

He stands up and grabs the paper off the table, folding it twice so that it's smaller and the ads he's circled are easy to see. "I should call some of these places in the paper."

"Oh. Okay. Thanks again."

He smiles, a splitting-face kind of smile that even reaches his eyebrows and makes them seem happy. "You're welcome."

I stand up too, and grab my backpack, then I pick up the rock and sweatshirt. "I have homework and stuff. Thank you again."

For a second his eyes go hard, mean, like a predator.

"You're welcome again," he says and sits on the stool by the wall phone. He puts the paper on the counter and picks up the yellow phone and puts his finger into the rotary part to dial numbers.

For a minute, I'm embarrassed that we still have a rotary phone. Other people have cell phones, or at least push-button and cordless phones. We have one of those in my mother's room, but the kitchen phone is a rotary. It's so old fashioned, but my mom insists on keeping it because she thinks it's "quaint." I have a cell phone but I'm on a limited minute plan, which means it's pointless and just for emergencies. It's for dialling 911 when strange men follow me down an alley or something, my mother says. She never says anything about strange men following me around in our house.

I head down our ugly hallway with its 1970s paisley

wallpaper and into my room to do my homework. I put the green rock that is exactly the color I imagine Ireland, green like hills and summer leaves that are wet from rain, into my pocket. I plop my pack on my bed and my sweatshirt on my bureau, and go back to shut my door.

✳

My Uncle Mark, he gave me a present too. Why is it that men think they can right everything wrong they've ever done, or are about to do, with a present?

Mark's present was a jade cross. As soon as he was gone, I ripped it off and ran across the backyard to the woods. I whipped it over my head, hanging onto the end of the chain. Then I let it go. The cross tumbled through the sky and disappeared into the woods, lost in dead leaves and pine needles. I never saw it again. I looked. Sometimes I imagine it glowing there, waiting.

✳

In my room, I open my closet and begin hauling things out, spreading them in piles on the floor. I stare at clothes like they hold secrets, secrets to a new Lily, a sexy Lily, a put-together musical star Lily, a Lily who is not twins with Mary Bilodeau.

The toilet flushes down the hall and all the water from the toilet whooshes through the pipes. I hear Mike

O'Donnell walk down the hall. He stands outside my door. I wait for a knock. There is no knock. I tiptoe to my door, real quiet, put my ear against it. I can hear him breathing. I no longer breathe.

I find the bread knife that I've stashed under my pillow and clench it in my fists, fat lot of good it'll do me, and then go back to my door.

I can smell him, that male smell, just on the other side. Not all men are hero men.

The knife is not sharp. It's not a good weapon. I don't know what I was thinking. I want to move away from the door and look for something better. My lamp. It's heavy. I will dart over there if he tries to come in, leap over the clothes on the floor, maybe throw a couple textbooks while I run for the better weapon.

I swallow, imagining it all.

Then I hear his feet go back down the hall.

Maybe he will go buy some Coke soon and I can go out into the kitchen and call Nicole and have something to eat and not have to worry about him listening to my phone call, or have to look at those sad watery eyes of his and worry about whether or not he's happy and if I'm not being thankful enough, or cold or mean. And I won't have to worry about why he stood outside my door.

Do you remember when you were Capt. Rockwell Torrey in *In Harm's Way* and you looked at your friend, right in the eyes and you said, "All battles are fought by scared men who'd rather be someplace else." That was truth, right there, Mr. Wayne, real truth.

✴

After a while I summon up my courage and leave my bedroom, and grab that green rock again. It's not the color of Ireland. It's the color of that jade cross my step-uncle gave me right before he left for California.

"Oh, that's so generous," my mother had cooed when he presented it, all tidied up in a fancy jewelry store box and everything. "Put it on, Lily."

I shook my head. My uncle glared at me, meaned up his lips into this tight line.

I put it on. It fell between my breasts. Well, where my breasts would have been if they'd started to grow yet. They hadn't. I hated the way it felt there. I hated my uncle's eyes staring at it.

My mother clapped her hands together. "Beautiful!"

He echoed her. "Beautiful."

She gave me a look and I knew I was supposed to go kiss him on the cheek or something, but I couldn't. I just couldn't do it. I was a block of soap and I couldn't move. I just was getting worn away from things rubbing against me.

"What do you say, Liliana?" she made big eyes at me and gave my name a few extra syllables.

"Thank you," I said.

When he left I threw the cross into the woods. It's still there somewhere unless a squirrel has stolen it. I keep thinking about it now, over and over again. I thought I had stashed that stuff away.

What was it you said in *Stagecoach*?

Well, there are some things a man just can't run away from.

That goes for women too.

Dear Mr. Wayne,

Paolo walks me out of study hall again.

"I've been brushing up on my John Wayne," he says.

"Really?"

"Yeah."

"Why?"

He smiles and does the little hip-bump thing. "I figure if you're so into him, he's got to be cool."

"Oh." A big swallow sticks in my throat. I'm afraid to look up at him. I look up at him. He smiles. He's shaved this morning, which is too bad, but good. I can smell his aftershave/shaving cream stuff. I inhale and smile at him. "John Wayne is amazing."

"Yeah." He looks up the hall where some girls are jumping up and down, shrieking. "Is that the kind of guy you like? The whole strong and silent thing?"

"Oh … I don't know. It's more—"

I don't have to answer because Nicole appears out of nowhere, which is so strange because her homeroom is nowhere near here. She smiles all big. She's wearing her favorite skirt. "Hey Lily! Hey Paolo!"

Her eyelashes flutter.

"Hey," Paolo says. He leans a little closer to me I think.

"You guys walking towards New England History?" she says in her ultra-chirpy version of her voice.

I eye her, trying to assess the situation. "Yeah."

"Cool. Paolo, have I told you that I have the worst assignment ever?"

She blabs and blabs and pushes her way next to him so I'm left trailing behind them the whole way, looking at their butts as they walk on. Paolo looks back at me, stops, waiting for me to catch up, but what's the point really? I mean, c'mon. Mini skirt vs. John Wayne. Give me a break.

At home, Mike has left me a note.

Went out with my sister.

It isn't very long. Short, quick, to the point, not like how he talks at all.

I am so happy that he's gone that I do a little two-step

line-dancing thing all around the kitchen. I kiss the refrigerator and pretend it's Paolo Mattias. I have obviously completely lost it.

"Settle down," I tell myself like I'm some uppity nervous horse. "Whoa."

A good yank opens the refrigerator door. There's been a Coke heist, again. Some cowardly thief has stolen all the Coke. A good fist slams the fridge door shut and knocks off a couple magnets holding up my eighth-grade report card.

"Damn him," I say and then I head into the family room. Sometimes my mother stores extra Cokes under the bar that we never use. I get on my knees to look for some and there isn't any. One sixteen-ounce bottle of ginger ale, but ginger ale doesn't have caffeine and I need caffeine if I'm going to be able to stay awake and do all my homework. My hands shake because I am already going through withdrawal. Chocolate has caffeine. Maybe I'll have chocolate milk to pep me up.

As I start to stand, I pivot a little bit and look at the ankle-high shelf behind the bar where my stepfather lined up all the bottles of booze he kept for when he and my mother had company. There are ten bottles, at least, maybe fifteen. The summer before eighth grade, Nicole and I tried some. I liked the Scotch the best, because it felt like what alcohol was supposed to feel like, hot and burning. It reminded me of damsels in distress who have just witnessed horrible, terrible, monstrous things in the hot, dusty streets of Durango and need some boosting as the bartender's helper runs to get them some dry tweed clothes.

Nicole's favorite was Bailey's Irish Cream, a girlie drink, like milk and sugar.

When I start to get up, I notice that the bottles don't look the same. Grabbing the first one that I see, Kahlua, I screw the top off of it and look inside. Nothing in it. I grab some Scotch, J&B. Twisting off the top I already know what I'll see when I look inside, but I look anyway. Nothing. Bottle after bottle. Scotch. Vermouth. Vodka. Gin. Tequila. Nothing in any of them. All of them empty. Every single one. Even the brandy.

Fact #1: It's been three years, and they are all gone.

Fact #2: My mom doesn't drink.

Fact #3: Mike does drink.

Fact #4: Mike puts booze in his Coke in the middle of the day.

Fact #5: Mike has only been here three days and there are twelve empty bottles, which would mean he's downing four bottles a day. Can you even survive that?

My hands place all the bottles back where they belong. My hands are shaking. I don't understand what's going on in most of my head. But this tiny little part of my tiny little brain might have something almost figured out and it's pushing my body into action.

Standing up, I stare down at the labels, at the caps. In the little garbage can that's been empty since my stepdad died are plastic seals that Mike O'Donnell must have taken off when he opened untouched bottles. The ginger brandy had never been opened, I remember, and the tequila.

✶

I try asking my mother about the whole Jessica-Brian beating up thing at dinner and she gives me a glare that means *stop talking*. She doesn't want Mike to hear.

So I lean across my pork chops, which are pale and dry and ugly and try to whisper to her, "What are we going to do about Jessica?"

She hushes me and says in a real loud voice, a fake happy voice, "Mike, sweetie, would you mind getting me some aspirin from the bathroom. I have an awful headache."

He jumps up, his face all concerned. "Of course. How many?"

"Two."

The moment he's gone, she pushes her chest forward and says, "There is nothing going on with Jessica."

My fork clatters to the floor, keeping company with my jaw. *What?*

"There is nothing going on with Jessica."

"He's beating her up!"

"Keep your voice down." She shoves herself up and gets me another fork from the kitchen. "Jessica is not your problem."

"She's my sister."

My mother cuts her meat with quick sharp slashes and whispers, "Not your problem."

"We have to save her." I stab my fork into the mashed potatoes. "Somebody has to save her."

My mother leans back in her chair, closes her eyes. "We can only save ourselves."

After dinner, Mike goes to watch TV and we clear off the table. He doesn't help, of course.

"I'm worried about Jessica," I say, grabbing two glasses.

"I'm sure she's fine." She takes the glasses from me and rinses them. I get some plates, load one on top of the other.

"But what about Brian?"

"She is fine." My mom accentuates each word. I put the plates on the counter. CNN blares in the background. Mike watches TV too loudly. The anchorman drones on about a man shooting up a Best Buy. Mike yells, "Yee-haw." And starts clapping. The pork chop solids up my stomach, weighing me down. What is it about some men? Do they think being stupid is cute?

I imagine going to Jessica's house. There's Brian with his fists, and his mouth, and his twisted face. He's going to hit her and I reach up and grab his arm, just like that.

What would I say?

I'd say, "Think again, partner."

I'd say, "Pick on someone your own size."

But with my mother, tonight, while she washes dishes, all this anger is burning inside me like strong gin. It just sizzles there in my esophagus. How can she pretend like things are fine? How can she pretend that?

"But what about her face?" I put a plate upside down on the counter. "Remember, Mom? Her face?"

My mother shoves her hands into the hot, sudsy sink water. "It was nothing."

She doesn't even look up.

So then I just pull out both barrels, all the big guns. "Don't you think Mike drinks a little too much?"

She throws down her dish rag. It plops into the sink. "What is wrong with you? Do you want everyone to be miserable? You want everybody to be just like you?"

I stand there. I do not stand there. I turn. I walk away.

Pow.

Dear Mr. Wayne,

Well, the first week that Mike O'Donnell stays with us stinks. At night there are moans. In the afternoon he is there. Everything is different. It smells like man socks and Wal-Mart cologne. At night my mother talks all prissy and giggles. I don't get to drink straight from the milk jug and I always have to remember to be polite and cover my mouth when I cough all the time, and sometimes I feel a little displaced, like I wonder if this house really is my house or whether or not I've been suddenly hurtled into this parallel universe where I'm actually good at something (acting) and maybe even have a boy who could possibly like me (Paolo Mattias) and where Nicole might not really be my best friend anymore. But mostly it feels as if I've been taken apart molecule by molecule and some of my molecules are lagging behind in my old life, maybe a second out of synch. It's the same way you feel when you have a cold.

Of course in this brave (!) new world, I have this strange man in my house and my mother is getting bootie all the time and taken to batting her eyelashes like some kind of saloon whore. I don't get to sleep much, and when I do I'm stuck dreaming about knife fights and bars and newspaper headlines: *One Man Dead*.

Each afternoon Mike O'Donnell sits at the kitchen table, a glass of Coke or ginger ale resting on the corner of the newspaper classifieds he's folded out in front of him. A ballpoint pen waits like a weapon in his hand. I go to my room. He goes to the bathroom. He stands outside my door and just breathes.

For a minute I imagine he bursts in, but I'm ready for him. I'm ready for those bloodshot eyes, like a werewolf's at night. I'm ready for those thick-fingered hands. I'm ready for that greedy mean mouth and I pull out a gun, release the safety and … and … and …

And I can't imagine any more.

I've got to tell you, Mr. Wayne, that I do not trust this character. He makes me think of shifty eyes even though his bug out a little. He makes me think of those men standing outside the saloon, leaning against the post acting all casual when you know their gun hands are twitching all over the place. What does he want? Why is he here? Why would he even like my mother? Why doesn't he have a job yet?

I fix a stare on him. I mosey over.

"Any luck?" I say.

And then he shakes his head so sadly it makes me want to hug him, but I don't trust it. It might be a trick to draw me in closer. My uncle did that. He pretended to be sad about my stepdad dying and then what does he do? He tries to get to second base with me even though I'm eleven. He scores a home run with my mother even though she was less than seven days a widow.

So, the week after Mike O'Donnell arrives passes, the weekend comes and goes. Time comes and goes. Sunsets I don't ride off into. There is a math quiz. A surprise. I get a ninety-eight. Two points off because in my hurry to get done and daydream, I put only one line in an equals sign instead of two. Stupid rookie mistake.

I have a new look now. That seems shallow, I know. But I was tired of looking like everyone else. Sasha wears long, swishy skirts and dangly earrings so she looks part gypsy part poet, but that's not me. So, I'm wearing jeans a lot. They ride sort of low, and then I wear one of my stepdad's old button-down shirts that I found in the base-ment. They're too big, so I tie them at the waist, and then I put in some new holes in his old belt. It's big and brown and thick and good like that, with a big ole silver buckle that has a picture of a boat on it.

Sasha and Olivia really like it, but Nicole rolls her eyes and so does my mom.

"What? Are you trying to be a cowboy now?" Nicole laughs so hard she covers her mouth because her fillings are showing. Fillings, she always says, are unattractive. "Oh my God. You are."

I shrug. I stand tall, but I want to crumple into a ball and roll down the hallway, past all the lockers and the gym and into the street and away, just a lonely tumbleweed. Stand back folks, nothing to see.

"You're turning into such a theater freak," she says, laughing still, doubled over. "Oh my God, I'm so sorry, but you are."

She says that, right? But at lunch one of the boys at the football table keeps staring at me with greedy eyes and everyone knows what that means. Then at play rehearsal Paolo Mattias goes, "I like your jeans."

I put my fingers into my belt loops. "Really?"

"Yeah." He stares at me hard and long and good. "I like your buckle too."

I finger it. I'm figuring that's not all he likes. Then I screw it all up and blurt out, "My dad's not gay, you know."

His eyes go blank and he leans against one of the theater chairs that are bolted to the floor. It squeaks. "It's okay if he is."

"He's not."

"Okay. There's a lot shittier things dads can be than gay. Or a cross-dresser. Is that what he is?"

"Really," I shoot at him.

He staggers from the blow, lifts up his hands to surrender. "You sure you're okay? You're wicked worked up about this."

I am not sure. I am not sure. He wears women's tights. I have no clue, but then I think it's pretty obvious, isn't it? I slam myself down into one of the seats. The whole row rocks.

Paolo sticks one shoulder higher than the other, makes

his back go rigid and says, "'Even grown men need under-standing'?"

His voice is all low and drawly.

"What?" I fire.

He stands posture-perfect tall, moves his head so that his chin is straighter than ever. "I said, 'Even grown men need understanding'?"

"Are you quoting John Wayne?"

He blushes and his posture goes back to normal. "Yeah. Did I get it wrong?"

"You're quoting John Wayne to me?"

He nods. "It's from *Cahill U.S. Marshall.*"

I shake my head. I don't know what to say. This boy blows me away, and he doesn't even have a gun. Quoting John Wayne.

"I know where it's from," I say, and my voice is soft again. "I just can't believe you know it."

"I thought you liked him."

"I do... but..." I eye him something good. "Are you pretending to like him?"

He loses his smile. "No."

I wait. His lip quivers for a second and my finger longs to touch that lip, make it strong again. My stomach twists. Why did I even ask him? I'm such a jerk.

He starts talking again. "It's not like he's my hero or anything. But he's cool."

"Who's your hero?"

His shoulders relax into broadness again. "David Belle."

I can't get a fix on David Belle, and Paolo must notice because he goes, "He founded parkour."

"I'm an ignorant dork obviously," I say, "but parkour..."

"Parkour is parkour."

"Funny."

"No, that's what they call it because it's so hard to define. It's like a martial arts thing, but instead of fighting, it's running. Like your body gets these super-efficient movements down and then you can just get over any obstacle, jump between buildings." His eyes light up his whole face. His whole face lights up his body. "You can scale walls. It's amazing."

I can see it. "Like in the James Bond movie with the new guy on the skyscraper."

"Exactly."

"That stuff is amazing."

"I know! Isn't it? It's brilliant."

"Can you do any of it?"

"I'm learning."

My breath whooshes out. "Really?"

"Life's not all about fighting. It's about flight, too, you know. And in parkour, it's like your only opponent is you. It's not very John Wayne, but I like it."

I nod. "I like it too."

He smiles all big and ambles away. He tips an imaginary hat at me and against my will, my faces blushes bright red. Sasha giggles, slips into the empty seat next to me and grabs my arm. "Somebody likes somebody."

"Shut up," I mumble, but I can't stop smiling.

"It's okay to like him. He's so long-legged cute and he moves ... have you noticed the way he moves?"

"Like he knows where every one of his muscles is?" I say.

"Yeah." Sasha squishes her eyes tight. "And he likes you. He's memorizing John Wayne lines for you. It's so cute."

"He keeps asking me if my dad is gay." When I say it, it's like all the good whooshes out of everything, like I'm jumping between buildings and I've missed the edge. I'm just whooshing down towards a concrete parking lot and a dumpster full of trash.

Sasha saves me. "Lily, *everyone* thinks your dad is gay. He's probably just trying to give you a way to talk about it."

I slam back in my theater seat. "They do?"

"Yeah."

I bend over, touch my face to my knees. "Oh God."

"It is so not a big deal." She rubs my back in little circles. "And Olivia thinks he might just have gender identification issues and cross-dress. And who cares? He is what he is. He's your dad first, anyway."

My jeans smell like honey from my bodywash or something. I breathe it in and say, "Nicole doesn't think he is."

"What?"

"She doesn't think he's gay."

Her hand starts rubbing again. "Oh, sweetie. Nicole is very good at seeing the world the way she wants to and ignoring the rest."

"People!" Mrs. Gallagher shouts. "Act One. Scene Two. Places."

I sit up. Sasha smiles. "It's okay."

I repeat, "It's okay."

But Sasha doesn't fall for it. "What are you thinking?"

"That I wish I could do parkour. That I could run up walls and leap things. Or that I could just stand my ground and fight."

She cocks her head at me. "But you can."

Play rehearsal starts and we all read the script. I shoot off glances at Paolo, who is all stretched out on the stage. I have so many lines. Most people highlight their lines but I don't. I highlight the lines around mine. Sasha taught me this. By highlighting your lines you focus only on your character, you become stilted, too focused on your own words. By highlighting the others' lines, you focus on interactions, interplay, the cause and effect of the movements, the beats of the play. Motivations.

Sasha's amazing. And right.

So as we read through the play, the entire cast sitting in a massive circle on the stage, most of us cross-legged, Sasha, yoga-style. Tyler Reed, the cute boy with the eyes, and Paolo lie on their stomachs. Stuart Silsby gets bored and tries to balance his body in weird pseudo-yoga poses until Mrs. Gallagher yells at him.

I sneak peeks at Paolo Mattias, who wears jeans and work boots, which aren't cowboy boots, but kind of close. I highlight with yellow all the lines of everyone around me.

My character is stupid. I can't stand her. She's bigoted, but comes through in the end. All she cares about is this Emile guy she's in love with. She's prissy and corny. You can see her smiling while scrubbing the greasy scum off the stove. That kind of person. The kind of person that would just say the Pledge of Allegiance and never think about the words, just repeat it every day, mindlessly.

I worry that I was picked to be Nellie because I'm like her.

"I hate Nellie," I say in the car, perched between Olivia and Sasha.

"Oh, no," Sasha says. Her hand covers her mouth.

"I can't stand her."

"Why?" she asks and takes a stick of gum out of her jacket. She breaks it in three and offers some to me and some to Olivia.

"Thanks." Olivia pops it into her mouth and drives the car with one hand, and that hand barely on the wheel, not gripping the wheel or anything, just floating on it.

"Thanks," I say. "It's just that she's so, she's so . . ."

"Stupid?" Sasha suggests.

"Yeah. Stupid and mindless and sappy."

"A man wrote *South Pacific*, right?" Olivia asks.

"You guessed it," Sasha says

Olivia snorts. "Figures."

"Why?" I ask, chewing my gum with my mouth closed, not like Olivia who opens her mouth wide and then clamps it shut on the gum like she's an alligator or a snapping turtle biting its prey, or a machine, each stop exact and hard.

"Men always made women stupid in musicals."

"Why?" I ask again.

"Because," Sasha says, "that's how men like women."

"Stupid?"

"Stupid in life. Smart in bed." Olivia laughs.

I don't know if this is true, but I don't follow up on it because then I would have to think about my mother and Mike O'Donnell. So instead I ask, "How am I suppose to play this woman if I don't like her?"

"Play her like a caricature. Make fun of the playwright's intentions. Then it's a statement. You know?" Sasha says. We are almost at my house. Mike will be waiting inside.

"Is that what you're doing?" I ask.

Sasha nods. She's Bloody Mary, an Asian woman who is the comic relief of the musical. Greedy with stilted English, but with a mystical part to her as well.

"What if no one gets it?" I ask as I climb out of the car.

She shrugs. "I don't know if they will. Maybe one person will get it, and that makes it worthwhile."

"Just one person," I say.

"All you need is one," Sasha and Olivia sing at me together before Sasha shuts the door and they turn around to go home.

I'm going to have to kiss Tyler, the other romantic lead. I haven't told Nicole. We haven't done it yet. Whenever we get to a kissing part Mrs. Gallagher yells, "KISS!" and Tyler and I look at each other and laugh. I can't imagine kissing him. What it will be like. Better than my pillow I'm sure, but what if it's too wet like a dog, or too dry like cardboard? I have to start eating more Certs. Thank God I don't like him that way. I'd never be able to do it.

I stop halfway up the rock path behind my house, grab a dandelion that's growing between the stones. I think of what Sasha said: All you need is one. Maybe that goes for kisses too, just one and then they'll be coming to me all the time, a whole life of kisses.

It sounds like a chant. *All you need is one. All you need is one. All you need is one.* I wonder if they've learned that at a protest somewhere. I mosey up the path to the house and worry about my character being a caricature and it makes me think of my uncle, the one who visited from California right after my stepfather died. And thinking of him makes me shudder and wonder if I'll ever be able to kiss a boy at all without my mind straying.

My chest feels hot where that cross would hang. My chest feels his hands there, feels them lower. I stagger against a tree and close my eyes, but that doesn't help. I open them and stare up at the leaves, all orange and yellow.

"Beautiful leaves," I say. "Beautiful leaves."

But that's what he said to me: "Lily, do you know how beautiful you are?"

And there were his fingers, moving back and forth, back and forth.

"Hello," I say to Mike when I muster up enough courage to go inside my own damn house.

"How was your day?" he asks and stands up, blocking my way out of the kitchen. He is big, big, big. He is just too tall and his shoulders are broad, like the doorframe or a guillotine.

"Good," I say, taking a step backwards into the kitchen even though I want to go forward to my room. "Long rehearsal. Lots of homework to do."

I nod past him towards my room. I wait for him to get the hint. He doesn't.

"I need to get to my room," I say, ambling forward. "Sorry."

He barely moves when I walk past him. We are so close that my shoulder almost touches his arm. He sways on the balls of his feet.

"Sorry," I mumble and it's all I can do not to run down the hall.

In my room, I shut the door. I think about it and then I shove my dresser up against it. The damn thing thumps against the rug, sounding like a bull about to rumble through the house, but I don't care. I can't make it quieter. I shake my head at myself, but I'm not moving it. No way.

He walks to the door. I hold my breath. I cross my fingers. What if he tries to get in?

I can hear him breathe.

"Lily?"

"Yep!" I yell, backing up to the window.

"Can I come in?"

"Um. Um. I'm kind of getting dressed," I lie.

There is silence. I hear his breath. "Okay, well, I'm going out to the store. You want anything?"

"Nope," I say even though I want more Coke since he keeps drinking it all. "Thanks."

He sighs and walks away. I pull back my white curtain that used to make me think of ghosts when I was little, and I watch him drive away in this car he's bought on the cheap. It's dented and rusty and more embarrassing than my father's beige Ford Escort.

"Big breaths," I tell myself. "Big, deep breaths."

I imagine the car exploding as it turns out of the driveway, vaporizing Mike O'Donnell instantly. My mother will be sad, of course. I will wear a black shirt with my jeans and big belt to the funeral. No such luck.

I move the dresser and go out to the kitchen and call Nicole. I tell her about the potential play kiss with Tyler Reed.

"I am so mad at myself," Nicole says.

"You should be," I tell her on the phone. "You said theater was for losers."

"I was wrong. Okay. Shut up." She chews so loud I can hear her teeth hit each other.

I can see her going to every single performance, chewing gum and drooling in one of those dinky auditorium chairs, not paying any attention to the musical but just thinking about him, Fire Man, Red Pants Boy, Tyler Reed. But who will she sit with all five shows? Who will listen to her rant about his calves, his eyes, his toenails? I wish I could be there for her as her hormones kick into overdrive, but I can't. I'll be up on stage with Fire Man, and you can bet, romantic lead or not, there will be no male Nicoles sitting below me fantasizing about my shins when I sing "I'm Gonna Wash That Man Right Outa My Hair."

Nicole wants me to invite her to the cast party. She tells me this on the phone. I pull the cord all the way and then sit in the coat closet to get some privacy, shutting the door behind me. It stinks in here like mothballs and mice, almost a death smell, but it feels safe.

"You have to invite me to the cast party," she says.

"I don't know if I can."

"What do you mean you don't know if you can?"

"I don't know if it's allowed."

"Well, break the rules."

"I don't even know if there *is* a cast party," I say, shoving a big, ugly duck boot from L.L.Bean out of the way. I was sitting on it and the ribbed toes were pretty uncomfortable beneath my butt.

"There's always a cast party."

"How do you know?"

Nicole thinks she knows everything.

"My brother told me."

"The same brother who put all your CDs in the microwave?"

"Yes," she grunts.

"The same brother who tied you up in phone cord and dragged you down the stairs?"

"Yes."

"The same brother who posted your picture on the

sexy singles page on the web and named you Fruity Pebbles and said you were looking for someone cuckoo for Cocoa Puffs?"

"Shut up," she says. "He's my brother."

"Some brother."

"At least my mother isn't living in sin with some freak from Oregon."

"Grow up."

"You."

"You just said 'living in sin,' get a grip."

"You get a grip. I'm not such a freak that I go around purring and writing letters to a dead movie star."

"Shut up."

"You do. You write letters to freaking John Wayne and now you're dressing like some sort of cowboy slut."

There's a big lump of lead in my throat, like a million slugs from an old gun and my words still explode past them into the phone. "At least my brother doesn't pop his pimples on me and then I pretend like he's some freaking genius."

"The only person you think is a freaking genius is you."

And then she hangs up. I wait for her to call back and she doesn't. I wait and wait for the phone to ring, just sit there in the closet, only getting up to shut off the kitchen light so that the closet can be as dark and blank as my head. Nicole always calls back. When we got in a fight over whether the President or the Pope was more masculine, she called back after I hung up. The phone rang after thirty seconds. After a while I give up. I call Sasha and I don't say anything about Nicole and our fight; instead, for some reason I say, "I'm worried about my sister."

I talk in hushed tones even though Mike still isn't back.

"Why?"

"I think her husband hits her."

I bite my lip. I've said it. That's what you'd do, right, Mr. Wayne? You wouldn't pretend like nothing happened, which is what we do in my family. Pretend. Pretend my sister isn't hurting. Pretend my father isn't gay or something. Pretend like nothing bad has ever happened to me. Pretend like Uncle Mark was some nice guy who made good taco salads.

There's silence for a second and then Sasha says, "Oh."

"Yeah."

"Oh."

I stare at the ceiling and refuse to cry.

"Oh."

Dear Mr. Wayne,

What did I think would happen? That Sasha would some-how magically know what to do?

No one knows what to do in real life. Real life is not the movies.

If it were, I would grab a gun and Sasha. We'd break into my sister's house, yank my brother-in-law off the couch by his shirt collar, throw him against the wall and say, real slow and menacing, but strong, we'd say it strong, "Listen pardner. You've got yourself a little problem with your fists. Now, here's what we're going to do about it..."

And then he'd listen. And then things would be sun-sets and ice cream and horses galloping free across the prairie.

Because everything is going so bad, I call my dad and ask him to go to the movies.

"The movies? Really?" he says, like I'm some hot babe asking him on a date.

"Yeah. If you don't want to that's okay."

"No, I want to."

We go see *North to Alaska,* which is still playing at the Alamo. It's been playing there a month. I look around for him, but Paolo Mattias is not in the theater. Like he would be. He's probably out there trying to scale the wall of the Masonic Temple or something. Instead, there's just a couple old ladies and the projectionist here.

My dad settles into his chair, giggles and says, "John Wayne is cute."

"I thought you'd prefer Tom Cruise," I say.

"No, Wayne is cuter."

I take his popcorn away from him and put it on the floor, and whisper, "What did you just say?"

My father shrugs and waves his hand around in the dark movie theater air. "Give me back my popcorn."

He sounds whiny, like a child. I stare and stare at his hand, wiggling there, and wonder how he could be my father, how I ever could have thought he'd keep me safe. When I was little and he'd come get me on Sundays, I'd be so happy to see him. He'd lift me above his head and twirl me around and tell me how much he missed me. I felt safe then, like he'd never drop me. Then my stepdad died. Then my step-uncle came with his hands. Then my dad wasn't there. Not like he could be, like he could magically know that I needed him, but I expected him to be, you know? Isn't that what dads are for? To scare the bad guys away? To fire the guns? To stand tall? To keep the children safe?

On the screen, Mr. Wayne, you realize that George Pratt's beloved is married to another and you won't be able to bring her back like you promised. You're stuck. But I know this movie, I've seen it a million times with my stepdad. I know that you find Capucine, the bar dancer, you bring her back instead. You figure things out.

I close my eyes, just listening to your voice, low and smooth and stable, and try not to think of my Uncle Mark, of Mike O'Donnell, of my sister's husband, of all the bad men out there. I close my eyes and listen to your voice, to the gun shots, and I wish so bad you were here to protect me. Why aren't you here?

Next to me is my dad. He grabs my hand with his sticky popcorn fingers. I let him.

Dear Mr. Wayne,

Let me tell you, that girl can be some stubborn. It's really not a good time for her to ditch out on the whole friendship thing. I mean, I've got a lot to deal with here: gay dad, beaten sister, mother's boyfriend is a freak. Still, Nicole and I don't talk. I have no notes to read from her in study hall, so I start the first page of my Hannah Dustin report. Then, bam, across the floor comes a Paolo Mattias note.

I take a couple big breaths. It's not like it's poison, but I'm afraid of the note. I am so dumb, sometimes I can't stand myself. I grab it and pull it open.

Going to the football game Friday?

I stare. I look around like maybe it's a big joke, you know, invite the loser to the football game so you can dump pig's blood on her. No one is laughing or even smirking.

I look at the note again. I think about Nicole. We've had an eternal promise to attend all football games together so she can scope out the best butts with a friend at her side. Since we aren't talking, that promise doesn't hold anymore, does it? She thinks I'm a theater geek anyway. Right?

Sure

I write back, fold the note, kick it over to him. A minute later, the note is at my feet again.

Me too. I'll see you there.

I stare at this a while. I'll see Paolo at rehearsal every day before then. Is he not going to be there?

yeah and at rehearsal too.

I give the note to the girl next to me who passes it to Paolo. He opens it up and smiles. Gives me a little wave. Then he scribbles frantically and shoots another note back at me.

*Why don't we go together?
I'll pick you up.*

I swallow. I swallow again. Maybe there are some secret cameras hiding behind people's book bags slumped on the floor, because this is all some super-big evil joke. There are no cameras anywhere.

Shrugging like this isn't a super big deal, I write,

Sure

The note slides back.

Paolo writes something down. I give up trying to appear casual about the whole thing, and watch the note glide across the floor and witness the horrible grass-stained sneaker of Mr. Farley stomp on top of it. He bends down, picks it up, and opens it.

Paolo's mouth drops open. I stand up. "Um, Mr. Far-ley ... that's ..."

Mr. Farley prances in place like one of those white stallions from Austria or Germany, you know the kind that dance and do circus tricks. His resemblance to a horse is made more apparent by the tightness of his green cords across his flanks.

"Well, well, well ... class, or should I say, brain-dead study hall attendees?" Mr. Farley struts back to the front of the class. "It seems we have a budding romance and a date, between our young jock friend Mr. Mattias and our bright little cowgirl, Ms. Faltin. A football game on Friday. How high school? How sweet?"

I gasp. I look around hopelessly and I spot Sasha in

the back row. She winks at me and then whoops, "Amen to that. Whoo-ee."

Everyone starts laughing, but at Sasha, not at us. She sacrifices herself and stands up, clapping her hands. "Let's hear it for the team!"

She runs over to Paolo, pinches his cheeks and acts like a cute grandmother. "Such a sweetie. Is this your first date?"

Paolo laughs.

Steam comes out of Mr. Farley's ears.

She trots over to me. "And Lily. Can you be more of a pint-sized babe than this? No way. Good cowgirl gear too."

She wiggles her eyes at me and winks. "Giddyup."

Mr. Farley has had enough and he's trying to shout over everyone's laughter. "Ms. Sandeman. Ms. Sandeman! Will you please sit down."

She puts her hands in her pockets and nods at him. "Sure, daddy-o. Sure."

She becomes some sort of beatnik/hippie hybrid and flashes us all a peace sign before slamming into a chair.

"Detention!" Mr. Farley announces, and then gives up and falls back into his chair at the front of the room. He throws the note in the trash. "There is no note writing in study hall!"

Sasha and I make eye contact. She's sacrificed herself for me. My heart flitter flutters around my ribs. I mouth, "I am *so* sorry."

She winks and mouths back, "I *love* detention."

"Seriously?" I mouth.

She nods.

"Ms. *Faltin*! Will you *please* sit down," Mr. Farley says. "Or do you want detention, too?"

I settle into my seat trying not to grin too hard, but my feet do happy little dances beneath the desk. A date! A date! Me on a date with Paolo Mattias! Will wonders never cease? Will pigs soon fly? Will my father start wearing muscle T-shirts and normal socks? Anything is possible.

Collapsing further into my chair, my shoulders down and shrugging, I imagine I'm a gold prospector like in *North to Alaska*. Study hall turns into Nome, Alaska. The sky sings blue, and gold weighs my fingers. Right next to me in his open-necked shirt, sleeves rolled up to reveal muscular forearms, is Paolo Mattias. He winks. I smile. In the river our fingers touch, heating up the cold, cold water.

Mr. Farley snaps *his* fingers in front of my face, real close, and I jump and give a stupid little scream. He swaggers there, his face all snarky and his voice taunting. "Dreaming of boys, Miss Faltin?"

Everyone laughs except me and Paolo. I spend the rest of study hall writing and trying to get my skin back to its normal non-blushing color.

I wait for Sasha at the door. "You didn't have to do that."

She beams. "I hate when teachers get all *The Man* on us, you know?"

We squeeze through the door. "Sure."

Paolo is waiting in the hallway. Sasha just keeps beaming. She grabs his hand. She grabs my hand. She makes our fingers intertwine. "If you're going to go out on a date you have to hold hands. Really."

She winks and runs off.

I use my free hand to cover my face. "Oh my God."

Paolo squeezes my fingers. "You don't want to?"

My fingers look like play toys next to his. I stare at them so I don't look at him. "No. Um. Yeah. I want to." He checks me with his hip. I check him back with my hip. Stuart comes bouncing by us and laughs. "Well, it's love! Love in the hallowed halls of high school. Oh, how lovely love loverly."

He kisses Paolo's cheek. Paolo laughs, lets go of my hand and wipes his cheek. Stuart then smacks a big one on my cheek too.

"I am in love with love," he yells and rushes away.

Paolo looks at me. I look at him and we both completely lose it. We just stand there in the middle of the hall with people swarming around us. We just stand there in the middle of the hall laughing. We just stand there in the middle of the hall until we double over and have to clutch each other's stomachs because everything is suddenly so funny and so good-weird.

When I get to lunch, Nicole sits down next to me and says like nothing's happened, "Want to go through the line?"

"Uh-huh."

It feels good, like I have my best friend back, and even

though Nicole is occasionally an idiot, I really do love her. I mean, who else would throw hula hoops at cars with me back in fourth grade? We buy our bagels and sit back down. I try to think of how to tell her that I'm going to the football game with Paolo. Nicole starts the ten-minute-spreading-of-the-cream-cheese ritual and before I can say anything, whispers, "You'll never guess what I heard."

"What?" I bite into my onion bagel. I'll have to get a Certs from Nicole like I always do or Martha, my biology lab partner, will faint when I breathe on her.

"It's weird."

"Uh-huh."

Nicole doesn't look at me, just her bagel. She digs into the cream cheese pack and scoops out some more to spread.

"It's about Olivia."

"Sasha's sister?" I ask.

Nicole nods.

"What about her?"

She motions for me to lean over. I do. She cups her hands around my ear after looking around to make sure that no one is listening. No one is. No one is even looking at us except for Nicole's brother and Travis Poppins.

"She's a lesbian."

I can feel Nicole's breath against my ear. My back hurts from leaning over so I straighten it, bite into my bagel. A lesbian. Okay. I try to digest this. I try to figure out if I care. I don't. If Olivia's a lesbian, big deal. No, it is a big deal, because Nicole is making it into something bad, something shameful. Nicole's acting like she's some sort of right winger, some ultra-conservative freak who thinks gay people should die, be dragged behind trucks, dropped off bridges, not allowed to teach. I chew my bagel and each bite makes me madder. I chew my bagel and the sound of my teeth grinding against the food, against each other, gives me the biggest headache of my life.

"Can you believe it?" Nicole asks. "I mean, once I heard I thought, 'Well, you can kind of tell.'"

I chomp my bagel, take a swig of my Coke. I count to ten to try to calm down and not commit homicide in the cafeteria with just a plastic cream cheese spreader and a bagel.

One. Two. Three. Four.

"I mean," Nicole continues and goes back to spreading, "I've never known anyone who actually was..."

Five.

"...before, other than possibly Mary."

Seven.

"Not that there's anything wrong with it."

Eight.

"It's just so, so gross really and..."

Nine.

"Well, I thought I should tell you because, because..."

Ten. I look at her, fix her with a real good stare, but she doesn't notice. My gun hand twitches but I don't have a gun. I believed in her. I thought we could go back to normal, but we can't. We can't. We're too different.

"Well, if you hang out with her a lot, people are probably going to think you are too," she finishes.

I put my Coke down and stand up. Saddle up.

"Nicole," I say, a parting shot before heading to the bathroom, "you must be one of the stupidest damn people in the whole damn world."

Before turning to walk away, I let myself watch her mouth drop. In the bathroom I throw up like a cat that eats too much, too fast. One splurting removal of all I've eaten and then my stomach is empty and free. I'm not sick, but it happens anyway. Nervous throw-up, my mother calls it. It's because I can't deal with confrontations. It's because I can't deal with yelling at the girl who used to be my best friend. It's because I can't deal with anything, really.

I wipe my mouth with one of the brown paper towels by the sink and get a drink of water from the water fountain before going back to the cafeteria. Nicole's moved to sit with her brother and Travis Poppins. She's crying, and Travis has his pimply arm around her shoulders. Her brother glares at me. I glare back. When the bell rings for biology, I make my way to class and worry about my breath and what my lab partner will think. Onion bagel barf breath. Yuck.

On my way through the hall, I walk alone. Usually I walk with Nicole because her earth science class is next door. It seems too quiet, despite all the other people around me. It's like all the innocent town folks just roaming about, going about their business before the outlaw gang comes through, rifles firing. And then Alyssa Cutler, queen of popularity Alyssa Cutler of all people, comes up to me and says, "Lily, I heard you're doing great in *South Pacific*. Congratulations."

"Thanks," I say and try to think of some compliment to give her, but I can't. I can't say, "Oh, you're so beautiful." Or, "How did your lips get to look like bacon?" Or "How could I be thin like you?" Or "God, will you please be my friend?"

Instead, my mouth somehow manages to smile, which is something at least. One working body part. That and my feet. It seems my tongue and brain have deserted me.

"I was wondering," Alyssa says, still beside me. "Is it too late to join Students for Social Justice?"

"No way. You can join anytime. We'd love to have you."

"Great." She smiles a cover-girl smile and says, "It's Mondays, right?"

"Uh-huh."

"Do you think you could give me a ride home?"

We stand outside the door for biology and I say, "I get a ride home with Sasha and Olivia. It's pretty squished, but I don't think it would be a big deal or anything."

"Good," Alyssa says before she walks away. "Will you ask for me? I love your belt."

"Thanks." I smile and wave as Alyssa saunters down the hallway, and it's only as I get in the classroom that I remember about Olivia maybe being a lesbian and wondering if Alyssa knows, if Alyssa thinks I'm one too, if Nicole was making it all up, if Alyssa would care if I was a lesbian, or if Olivia was, or if she's just so cool that she doesn't care about anyone's sexual preferences.

Alyssa Cutler likes my belt. But I still feel all hollow because Nicole's such an idiot and I'm so mad at her for always, always, always caring more about what people think than what they do, and for how she flirted with Paolo when she knows I like him, but still there's an empty space inside me where a *Cosmo*-loving, boy-luster should go.

In biology, I sit next to Martha and try not to breathe on her.

"Lily?" she asks, taking out her notebook and placing it on the black top of the lab table we share. "What's that sound?"

"What sound?"

"Like purring?"

I lift up my shoulders to show her I have no idea what she's talking about, and then I reach down to get a notebook and pen out of my backpack.

"Oh," she says, opening her notebook to the next blank page. "It stopped."

✦

I hate fighting.

I hate fighting with my mom.

But I really hate fighting with Nicole.

My head throbs because there isn't anyone to talk to, because there isn't anyone I can call and cry to and not have them think badly of me after. Sometimes if you tell people your sorrows they want nothing to do with you, afterwards they'll almost ignore you, give you vague smiles that don't go past their teeth, little nods and small talk and then you know you've gone too far, told too much, exposed yourself to someone who couldn't or didn't want to see.

I pick up the phone. Dial the numbers and call my dad, who should be home from work by now.

"How about I bring my homework? And come over tonight," I say. It will be musty smelling there and his voice already sounds weepy, but it has to be better than another night at this house with my mom and her man.

"Oh goody! I'll come get you," he says.

"I'm sleeping over at dad's," I announce when my mom gets home. I grab some stuff and call Sasha to tell her I won't need a ride tomorrow morning, that my dad will bring me to school. My mother goes into the TV room and turns it on. She seems happy to have me gone. She probably figures it means more alone time with her man, her hard-drinking, got-no-job man.

Yeah, get rid of the kid, she's probably thinking, *then we can do it doggy-style on the kitchen floor.*

I shudder. I sit there by the counter, I just sit there on the stool for a while because I don't have enough energy to move. I'm sort of hunkered down and rocking back and forth, feeling like the gray or lightish purple color in front of my eyes is the color of my soul. Blah. Bleak. Sad. I hate my mother.

The sliding noise and creak that the doorknob makes when it turns forces me to lift my head up for a second, startled. Great, Mike O'Donnell. I wipe the back of my hand against my eyes, so he doesn't know what it's all about. Maybe he won't notice anything. I try to smile but it comes out all crooked, and my lips just don't make it into the upturn.

"Lily?" he asks. "What's happened, honey? Do you want me to get your mother?"

I shake my head no. That's the last thing I need.

He kneels down and grabs my hand. I try to pull mine away, but he just grips harder. Trapped. I take big breaths, but it makes me start tearing up more and I almost start to panic because I can't get my hand away, and then the sobs just come, whoosh right out of me and I try to pull away but he heaves me into his arms. My head presses into his ugly, tan, old-man jacket, smelling him, pipes and aftershave and steak. He holds me against him, patting my hair with his hand. I can't breathe. I push away.

He smiles at me and says, "Let's go outside. I have some things to tell you."

"No," I say. "My dad's coming. I have homework to do."

"Soon then?"

"Sure," I say. "Soon."

But I say it just to make him go away, which makes me a liar, which is something a hero never is. But we all know I'm no hero, don't we?

Dear Mr. Wayne,

On the table, Grammy has placed cut tomatoes, acorn squash filled with pools of butter, pot roast, potatoes cut in squares and covered with gravy, sweet potatoes, butter, homemade bread, carrots rolled in brown sugar and butter, and carrots in gravy cut in circles.

"Did you make all of this?" I ask, pretty much drooling.

"Don't I always?" Grammy answers. "Can't expect your father to cook well."

"I helped," my dad says, pouring whole milk, not skim, from a pitcher into my glass and then his. "I turned the pot roast over."

"And talked on the phone. He's always talking on the phone to his friends," Grammy says. "Liliana, have some tomatoes."

I watch Grammy fork some tomato slices onto my plate. One. Two. Three.

"That's enough. Thank you."

"A couple more. These are good for you. They're fruit. Did you know that tomatoes are fruit?"

I nod and worry about getting all my homework done.

"That's the strangest thing," my father says, sprinkling salt on one of his tomato slices. "Tomatoes are like apples and oranges."

"They're sweet," Grammy says, sucking on one.

"But could you imagine putting salt on an apple?" my father asks.

"You shouldn't put salt on anything. It's bad for your blood pressure," I say, biting into a tomato. It squirts into my mouth. It *is* sweet. I smile at Grammy. She smiles back.

"Good?" she asks me.

"Good." I stab into another one.

"Oh, my pills!" My father rushes up, nearly knocking his chair over as he goes to get his pills off the counter. His baby blue sock has sagged down because the elastic is gone and a gold chain hugs his ankle in between the dark hairs. Sparkly little gems stick to the chain. These too are baby blue.

Grammy sees me looking and whispers, "He should have been a girl."

"He's a truck driver."

"Women can drive trucks. Your great grandmother was the first female doctor in Czechoslovakia. Of course, it was Moravia then. Czechoslovakia, what sort of horrid name is that?"

I nod. I've heard it before. My father comes back and

sits at the table. "So how are things going with your house guest?"

"Mike O'Donnell?" My knife freezes in midair.

"Yes."

"Okay, I guess." I breathe out and cut into my pot roast. It's tender and I can use a bread knife. "Good roast, Grammy."

"I turned it," my father says, drinking some more milk.

"Good roast, Dad."

My father smiles and nods and cuts into his meat. His hands are large and delicate like his father's were. In pictures of Grandpa, it is his hands that always stick out, long and white and thin beneath the elegant and practical black overcoat that he always wore. He was a stock broker and an existentialist. Everyone says he was a brilliant man, but cruel. My father can barely read or use a calculator so I don't think he takes much after his father. But when you talk to him, he seems smart. He knows about all kinds of things, like you do, Mr. Wayne.

You, of course, were a straight-A student.

"Dad," I ask, thinking and talking simultaneously, not to mention chewing. "When you call people up on the phone you get the numbers wrong a lot, don't you?"

"All the time."

"Is it off by two digits usually? Do you dial 3391 instead of 3319 and stuff like that?"

He looks up from his sugar carrots, chews for a moment before answering because his mother makes sure his manners are impeccable, and says, "Yes, I do. How did you know that?"

I think about the birthday cards he has given me and how often he writes *p*'s instead of *b*'s and writes *q*'s for *d*'s and how he writes over these mistakes.

"I think maybe you're dyslexic."

Both he and Grammy stare at me like I'm crazy.

"No offense," I say and spear a cubed potato with my fork.

I have recently seen a talk show about this, if you can't tell. And it's all coming together now. Like a bullet into my back; I didn't see it coming. I don't know where it came from, but suddenly my whole idea of the world shifts as it penetrates.

"Dyslexic?" Grammy asks me and her voice loses its elegant timber, becomes croaky like an old woman's voice always seems, but hers never is. She drinks lemon water all day. One of her vanities.

"Uh-huh."

"I suppose that might make some sense," my dad says, not eating at all now, just staring at me with those blue eyes of his, waiting for me to go on.

"Well, you aren't a stupid person. I mean you're always asking people questions and watching PBS and learning things. You know tons of facts about everything, right?" I say.

"Your father is the king of trivia," Grammy says. "Ask him anything. But he was never as bright as his brother."

My dad frowns and starts eating again.

"That's where you're wrong, Grammy. I think Dad is smart. It's just that his brain works differently. Dyslexics transpose numbers. They have a hard time reading. Even using the calculator can be difficult because they switch the numbers they see on a page around before they get them into the calculator. It isn't something bad. It's just that their brains process things in different ways."

My dad swallows some more roast, washes it down with some milk and keeps staring at me, waiting for more. I think about the bracelet on his ankle. That has nothing to do with being dyslexic. Being dyslexic does not make you want to wear anklets or pierce your belly button (not that my dad has; thank you, God). I guess what I mean is, I think about all the ways my dad is different, and how hard that must be for him.

"Einstein was dyslexic, wasn't he?" he asks, smiling.

"He had some sort of learning disability," I say.

"Brilliant man." Grammy plucks a few tomatoes off her plate and puts them on mine. They are the same firehouse red that I once painted my dad's toenails. That was a long time ago, when he still lived at home and I was only three or so. I didn't stay on the nails, and colored the hair on his toes, everywhere. When my mother saw what we had done she flipped, dumped a bottle of nail polish remover on his feet and got it all over the rug. The color of the carpet leached right out and I couldn't understand where it went.

They got divorced pretty soon after that.

"A lot of dyslexics are brilliant," I say, "but a lot of them are so upset about their reading capabilities, their transposing of letters and numbers, that they never realize that they are."

My dad's smile slows across his face and his hand shakes a little bit. He changes the subject. "How are Mike O'Donnell and your mother? Is he going to find a place soon?"

I shrug and lift some potato onto my fork. "He's still looking for a job."

"She needs more milk," Grammy says and motions for my father to refill my glass.

My dad gets up with the pitcher and pours the milk into my glass. I can smell his clean smell, a soap and lemon detergent kind of smell. Very different than Mike's.

"He used to be quite a drinker," my father says.

Grammy scowls. She is still, more than half a century after the movement passed, a prohibitionist. "Who?"

"This friend of Rita's," he says, sitting back down.

"Mike O'Donnell," I say, giving him a name. "Thanks."

"Irish. All of them are drinkers."

"Grammy!" I say. "That's offensive."

"It's true," she says. "Just like the Moravians are all depressed."

"I'm not depressed," I say and plunk a tomato into my mouth, feeling the juices of it spurt against my teeth.

"The young," Grammy says to my father, completely ignoring me, "are all such liars."

✳

When he tucks me in, my father puts his hand on my knee where it's upraised under the covers and says, "I'm sorry I forget to feed you on Sundays and about the child support checks and all that."

I look straight ahead at the double circles of light on the ceiling. "It's okay."

He squeezes my knee. "No. No, it isn't. I know I'm not perfect, that I'm not the perfect dad. Thanks for sleeping over. I wish you'd do it more often."

"Maybe I will." Sometimes he is a such sweet man. After a second, I ask him, "What's up with the ankle bracelet thing?"

"You saw that?"

"Uh-huh."

He laughs. "It brings out my eyes."

He blinks them really fast and flirty, and then rolls them.

I laugh too, and our giggles echo against walls of this tiny bedroom and join the sound of the classical music Grammy always plays at night, reverberating in the darkness. One car comes down the road and then another, each shining their lights inside the room for a few moments, and during these seconds I sneak a glance at my dad. He looks happy.

"Do any of your trucker friends know about it?"

Laughing again, he spreads his arms wide open and says, "What do you think?"

"I think some of your trucker friends might knock you some good," I say.

"Either that or ask me home."

He fluffs the bed covers, pulls the comforter to my chin like I'm a little girl. The soft weight of it makes me feel all cozy safe. The smell of clean sheets is comforting, so I smile, and then he asks, "Do you really think I'm dyslexic?"

I tell him yes, and then I spend the rest of the night wondering about how people can be so many things that they don't even know. How my dad could be dyslexic all his life and not realize it. How my mom could be selfish and not know it. How about me? What could I be and not realize? God, I hope it's something good, and not like World Champion Bratwurst Eater.

Dear Mr. Wayne,

Of course, at play rehearsal, every time Sasha and I sit down she wants to talk about my sister. It's her new mission. We scrunch up in the auditorium seats. I hug my hands across my chest and we talk.

"We have to do something," she says. "It's ridiculous. It's like, oh yeah, we can do stuff about women in Sudan but not your sister?"

I bite my lip and scrunch down lower. I stare at the ceiling. It has water stains. Someone shot a pencil up there and it hangs, waiting to fall.

"We have to tell people," Sasha insists. She looks at me all earnest. "We have to."

I nod. "But what?"

"That," she sighs dramatically. "I don't know."

Everything is high drama with Sasha, which is good because it's interesting. But sometimes I wish she were a little more like Nicole and we didn't have to save the world or be amazing actresses or deep thinkers for just a minute or two.

"I don't know either," I say. I imagine lassoing Brian and dumping him in a pig's pen. I imagine branding his big beefy Budweiser butt with a WB for wife beater. "But we've got to do something."

During a break in the action Stuart Silsby yells, "It smells like feet in here."

Up on the stage, Paolo looks at me and I can tell he's trying not to laugh. I look away first. He has a hula skirt on over his jeans. He looks mortified. Stuart lifts it up and looks under it.

"Enough, Stuart." Mrs. Gallagher stops consulting with the boys on how to dance the hula without looking girlie for a long enough time to point her long, crooked finger at Stuart. He shrugs.

He trots over to us, and Sasha makes a big sweet look and says, "I'm sorry Stuart, we can't talk right now. Personal stuff."

"Oh, the rejection," he croons and skips away.

I sort of wish Stuart would stay. I draw a heart on my jeans. It's lopsided. "There's no one to tell."

"How about your dad?"

I shrug.

"Your mom's boyfriend?"

"I don't know," I say. "He's a little weird."

I almost tell Sasha about the empty bottles and how he stands outside my door, but she's already worried about my sister's cheek and I don't want her to think we're total trash, all talk show and stuff, because we aren't. Not really. We just are right now. Fortunately, Mrs. Gallagher's scream saves me.

"Enough! Can't you be secure enough in your masculinity to wear a goddamn hula skirt? Jesus!" she yells, then throws up her hands. "Get off my stage!"

The boys all hoot and celebrate and yank off their hula skirts, throwing them into the air. She calls Sasha up on stage. Paolo jumps down and I gulp when he heads directly towards me.

He plops into the seat next to me, slings one leg over the seat in front of him. "You okay? You look sad."

I shrug, tilt my head a little and look into his big eyes. I'd like to tell him, Mr. Wayne, I really would, but it's like my mom said, there are no hero men. We've got to be hero women now.

"I'm good," I lie.

He gives me the look of scrutiny, squinting a little at me, and then he decides to accept things I guess, because his shoulders relax. He has big shoulders like you. I can see him walking down those western streets. I start to blush.

"I'll pick you up for the game Friday, okay?" He shifts his weight so that he leans back against the chair. One hand crosses in front of his belt and the other hand kind of rests under it like he's some sort of Latin American movie star posing for a shot. Only Paolo is not posing.

And me? I want to touch him, sneak my hand under his, grab the belt loop of his jeans and pull him closer. It's all warm and gooey inside me like I'm just one big want. My face must be bright red. "You can drive?"

He blushes now. "Not officially."

Imagine with me, Mr. Wayne. There he is, Paolo Mattias, with a black baseball cap, yee-hawing down the streets of Merrimack. He's got one hand on the wheel, the other around my shoulders and he's driving free with fourteen lawmen behind him, all ready to take him to the brig because he doesn't have a license. The car leaps over the top of a hill, careens down a dirt road kicking up dust behind us, but the way ahead is clear.

"My brother's going to drive us," he says, chasing my thoughts away.

He has little dimples in his cheeks when he smiles. Sometimes he looks like you, Mr. Wayne, all man-confident and able, and sometimes he doesn't. Sometimes he looks like a boy.

✦

Paolo and I both have nothing to do for the last hour of rehearsal. He's waiting on his brother for a ride. I'm waiting on Sasha and Olivia. Sasha's up on stage, waddling like she weighs 875 pounds or something and hamming it up. She's so brilliant even Mrs. Gallagher cracks up. Stuart keeps forgetting his lines.

"Stuart!" Mrs. Gallagher yells. "Have you read the script?"

He sulks into himself and goes, "Yeah. I have."

She points at him. "Then prove it to me."

Sasha jumps out of character. "They're difficult lines. I'll practice with him. Lily will too. Right Lily? Maybe this weekend?"

"Yep!" I yell from where I'm sitting in the bleachers cranking out the geometry homework. I alpha-dog stare at Mrs. Gallagher. She surrenders.

"Fine, try it again. Stuart, go get your g-d script."

Stuart hustles off stage right to get his g-d script. Paolo leans over my shoulder. "You want to leave?"

I'm slamming my math book and notebook into my bag before I can even answer. "You bet."

As soon as we mosey through the big green auditorium doors and hit the hallways, it's like being released from prison. The air loses its gross damp theater smell. We stop in the center of the hallway.

"Want to go outside?"

I nod.

Outside it's even better—fresh air, blue skies. We head down towards the back of the building and we aren't really saying anything, which makes me feel kind of awkward once I realize it, so I say, "Tell me more about this parkour stuff."

"How about I show you?" He sets his pack on the ground. The straps flap and still. I put my bag next to it and it kind of leans in, like they are meant to be there resting together.

I flop on the grass with the bags. My hands brush against the soft blades of it.

"Grass in New England is different from grass in Florida," Paolo says.

"When did you live in Florida?"

"Till I was eight. I moved here. Remember?"

I nod. I lie. I don't remember.

Wind brushes a dark wave of hair across his forehead. "You ready?"

"Show me what you got," I say and then realize I sound too John Wayney, too much like you and not enough like Lily, so I say in a more normal, too soft voice, "Don't get hurt."

Paolo laughs. "Trust me."

And then he moves. He runs, springs, dashes right at the brick wall so fast I know he's going to smash into it. I jump up ready to scream "stop" but I don't get to, because he's already conquered the wall, not by crashing into it, but by kicking off of it. It's like all the push of him going forward has pushed him up instead, and with two steps he's standing on the roof.

"Oh my God."

He turns around and smiles.

"I can't believe you just did that."

"Breathe, Lily."

"Oh my God."

He keeps smiling, soul-splitting heart-shattering smiles. I breathe. And then he jumps off the roof with a front tuck somersault thing and lands on his feet.

I walk over to him, right next to him, and bash him in the arm. "You could have killed yourself."

He shakes his head. "I've practiced this a lot. I've practiced it forever."

"You scared me." My hands cross in front of my chest. He takes a step closer.

"No I didn't."

"Yes, you did."

"You weren't scared. You're jealous."

My eyes meet his eyes. His eyes intensify. I swallow. "Can you teach me?"

"You can't do that kind of thing right away."

"I know."

He bumps me with his shoulder. "Of course, I'll teach you. Let's go."

We spend the next forty-five minutes walking on the bleachers. Then I walk on one of the old railroad rails behind the school. Then I do it with my eyes closed. Then I graduate to walking on the bike rack outside of school.

"I can so not do this," I say, eyeing the thin metal that's rounded and so slippery.

"Jump up and I'll hold your hands."

"What if I miss?"

"I'll catch you."

I jump. My body rocks and almost falls but I make it. My feet balance on the edges of it. Paolo grabs my hand. "That was actually the hard part. The jumping. Now walk."

My fingers hang onto his fingers. I look over at his face, dimple-less now, his lips that are open just a little bit like he's ready to kiss someone or say something. No, kiss someone.

"It's fun being tall," I say.

His fingers tighten. "I can't believe you got right up there. It's amazing."

I walk forward and jump off. Then I do it again and again and again until his brother drives up and honks the horn.

I smile up at Paolo again as he grabs his bag. "You have to promise me, no videos where you like fall and crack open your skull or anything."

"I'm not into that. I'm serious about this."

"I can tell."

"That video stuff is not what I'm about."

"What are you about?"

He doesn't answer. Not with words. Instead he just opens his arms wide. Then he winks and runs over to his brother's car, opens the door and rides off, not into the sunset because it's still light out, but somewhere. The good thing, Mr. Wayne? The good thing is I think he'll be back.

Dear Mr. Wayne,

After Olivia drops me off, Mike O'Donnell and I walk side by side down the trail that cuts through the woods. We stroll ten feet into the trees, twenty, thirty, fifty, a hundred. Beautiful leaves crunch beneath our feet. Some leaves still hang onto the trees but you can see through those leaves, see the patches of blue. Blue, the color of my eyes, my father's and Mike's. The fall winds swoop across the great lakes over Canada, across the Appalachian Mountains and to us, making it cold.

How I get myself into these situations, I do not know. I glance at him with my peripheral vision. I can't believe this. This is the perfect place to kill me. Hide the body in the swamp. Yep, brilliant move Lily, walking out here with him. The tiny hairs on my arms bristle.

If my life were a horror movie, people would throw

popcorn at me, yelling, "You deserve to die, idiot! Walking in the woods! Remember those headlines."

If my life were one of your westerns, he'd make a pass at me and you'd swoop in, jump off the granite boulder over there and pull out your gun or your fist and say, "Let's get a couple things straight, fella."

If my life were my life, which unfortunately it is, no one would come to help at all and I would be some stupid, numb, short girl caught without a plan.

So, here's my plan. If he tries anything I run. If he tries anything I trip him. He's probably already so plastered he'll fall. I trip him. Run. Parkour it and scramble up a tree. When it's safe I'll hike out to the highway, stick out my thumb and hitch a ride to my dad's. That's it. That's my plan.

Trip. Run. Scramble. Hike. Stick. Hitch.

Trip. Run. Scramble. Hike. Stick. Hitch.

My stomach hurts. I wrap my arms around it. His weight shifts closer to me. I shift away.

Trip. Run. Scramble. Hike. Stick. Hitch.

He hums a little bit and then says, "There are things you need to know."

I keep walking, looking at the ground. The thing with Mike is that you never have to say much, he just keeps talking. It's all very low impact. You nod or make a small "mmm" noise and he will go on. I hope he will hurry up with this, because I really want to just run into my bedroom, slam the door and hide. Or maybe go ride my bike, really hard, really far.

"Your mother should probably be the one to tell you

this. Actually, we should tell you together. That's what we planned to do, but I think that the time to do this is now, right now. I think you're ready to know."

Know? Know what? There's something like a fur ball stuck in my throat; my stomach knots up. Please, do not let him tell me he killed that guy. Do not let him tell me he's proposed to my mother. Do not let him tell me anything.

"Well, maybe Mom *should* tell me then," I say, but my voice comes out like a whisper. I hate my voice. I make it bigger. "Okay? Why don't we let Mom tell me?"

He stops walking. I stop walking and ready myself.

Trip. Run. Scramble. Hike. Stick. Hitch.

Above me the pine needles and limbs block most of the sky. His eyes and the sky really are the same color, and both of them look a little cold. I know that he's trying to tell me something he thinks is important, trying to muster up some pseudo male-role-model affection or something, some seriousness that he feels is required because I cried like an idiot the other day, cried like an idiot and he saw. Lord. That's what happened with my mother and Uncle Mark. She cried. He took advantage. Why do I not learn? Aren't you supposed to learn from your mother's mistakes?

Just thinking about Uncle Mark makes me woozy. I sway. I sway and Mike O'Donnell reaches out and grabs my arm. His hand. It is right there. On. My. Arm.

He smells like booze. He's got that swagger too, that insecurity behind his eyes.

"We can wait for Mom." I start forward again. His hand topples off my arm. I head towards the swamp.

Decaying leaves make it smell of muck. I caught a turtle once there and kept it in a box for two days before I realized how cruel that was, tethering the turtle to me just because I thought it was neat, instead of letting it go free.

"No, I want to do this now," he says and takes just one stride to catch up with me. He clears his throat, a rumble of phlegm. "Now, I know that you know that your mother and I were friends before. Before I moved away. Before you were born."

I nod. The turtle moved so slowly out of the cardboard box when I decided to let him free. Somehow, I thought he would run for freedom, for the swamp. Instead he barely moved. Like me. I know a person's supposed to buck up and face it when they're afraid, like what you said in that Barbara Walters interview: "When the road looks rough ahead, remember the Man Upstairs and the word Hope. Hang onto both and tough it out."

My stepdad's face comes to me for a second. The smell of Old Spice cologne. He said he was proud of me when I let that turtle go. That's the kind of thing that makes fathers proud, isn't it, Mr. Wayne?

I grab a branch of a tree, break it off, hold it in my hand and pretend it's Hope. Mike doesn't even notice.

I am going to hold onto Hope and tough it out. So I nod at this Mike O'Donnell, this man who shares my mother's bed, this man with a past that leaks out with his breath.

"Now, what you don't know is that... Well, people make mistakes in their lives. Not mistakes, but bad decisions. Sometimes they're just carried away by things, like when you're driving along, coming home from work and you see a sunset and it's purple and all you can see is that purple, and it's so amazing, so out-and-out beautiful, that you forget you're driving a car and at the last minute you remember, right before you go off the embankment and hit someone's mailbox, you remember and then you swerve back onto the road."

The palms of my hand start to tingle. We are almost at the swamp.

"Now, looking at that sunset wasn't a mistake, really, or even a bad decision. It was just an intense moment, something so beautiful and passionate you got swept away with it. That's what I'm talking about. Am I making sense?"

"Yep," I say, and I start shuffling my feet through the leaves and my sneakers become wet from the water hidden on the undersides, water caught between the leaves and the ground from when it rained on the weekend.

"Now, these moments can be about sunsets or anger or men and women," he says.

I nod again and my belly is fire. My tingling palms are fire. The only thing that's cold and calm are my wet feet, uncomfortable, yeah, but ready to run.

"What I'm trying to say, Lily, is that when your mother was married to your father and when I was married to Jane, your mother and I had an affair."

He pauses. The entire world stops with him. Whoosh. The birds are gone. The trees are gone. I am gone.

The thing is, even if you guess something deep down,

even if you almost know ... the saying of it, the saying of it just annihilates you, stops you and you flap off into whiteness like an old-time film that's been spliced in two. You are nothing. Just gone.

"Lily?"

His voice smacks into my chest and my heart starts bumping along inside it. The world begins again. I begin again.

I ignore him and drop a stick called Hope.

I walk right to the edge of the swamp and grab a new stick, a long stick that's fallen off one of the pine trees, chewed off by something, it looks like. The end is pointed and there are tiny bites on the bark. The twigs with pine needles are easy to break off, and when this is done I take the branch and poke it into the swamp, stirring up the mud, looking for turtles or even snakes, just something alive to remind me how to breathe.

I hit at the swamp, smacking up the muck, and each time there's a mucky splash my mind whimpers with it, with what I've always known, *My mother is a whore.*

I remember my uncle on the boat. I remember how she didn't believe me. I remember the cross. A turtle head peeks out from the far edge of the swamp, watching. Whack. Splash.

My mother is a whore. My mother is ...

Mike O'Donnell puts his hand on my shoulder, pushing on me.

"Lily, you are the product of our affair."

I drop the stick into the mud. The turtle dives below

the surface. This man's hand is heavy. He was right. My mother should have been here to tell me this; she should have been the one.

Keep moving. Keep moving.

He won't stop talking, just comes right after me. "You are our love child, our child of love."

Child of love. I am nothing. I am a child of love. A product. I am a big gaping hole. I am a mucky swamp that turtles hide in. My stomach returns, a burning pit.

I hop onto a stump. My balance fails. I fall. Mike O'Donnell's hands try to catch me. He fails. The mud squishes all around me. I stand up quickly. Leaches live in here with the turtles. Leaches suck your blood. They suck and suck at you until there is nothing left.

He reaches out a hand for me to grab, laughs. "You're wet through."

I don't take his hand to get out of the muck. But he's a sucker, this man. He grabs me by the shoulders and hauls me up and I scream, "Don't touch me!"

He drops his hands like I'm fire.

When I am up on the bank again, I check for leaches, try to calm down. This is not how heroes act. This is how victims react. Big breaths. Isn't that supposed to calm you down? I try it and then I say in a voice much calmer than I feel, "I've got to go change."

He nods. "Your mother wants to keep this quiet."

"What quiet?" I spit out the words like they are swamp mud. I spit out the words like they're evil things. They are. Words are. "Keep what quiet?"

"That I'm your father."

It seems to me she's been keeping this quiet for a decade and a half, but I don't say that. Instead I just say, "Uh-huh."

"And..." He looks into my eyes and I can't look away. It's like there are magnets there, or that he's Superman or a magician, someone with those kind of hypnotic eyes. "I don't know if you should tell your mother about this."

It's Uncle Mark again. It's the line. The line the bad guys feed you to keep you quiet, keep you theirs: Don't tell your mother.

My voice is slow and quiet and shaking. "You don't know if I should tell my mother."

"She wanted to tell you this herself. We don't want your pa in the dog house already, do we?"

"My pa?"

"You don't have to call me that. Keep calling me Mike, if you want."

He looks over at a blow-down on the right, and this time I grab his eyes when he looks back at me and I force him to keep staring. My voice is cold like a monster, like my skin wet from the swamp. "It doesn't seem logical for me to call you Pa if it's supposed to be a big secret, does it?"

"True."

"Then I guess I'll just have to keep calling you Mike."

And then I turn and start running back to the house, tripping over roots and rocks but managing not to fall again.

Dear Mr. Wayne,

How could she lie all these years, Mr. Wayne?

How could she make me think my dad didn't love me because he forgot to pay child support? That he was too stupid to remember to feed me? How could she make me love him? All those times, she said over and over again, "He's your father, Liliana. You have to go." "He's your father, Liliana. Be patient with him." All those lies!

Up in the sky, the sun moves so slowly you can't tell it's gone anywhere unless you pay attention, until the dark at the end of the day grabs you by surprise.

I am Irish.

My name should be Liliana O'Donnell.

I should be tall.

Hannah Dustin is not my ancestor. There are no Moravian depression chromosomes in my DNA. My grammy isn't my grammy.

My real father doesn't wear blue tights or ankle bracelets.

How could she lie to me?

Am I a bastard or is that just a name for boys who are
in line for the throne? Can girls be bastards? Or are we just
illegitimate? How does that work?

Unless it's not true. I've seen enough movies to know
that people lie. I've watched enough awful uncle types to
know that men lie. But why would he lie?

A real father doesn't lie. A real mother doesn't lie. Do
they, Mr. Wayne? Real parents are there for you and they
believe you when you tell them about horrible things. A
real father doesn't tell you he's yours and then tell you to
keep it quiet.

I pull off my boots at the back porch so I don't track
mud into the house. I shiver and pant. Mike's still making
his way back to my house. He struts along like he belongs
here. He doesn't. He doesn't move like a turtle. He doesn't
hide in his shell to deal with things. He doesn't think
things over, does he? He just walks into lives and doesn't
care who he steps on, like some sort of thudding dinosaur.
He just lives in their houses and drinks their Cokes and
sucks away at their lives. I stare at him. I stare at his ugly
jeans that are up just a bit too high like he's some kind of
cowboy. Who is he trying to fool?

He isn't my Uncle Mark, but he reminds me of him.
They look. They take. They don't care. They move too
quick to think of consequences. They say don't tell.

But I am a turtle. I can hide if I want, or I can move forward. I can think and then act.

I grab some clothes from my room and carry the bundle of them in my arms as I run to the bathroom. I want to get in there before Mike gets inside. I need time to think. I turn the shower on and strip, shove my clothes into the hamper. The shower water falls hot and heavy onto my shoulders and head. I check for leaches. I scrub my calves with Irish Spring soap. How appropriate it seems. How appropriate everything seems. My whole life is a lie.

Well Mr. Wayne,

I don't know what to think, and I'm not sure what to write either. I feel as if I've been in a saloon and some low-down dude has just klonked me over the head with a whiskey bottle and I'm out for the count.

And you know, Mr. Wayne, it's no good to be out for the count.

So, I take a shower, thinking that will fix my head.

The water from the shower steams as it flows down and turns my body red. It runs over me so hot that it takes all of my willpower to stay under it, to stay still beneath it for as long as I can, but I do. I have to.

What did you say in *Hondo*?

You said something when you knew it was all different, that nothing would be the way it was, something like: *Yup. The end of a way of life. Too bad. It's a good way. Wagons forward! Yo!*

I stand under the water until it washes every loose skin cell off of me and down the drain. After I prove to myself that I can take this scorching, I turn the faucet a centimeter towards cold and pick up the bar of Irish Spring soap. Their motto is, *fresh and (whoo-whoo) clean as a whistle*, which is what I want to be, clean as a whistle.

I give it a try; I say it.

"Wagons forward!"

My voice resonates off the shower wall, sounds deeper, somehow.

"Wagons forward!"

I grab my mother's loofah sponge, which I never use because it's so ugly and scratchy until it gets wet. I scrub myself, in circles, little circles all over the place, my shoulders and belly and breasts. My breasts are too big, like my mother's, only I don't have the belly to go with them. They make me look ridiculous, like I'm going to topple over. I try to scrub them away, circles and circles and circles, until my skin starts to bleed.

Then, when I see the blood, I do something completely shameful. I step out of the shower, drip all over the pink bath mat and wrap one of the peach towels around me. My mother bought these towels when she knew for sure Mike O'Donnell was coming. She thought our old towels were embarrassing, which they were, thin and green and dark. These towels are fluffy and bigger. Not that I care. I just wrap it around me and let the shower run so that Mike thinks I'm still washing. I waste gallons and gallons of water, some environmentalist I am. Sasha and Olivia must never know.

Steam fogs the mirror and I wipe a circle off with the edge of my palm so I don't leave fingerprints I'll have to clean off later. Through the streaks, I examine my face. A long face. Does it look Irish? What do Irish people look like? All I see is my mother's lips, absolutely normal size. All I see is a nose that isn't too big or too small, a little upturned. Mike O'Donnell's nose is thin and straight. My father's is large like an eagle's beak. My mother's is small, much smaller than mine, the kind of nose that is practically nonexistent, a pug nose that sits in her round face. My mother looks more Irish than I do, with her thinning reddish hair. My hair is thick, even when wet, and curly a bit. Where did my hair come from?

And my eyes. They are blue. So are Mike's. So are my mother's. So are my father's. Blue eyes all around.

This tells me nothing.

The steam from the shower clouds up the mirror and I open the shower door back up, reach my hand in and turn the water all the way to cold. Back at the mirror, my hand wipes away another circle that I can stare at, wondering who the person is that looks back at me, wondering about lies and truth and stories.

Then I give up. I hate to admit it, Mr. Wayne, but I do.

I lean my forehead against the cold mirror and start to whisper, "Wagons forward. Wagons forward."

But somehow, that gets mixed up with these stupid crying noises, and one word, "Daddy."

I whisper-cry it again, "Daddy."

And I don't know if I mean my father or my stepfather, who I used to call daddy, and I'm not even sure if I mean you. There's too many men I've lost, Mr. Wayne, too many men.

I do know one thing. Daddy isn't Mike O'Donnell. That's for damn sure.

You never doubted who you were, did you, Mr. Wayne? Even when your name was Marion, you knew who you were. You were the Duke. You were John Wayne. You were you.

And then there's me.

Dear Mr. Wayne,

Thomas Dustin married Hannah Emerson. Their daughter, Hannah, married Daniel Cheney. They had a child who gave birth to Anna. Anna married a Kilton who married a Faltin. That's the connection.

I am nothing like Hannah Emerson Dustin. I cannot imagine having so many children, killing so many people.

I am a weak, cowardly person.

That's all.

All those Faltins who married and gave birth until it came to me, did not in fact make me. They are not my DNA. I have no warrior woman in my chromosomes.

But I thought it was true. I thought, but it might not be. I thought, but I may just be a lie. I thought, and so now I have to talk to my mother.

Why do I write you these letters, Mr. Wayne?

Dear Mr. Wayne,

I get out of the shower officially and turn off the water,
but it drips. I put on my clothes even though I'm not
completely dry and step out into the house. My mother
is there, but so is my sister. They both sit on the couch,
huddled together and crying. Mike O'Donnell is nowhere
that I can see.

"What's going on?" I ask, arms around my chest to
keep out the cold. Maybe my mother has told my sister
the truth about who I am. Then I think: *What if Sasha has
called somebody? Told about Brian?*

"Nothing," my mother says, looking up at me and half
smiling. She smooths her skirt across her lap. I hate that
skirt with its big gaudy flowers in hot pink on top of a
black background.

"Everything's okay," my sister says but she doesn't smile,

just wipes some water from her face and looks away as if I'm not even there.

My mother looks away, too.

I glare at them. "Why is it that no one tells me anything?"

The storm door slams as I leave and I can barely make myself yell, "I'm riding my bike to Sasha's."

I yell this so they won't worry, but I really don't go to Sasha's. I don't even ride my bike. Instead I run, the thing I hate. I run really hard up and down the hills of Jenkins Road, passing all the trees that are almost barren. My running shoes bounce into the potholes the town never got around to fixing last spring. Running until it gets dark, I forget everything except the wind that whizzes past my ears as I speed down a decline, the wind that erases the entire day with its whisper: *Forget it. Forget it.*

But how can I forget when I'm not even sure I want to? Who do I want my father to be? How can I forget when it has everything to do with who I am, or who I'm not?

I walk down the length of the road when I know that it's time to go home. The time for forgetting is over. Mary Bilodeau and her parents drive by and honk their happy horn at me, three quick toots, and pull up ahead. Mary sticks her head out of the station wagon and asks, "Do you want a ride home?"

Thinking of Mary and her moony eyes, thinking I'm

all perfect when she's the one who knows who her father is, even if she is such a weenie she spills her lunch every day, I shake my head. "No. Thanks anyways."

They all wave and drive off, tooting again. Dusk comes and goes and by the time I come close to home it's dark. This is the time my stepdad—my dad—always came home.

The summer before my dad died we went to the Four Corners, flew into Sante Fe and rented a car. My dad just wanted to go to the corners where four states meet, but my mom insisted we see the Grand Canyon too, and Monument Valley since it was on Route 160, but it was the Four Corners that stuck in my memory because we stopped there first, stopped there first and took a big pause.

It's a slab of concrete with the seals of four states on it, and you can walk around from one state to another to another. My dad told me that Ernie Pyle, a reporter, once said about the Four Corners that seeing and hearing and knowing are what people solve their problems by. Seeing and hearing and knowing, and we are full of that. But really, once you're in the desert you realize that everything you see and hear and know and worry about is just a crock of shit, not important at all, and it's in the desert that you realize this.

And that is what I wish, as I walk back up my driveway. I wish that inside of me was the desert surrounding the Four Corners, mesas and plateaus, layers of sedimentation and beauty, hawks circling within me to admire it all. I wish that the wind-pushed sand was forming crevices and canyons inside of my soul so that I could look at it and be reminded that seeing and knowing and worrying and hearing are nothing, nothing, compared to the beauty of the desert.

The first time I every saw one of your movies, Mr. Wayne, was before that trip. My stepdad bought a whole bunch of them and we had a marathon. We ate nachos and popcorn. We ate ice cream and did nothing for the whole weekend, except watch you.

He loved your movies.

He would let me sit next to him, snuggle in beneath his arm and we'd watch you.

"That's a hero," he said when you saved everyone in *Sands of Iwo Jima*.

"That's a real man," he said when you swaggered in *The Horse Soldiers* while William Holden played the goody-goody.

My poor neglected bike hangs out in the garage. I pull a rope around its neck like it's a horse. I stare at it and wish it wasn't a bike, but something I could hug.

If my stepdad were here, he'd know what to do, I think. Do you?

Dear Mr. Wayne,

My mother waits for me. Her foot taps against the floor. I shut the door and breathe out slow to try to calm down my itchy trigger finger. I'm not ready to spill out what I know. I'm keeping it close to the hip.

She's not.

"Where have you been? I was worried sick." She pulls her turquoise bathrobe tighter around her waist. The robe is cheap and meant to look like terry cloth but when you touch it you realize that it is imitation terry cloth, of all things, and as thin as paper.

"Running."

"Not at Sasha's?"

"No."

"I called her, you know."

I nod and start unlacing my sneakers. I can't look at her. I just can't. I might lose it.

"I felt like a fool."

"Sorry."

I pick a dead leaf off my arm. It crumbles between my fingers, disintegrates even though a second before it was fine.

My mother bangs her fist on the counter. "What did you say?"

"Sorry."

"Say it like you mean it. If you're going to say sorry, young lady, say it like you damn well mean it."

"Sorry."

Both my feet wriggle free and I walk past her towards the hall.

She grabs my arm. "Where do you think you're going?"

"To do my homework," I say. In her eyes fear mixes with anger. I shake her hand away, wonder if she'll crumble beneath that cheap robe. She stands straighter as I keep walking.

Mike O'Donnell sits on the couch as I stomp by. A beer nestles in his hand. He must have gone out to buy it. We never have beer.

"You worried your mother," he says.

I nod and keep walking.

"I said you worried your mother!" His voice is like a boxer's fist, banging away at me.

He stands up and rushes behind me, right at the entrance of the hallway. I whirl around, arms ready to push him away. "I told her I was sorry."

"What about me?" he asks.

My hands sink to my sides, balled into fists, and I look at this man who says he's my father, who says my blood, my genes, are all partially determined by him. This is the man who has gone missing all my life, letting me live some big fat lie and now he suddenly appears and expects *me* to apologize to *him*. Spitting in his face would be preferable, but that is not how I was raised and I still have homework to do.

"I'm sorry," I say with a quiet rattle and before I walk away I watch a smile spread across his face, like a canyon breaking, forming on top of stone ruins, creasing.

He thinks I'm a wild horse. He thinks he has broken me. But I can still buck and throw him off, I'm betting on it.

"Some boy called," he grunts. "I told him you were grounded."

I whirl around. "Who?"

He shrugs. "You shouldn't be getting calls from boys anyway. They just got one thing on their mind."

Shaking my head, I can't even get one word out. Then finally I manage, "Maybe boys like you."

I fly out and away, rushing down the hall before he can even think to react. My mother's voice echoes after me. "Liliana!"

I slam my bedroom door, push the bureau against it, turn on my music, get my ear buds in and pretend no one else in the whole damn world exists.

Dear Mr. Wayne,

In the morning my mom acts like nothing happened. So
do I. What else is there to do? To open my mouth is to
make it all real. I don't know why she and my sister were
crying. I don't know if Mike told her that he told me. Not
knowing whether she knows is hard, but I'm not going to
bring it up. It's up to her. It's her sin, or fault, or whatever.
I mean, she's the grown-up, right?

Anyway, I'm just glad she isn't going off about me running at night the way she normally would. She used to freak
out about me riding my bike across the highway in the middle of the day. Was your mother like that? Maybe all mothers are like that.

She has sweet lips, my mother. She used to put wet
facecloths on my head when I was little and had a fever. I
wish I had a fever and she'd do that now.

✦

"Do you remember when we went with Daddy to the desert?" I ask while Mike O'Donnell's, aka Pa's, sleep-snores echo down the hall. I ask while my mother rushes around with her turquoise robe over her work outfit because she's cold and trying to save money by keeping the heat off until Mike gets up. Truth is, Mike cranks the heat up to eighty and since the days have been too cold for early fall we're wasting a lot of money that way. She's worried about making it through the winter.

"Yes. What about it?" She pours skim milk into her coffee mug. She likes her coffee as white as her skin, she likes to say, and so she always pours a lot in, only this time she isn't paying attention and spills it over the rim and it sloshes all over the counter.

"Sugar diabetes," she swears while going to the sink to get the green sponge to wipe up the mess.

"Do you remember the West Mitten Butte? It looked like a hand reaching up towards the sky?"

Her eyes shift left, the way they always do when she is thinking. "A big, big rock, right? In that Navajo place?"

"Monument Valley," I say. "*Tsé Bii Ndzisgaii.*"

It is hard trying to remember how to pronounce it. But I try anyways. She won't know if I say it wrong.

"Uh-huh…" She wipes at the spilled milk so haphazardly that it drips off the counter and onto the floor.

It is such a mom thing to do that I calm down for a minute. I take a big breath to ask her about Mike and my father. Paolo said the secret and skill of parkour is to plan out every move towards your escape, but my mom is a quick one and beats me to the punch, Mr. Wayne.

"I am still disappointed with your behavior last night and if I didn't have other things on my mind—"

"Do you remember it? Do you remember how Daddy said it was a water basket and sacred? Do you remember how beautiful it was?" I gush out. Monument Valley is safe, I think. Safe. It was back when things were good and it was just my mom, my stepdad and me.

She squats down to wipe up the milk drops on the floor and the long line where it's dripped down the side of the counter. Standing up she says, "Sure I do. Of course."

But her eyes are looking left again, searching for something.

"Sometimes I don't think you remember anything," I say and wait for her to make the next move, cock her pistol and aim. She doesn't, just goes and gets a dish towel to mop up the wetness the sponge left when she wiped the milk.

Leaving to go outside before Olivia and Sasha are even here, I don't say goodbye and she doesn't even notice, so busy she is with all these other things that are on her mind.

While I wait for them to come, I sit on the stone wall, swinging my legs above the gravel driveway and trying to get that desert feeling back into my soul. Right now, I don't know what's what but I know that I was in that desert. I know its truth. I know the red and yellow coils of Raplee Ridge in Utah, where it was sand art in earth tones come to life, zigzags of subdued color coils. And I know the way at night the wind turned cold and whipped my hair into my face as I held my dad's hand as we watched the sunset. And I remember my dad's hand, calloused and hard against mine, holding me to him, tight. My dead dad. Stepdad.

How many does that make? Three? Three dads. One dead. One in name. One biological. Maybe.

Wagons forward, Mr. Wayne, wagons forward.

You know, the desert is like the bones of the world jutting up to the sky, showing what it is that makes the land stay together, unmarred by the expectation of show-boaty foliage. It shows what really is strength. How can I be that strong?

✦

At bus room in the cafeteria, Paolo winks at me.

Sasha goes all chirpy singsong, nudging me with her side. "I think he likes you."

"No? Really?" I say, and she laughs and laughs because I'm so cranky I barely talked in the car while she and Olivia railed about Sudan and the woman murdered there.

She tweaks my nose. She smiles. "You don't know how cute you are."

I roll my eyes.

She cocks her head. "Really."

In study hall Paolo risks it and passes me a note:

Are you okay?

I turn around really quick and give him a thumbs-up sign that's totally fake. He frowns. And another note comes over.

Liar.

After study hall, he pulls me into a little dip in the hallway so people don't ram into us while we talk. He bends his back so our faces are closer than they normally are. Little eyebrow hairs, dark and interesting, weave together to make the straightness of his eyebrow. I've never noticed all those little hairs before, all working together to make these two beautiful eyebrows.

"Lily?" His hand sashays up to the side of my face, gently presses into my skin. His skin touches my skin. "Do you want to tell me what's going on?"

My mouth forms the word "no," but no sound comes out.

"I'm right here, you know. You can tell me anything." His voice is strong and gruff but steady, so steady I'm almost jealous of it, of how he knows who he is, what he is.

My voice? It breaks. "If I told you, you might not—"

Like me. Agh. Was I really going to say that? I am so pathetic.

His thumb moves, gently touching my skin. "That's not going to happen."

His eyes brown their way into me somehow. I reach up and wrap my fingers around his wrist. They don't quite make it all the way around. I move his hand away, but keep hold. "We're going to be late."

He flips his hand in a way that makes his fingers twine into my fingers. Fingers meet fingers as we walk to our classes. So I feel a little better, but it doesn't last. Nicole glares at me in the hall. Some druggie boy stole Stuart's homework and was holding it for ten dollars ransom. Stuart didn't even have five dollars. I let him copy my homework.

Nicole avoids me in the cafeteria, waits until I've already gone through the lunch line before she gets up from where she sits with Christopher and Travis Poppins. She ducks her face behind her hair and avoids my eyes when I walk by. So I sit with Alyssa Cutler, who actually calls me over and asks if I want to sit with her. She raises her hand the way people do when they're greeting someone at the airport and sings out my name like she's one of those old jazz singers, Ella Fitzgerald or Billie Holiday, someone who can sing deep and low. I'm glad I don't see Nicole's face when I sit at what she calls the popular table, because I think it would have ruined my joy. The day is over before I have a chance to ask anybody about anything or to even think much about anything myself. German tests and math quizzes. A thrilling badminton lecture in PE.

At rehearsal after school, I'm so down that I can't be peppy even when I sing about being corny and happy like Kansas in August and in love despite the fact that it's World War II. Tra-la-la.

"Lily, pretend to be happy! Remember the joy of Kansas in August and how happy you were there! Remember how proud you are to be corny and fun!" Ms. Gallagher yells. I try again, shuffling through the words, and she throws her hands up in the air. "Jesus!"

I have a new respect for you as an actor, Mr. Wayne.

I close my eyes, remember Paolo's fingers around mine, his thumb caressing my face, and I do a little better.

And when Olivia drops me off in my driveway, my father's car waits there and I have to jump right in, and off he takes me to Hancock.

In his beige ranch house I hang out with Grammy, sitting in her upholstered, almost tapestry-like chair that has tiny wheels attached to the bottom of it. Her fingers pick the dry skin of her foot, peeling layers off until her foot bleeds and the look of it reminds me of the desert where layer after layer of the earth is revealed.

"If I do this," she says, dropping a slice of skin into the trash, "I have a better chance of getting an infection and dying quick."

I nod. She stops for a moment and leans back into the tapestry. "Our family is known for depression. We're Moravian, all those dark valleys where the mountains block the sun. You mustn't look at me that way."

"Sorry," I say and try not to look at her feet. She notices and puts her knee-high nylon back on. The dry skin catches on the weave of the nylon and makes a horrible sound, a sound that grates the soul. I stop myself before I hiss.

She smiles and says, "You are young and beautiful and your skin is wrinkle free, but one day you'll be old like your grandmother here and if you are the sort, which I doubt you are because none of us are that sort, but if you are the praying sort, you will pray to die."

"You're still beautiful, Grammy," I say, looking at her eyes as sharp as a cat's.

She blushes and waves a wrinkled hand at me. "Bless you for a liar, child."

Grammy *is* beautiful in an elegant way. She still wears silks and her hair shines a beautiful shade of white and her eyes sparkle when she talks about dying, like she's a child who has just smooshed playdough into the rug on purpose. She used to be a painter, and her grandfather was the son of a duke who escaped Europe when Napoleon went on his walks across the continent hunting down noblemen to kill.

"Do you know how old I am?" she asks.

"Ninety-four."

She nods, puts her orthopedic shoe over her stocking and says, "I hope you never get to be this old."

And then she starts to cry. I look around for my dad but he's in the kitchen turning over another pot roast and talking on the phone to his brother, Uncle Kilton, who lives in another town.

The smell of meat makes me think of cattle and Westerns and you.

"I hate these ugly shoes. They're hideous," Grammy says, pulling me back in.

"Grammy, you are beautiful," I say and she looks up. I gasp because she is so beautiful, this lady who may not be my grandmother.

"Beauty is a flower or smooth skin. It's in the new bloom of life. I'm a painter, I know this. Beauty is youth," she says.

I sigh and shift on the couch. Reaching over, I pat her on the shoulder and then feel stupid patting her like that. What I'd like to do is rub her with my head, to smooth her wrinkles down with my own skin, to give her the type of beauty she desires. The beauty of flatness. My back hurts from sitting up straight. Grammy gets so angry if people don't sit up straight. I think of things that are straight and rough.

"What about trees?" I ask.

Grammy takes a lace handkerchief out of her pocket, wipes her eyes and says, "I'm sorry, Liliana. What about trees?"

"As they get older they get more beautiful."

I watch Grammy imagine with her artist's eye the blooming strength of an old tree.

"Then they become diseased and lose their leaves. Their limbs twist and their wood rots." She shakes her head at me. I suppose she's disappointed that I've almost gotten her to believe.

"What about the desert!" I lean forward on the couch. "The desert is as old as you can get. The bones of the country,

and it's so beautiful, with the canyons and peaks, the rap-
tors circling above, the cascade of colors."

Grammy smiles, folds her handkerchief, tucks it away.
"You're determined to prove me wrong, aren't you?"

"Yes."

"That's your prerogative."

She leans back in her chair and closes her eyes.

"Are you imagining the desert?" I ask.

She nods.

"You're like that desert, Grammy."

She opens her eyes and looks at me like I might actually know something. "I am?"

"Yes," I say, "if you'd just stop picking at your feet."

She laughs and starts pushing her chair into the kitchen
where she can oversee the final stages of dinner and force my
father off the telephone. "Just imagine I'm the Utah Specu-
lation Company, mining for minerals in the canyon."

At home, after I give my mother the run-through about
what we ate and what was said, with all the death stuff
edited a bit of course, I finish my homework and then I
head into the bathroom.

"Gonna take a shower!" I yell.

From the living room my mother hollers back, "We're
going out to see a nine o'clock movie."

I step away from the bathroom door and go to the end
of the hall where I poke my head out the hallway door. My

mother and Mike sit close together on the couch. His arm hangs around her shoulders. Some sitcom fills the room with forced laughter, like you aren't intelligent enough yourself to know when to laugh. Movies aren't like that. When my mom sees my head stick out the doorway she pulls away from Mike a bit, slightly. So slight he doesn't even notice, but I notice because I know my mom.

"Have fun," I say, about as authentic as a sitcom actor, totally as fake.

"We will," Mike says. "Too bad it's a school night. You could come along."

The phone rings.

"That better not be a boy," he grumbles, sitting up straighter.

"So what if it is?" I say as it rings again.

"Oh, Lily," my mom sighs. "Could you answer it? If it's Nana tell her we've already left."

I groan and walk to pick up the phone. "Hello."

"Lily?" my sister asks. "Is Mom there?"

"Uh-huh."

"Well, can I talk to her?"

"Why are you whispering?"

"I don't want to wake up Brian."

"He's asleep?"

"Yeah. Could you get Mom?"

I twirl the phone cord. "Isn't it a little early for him to be asleep?" I know he must have gotten drunk and passed out.

"Just get Mom."

"Does she know you're pregnant yet?"

Her voice is the angriest whisper I've ever heard. "Just get her."

"Mom!" I yell into the phone. "It's for you!"

When my mother gets up off the couch and slumps into the kitchen, she hisses, "It isn't Nana, is it?"

"No. It's the other daughter. The one you like."

My mom looks at the clock, bites her lip. "He never lets her call this late."

She snatches the phone from me and says, "What is it? What's wrong?"

She shoos me away with her hand. I take the hint and head to the shower once more.

From the living room Mike yells, "You've been taking a lot of showers lately. People are gonna start to wonder."

I don't say anything or turn around. I put my hand in front of me as I step into the bathroom and flip up my middle finger. Part of me wishes he could see it, wishes I were brave enough to show him what I really think.

I cannot believe he's my father.

In the bathroom, I make my hand into a gun and face off with myself in the mirror.

"Pow," I say. "Pow. Pow."

Mr. Wayne,

My sister shows up after they've left. A new bruise colors the side of her face. She's tried to put foundation on to conceal it, but the makeup isn't thick enough and a round purple circle colors her face beneath the orange.

"Don't ask," she says, walking past me and into the living room. She flops into a chair.

"My bag is in the car," she says. "Can you get it for me?"

"Your bag?"

"I'm sleeping over."

"Oh. Okay."

She shrugs off her jacket. On her forearms, four dots the size of fingertips make themselves at home. My breath scissors my lungs in half. She hears me and shoves her jacket back on, hiding.

"Jessica..."

She waves my words away before they even make it out of my mouth.

"But—"

She shakes her head at me and says, "Please. Don't, Lily."

I cringe and wonder where she'll sleep. I guess in the room Mike pretends to sleep in. I guess since my sister is here, most of our pretending is over. Except for when it comes to who I am.

"Can you get my bag?" she asks again as I stare too long at her face.

"He hit you," I say, not going to the door, looking at her instead.

She nods, looks away, fiddles with the fleece throw on the back of the couch and then gives up and throws it over her head. She's crying. "Don't, Lily ... "

I walk to the chair, bend down and touch her knee, and she seems so small, my big sister. "We have to call someone. The police."

"No."

From beneath the fleece throw, I can see her head shaking.

"We have to. It's illegal."

"No."

"Why not?" I ask, my voice rising, frustrated.

"It'll be in the paper. I won't have my name in the paper."

"In the paper?" This makes no sense.

"Under the police report," she says.

I have no idea, no idea what she's talking about, but I just move on ahead because I can tell by the way she's sitting, so still, that she is just beyond. She isn't twitching like she normally is. She isn't moving back and forth. Even her hands are still.

"Do you want me to call him? To yell at him?" I ask. I tap her knee to get her attention. She doesn't answer so I ask again. "I'll call him."

"No, just go get my bag."

I take my hand off her knee and stand up. "Should I call Mom? She's at the movies."

"She already knows."

"She knows and she went to the movies!" I yell. I slam my fist into the end table. The lamp wobbles. I catch it. "She knows?"

My voice makes my sister cringe. Her own voice comes out low and solid, like a person who has seen their wagon go up in flames on the prairie, a person who has lost it all and still has to go on.

"I asked her to. I didn't want to come in with Mike here. I don't want to have to keep explaining, at least not tonight. I'm too tired. Please, just go get my bag, Lily. Please."

I turn and leave through the kitchen door, turning to glance back at Jessica with the blanket over her head like it will hide her, like she's a three-year-old who doesn't know that people still know she's there even though she's not looking at them.

"Have you ever seen *The Shootist?*" I ask.

There's no sound from under the blanket. My poor sister,

my heart goes out to her in one big rush. She used to carry me around the house on her shoulders when I was little. Have I already mentioned that? She's nice, usually; kind.

"In *The Shootist,* John Wayne plays John Bernard Books, right? And people are not being too cool to him," I say. "So he goes, 'I won't be wronged, I won't be insulted, and I won't be laid a hand on. I don't do these things to other people and I expect the same from them.' Everyone should expect that, Jessica."

There's silence, then a sigh. She curls her feet up to her chest and from beneath the blanket she says in a trembling voice, "Please Lily, just get my bag."

I can't believe it. Even one of the best lines in movie history does nothing for her, so I trot out into the night and look at the stars and pull her bag out of the passenger seat of her car. It's light and easy to carry. The stars must like being so far away from all this earth stuff, all this suffering. I'm not talking just about my sister but about everyone, all those people in the Sudan, the people sold for sex slaves in Asia, the people in our own country getting abused, hurt.

What good am I if I can't even help my sister, Mr. Wayne? What kind of cowpoke am I? I'm not worthy enough to haul on my boots.

Staring at the stars, I plan out what to say next to her. I will tell her it's not her fault. I will tell her that no woman deserves to be hurt or scared. I will tell her that I love her. That's what I can do.

When I come back in, the chair is empty. She hightailed it to the shower. She does that like I do, to be alone to think. I sit on the big couch in the living room and count cars on the highway. I count and count and count, but when she's done with the shower she doesn't come back out to the living room. She grabs the duffel bag where I've left it in the hall and then goes into the guest room and shuts the door. Mike will be officially sleeping with Mom tonight, I think. Have I said that before?

I'm sorry. This is not much of a letter, but I guess what I'm trying to say is that nobody is going to be fooled tonight. I get up and go into my room. I pull my bed-spread up. It's scratchy. I bet Alyssa Cutler has a puffy comforter. I bet she has pillows made with feathers.

I can't have feather pillows because my mother is afraid of birds. Each year blackbirds come and stop on our front lawn when they migrate. There are hundreds of them. They fill the tree branches and make them black. They line the wires on the utility poles. They make everything black but full of life. I like to imagine that they all have names and know each other.

I like to imagine that if one of them goes missing they all notice, and that's when the squawks start, a sort of alarm system.

Where's Harry? Squawk. Where's Harry?
Is Harry by Brad? By Brad?
Bad bird coming east. Bad bird coming.
Hide. Hide. Hide.

My bedroom is lonely and cold and as dark as the desert at night. Only there are no stars. I wish there were stars and then there would be something to count as I stare up at the ceiling, wondering how everything in the world could be so wrong.

Maybe I should get up and stare out the window, rest my head against the cold pane of the glass and count cars again, but it's night and people are running out of places to go so there wouldn't be that many to count anymore.

I can hear my sister crying through the wall. I touch the wallpaper where her head might be. I just feel the lump of old wallpaper underneath the new.

It isn't like I've never heard about people hitting women. I know all about it. I've watched the talk shows and the news and seen the women cry and the husbands in their orange jail clothes saying that they are sorry, but this is my sister. My half sister, I remember, and wonder if it's the same thing.

So, this is what I do. Later, when she's asleep, I sneak into her room with my camera. The flash goes off, but she's out cold. I take a picture of her face. I take a picture of her arm. Then I sneak out of the house. I untether my bike and start pumping it down the highway, straight towards Bangor. Cars pass me and dirt kicks into my face. I pass acres and then a brick house. The lights of the Merrimack houses seem too bright, too happy.

I close my eyes when I get too close to a house. I don't want to hear what's happening inside the walls. I don't want to know anything anymore, you know.

Houses look so good from the outside, at least the Merrimack houses do. They have nice lawns and pretty shrubs and the roof tiles are all neat in place against the wind. The trees by them reach towards the sky.

I ride right past them and I head for Bangor, riding in the darkness, not into a sunset, but into black.

I'm not sure why I'm riding in this direction, other than it seems right, somehow. It's just the right way to go, I guess. I think of all the two-story apartments. I think of the sidewalks.

Bangor isn't my city, not really. When I get to the line between Merrimack and Bangor, I stop at the sign. It says, *Welcome to Bangor.*

It's meant for cars to see. I reach up and touch it. Then I turn my bike around and head home.

Welcome. Welcome.

There's no sunset there either. Just dark.

At home, I crawl into my sister's bed and lean into her back. I wrap my arms around her. She grabs my hands in hers. She cries and then she sleeps. I stay awake. I think of those newspaper headlines: *One Man Dead.*

I think of statistics about domestic violence.

I think of how Hannah Dustin did everything to get back to her children and how my mother's right here, giggling across the hall, but she couldn't be farther away.

Dear Mr. Wayne,

In case you were wondering or worried by the last letter, let me tell you that I'm out of bed and ready for school before anyone else even wakes up. Even my mother is still in her room with Mike. The door is shut when I walk down the hall, but his snores come through wood and drywall, announcing he's here.

I put a Pop-Tart into the toaster and wait for it to come up. I eat the corners off and not the middle, just nibble around the edges so that I can lose weight.

The phone rings. No one calls this early, at ten past six. Someone must be dead. Grammy?

I snatch the receiver off the wall. "Hello?"

"Lily?"

His voice comes out as a grunt. How fitting.

"Hello, Brian," I mutter and my stomach threatens to do a toaster and violently expel the Pop-Tart. I keep it down.

"Let me talk to Jessica."

"She's not here."

The hair on my back starts to stand up, not that I have hair on my back, just little fuzz that no one can see, but I can feel it, moving.

"Don't give me that crap. Let me talk to her," he says.

I don't say anything. I just listen to him breathe into the phone. The kitchen looks so calm and normal like it always is, just counters and a yellow refrigerator and a stove. Dishtowels hang off the handles of the pine cabinets. My stepdad built those. My breath comes out like a hiss, my tongue in the center of my mouth. I put the receiver back on the hook.

My hands shake.

The phone rings again.

"Liliana," he says, his voice much calmer, the fake calm after a blizzard. This is the calm that tries to lull you into forgetting how frigid the snow can be, and makes you think only of how pretty the white is. "Let me talk to my wife."

Brian is a man with a body like an old stove, hefty. He always had a beer gut even in high school. He wears blue T-shirts with a pocket in front. He keeps his cigarettes there, and the top of the carton peeks out to show the red top and name of the brand he smokes: Marlboro. He is no Marlboro man, roping and riding in my desert with a bottom like a runner's. He won't be roping in my sister's desert either. Not if I have anything to do with it. I think of what you said when you were Capt. Rockwell Torrey in *In Harm's Way: All battles are fought by scared men who'd rather be someplace else.*

I imagine that Brian must be smoking right now, sitting in their kitchen by their table that never has a cloth over it. I imagine him flicking an ash into one of his glass ashtrays. I aim and shoot.

"I've got pictures, pictures of her bruises. So you listen to me—you call here, you come on this property and we'll have the police here faster than you can spit. No one messes with my sister."

Bang.

I hang up the phone again and switch the lever on the bottom, which controls the ringer. No one will hear the phone today. Imagining how angry Brian will get, when he dials and hears it ring five hundred million times, doesn't make me happier. Actually, I feel a little scared, and when Olivia and Sasha come I don't want to get in the car and leave my sleeping house. I stash my shaking hands in my pockets and listen to them discuss bipolar systems of sexuality, but I can't stop worrying.

"It's not gay or straight," Sasha says. "It's not one or the other on a straight line, it's more like a circle, or like you can be different spots on the line, instead of just all one thing. Right? Like I'm not totally straight because I can think girls are cute, but I don't want to kiss them or anything."

"That's still pretty straight," Olivia says, shaking her head and turning off the highway.

Sasha pouts and then mocks herself. "No. No. I'm not a straight, boring person. I'm not!"

She rips on a trying-not-to-be-straight monologue for a while. Sometimes I think she'll do stand-up comedy and just blast out of Maine and high school early, leaving us all behind. Maybe she could make my life into something funny. *There was this girl who wanted to be John Wayne because she wanted to be a hero... Only she was like five feet tall and had these really great boobs...*

"Lily? You want to help us with our Darfur campaign?" Olivia asks.

"Sure," I surprise myself by answering. "Sure, I'll help."

"Cool." Sasha bounces in the front seat. "You okay?"

"Yep."

Sasha and Olivia give each other looks.

"She's lying," Sasha announces.

"No shit, Sherlock," Olivia says and we all laugh. Sasha turns the radio up because she knows I'm not in a talking mood. Instead, she and Olivia make up fake rap lyrics to the song that's on.

"I oppress my woman, I oppress her good, 'cause if I didn't, I'd never get wood," Sasha sings. Olivia laughs.

I imagine Brian barging into the house.

Mike is there, I tell myself. He's a man. He could beat Brian up probably, if he doesn't fall over drunk first. It's awful to think this way, but I can't help it. I'm only a pacifist when it comes to myself, not my sister.

"Uh, can I tell you guys something?" I ask.

Click. The moment they've been waiting for, my sweet, goody-goody activist friends. The radio goes silent.

Telling Olivia and Sasha what happened is easy, but

listening to them talk about protection orders and women's rights and survivor syndrome is hard, almost annoying, and when I get to school it's a relief to sit in study hall and have Paolo Mattias smile at me. He doesn't know anything about me and I'm so glad.

He kicks a note at me and it says,

Are we still on for tonight?

I stare at the note for a minute. The Bic pen in my hand leaks a bit on my finger.

Sure

Meet me after study hall.

I don't write back. I nod instead and smile, little butterflies trapped in my throat, and wait for study hall to be over, amazed that I'm going on a real date with Paolo Mattias.

There are all these other people around me, sitting at their desks with the chairs attached, looking into their Calculus books or trying to read *Othello* for English class. I don't think any of them know anything about what is happening, about how my life is so bad and so good at the same time and the crazy Ferris wheel of it makes me feel like my head is spinning in endless circles, high and low and high again.

I want to tell somebody, and then I realize that the person I want to tell is my dad, the Faltin one, the one with blue tights and silliness.

He would definitely think Paolo was cute.

Paolo's all smiling-happy when we get out of study hall.

"I'll walk you to class," he says, leaning in, trying to carry my books.

I back away. "What are you doing?"

"Trying to carry your books."

"That's so old school."

"What? What's wrong with old school? I like old school."

I shake my head. "I'm a big girl. I can carry my own books."

He scowls at me, but the scowl doesn't reach his eyes. Still, I feel bad, so I say, "If zombies were chasing you and you had to run away, parkour style, what would you do?"

A Britney girl jostles by me. Tyler yells to us. We wave.

Paolo thinks for a second, still walking. "Are you with me?"

"Why?"

"Because then I'd have to take care of you, too."

"No. You don't have to worry about me, just rescuing yourself."

His lips relax a little bit. "Are they hyperactive zombies, or just regular slow-moving zombies?"

"Hyperactive, definitely," I say and my heart feels a little bit lighter.

He steers me around a group of senior girls standing in the middle of the hall, messaging frantically. He nods towards the corner of the hallway and says, "I'd run full force, scale the wall, break through those Styrofoam ceiling tiles and scurry through the top really fast, drop down at the fire stairs, rush up to the roof, and jump."

"Jump? It's like three stories."

"Not down. I'd jump from this building to the garage. That's one story down."

"You couldn't do that."

He smiles, all handsome confident guy. "I've done it before."

"That's insane!" I yell, and his lips relax. The tiniest flash of white teeth appear between them. I stop walking. "Could you teach me to do that?"

"Not right away."

"But eventually?"

His free hand swipes a piece of dark hair off his forehead, pushing it back. It flops down again. "Yeah. I could teach you."

"So, in case of a hyperactive-zombie invasion someday?" I ask, moving closer to the warmth of him, away from the bumping people hustling to class.

"You'll be able to save yourself."

I smile up at him. How can I not smile? "You are too cool."

He laughs. "Right."

Dear Mr. Wayne,

At home, I put on lip gloss. It's my mother's. In front of the mirror I stand, lips puckered, one finger full of the globby stuff even after I've swabbed it on my lips. My finger needs to be wiped off. Nicole told me once that if you put lip gloss above your eyes it makes your eyes look bigger. I can't remember if you're supposed to put the lip gloss on your actual eyelid or above it. If you put it on the eyelid it might get sticky, so I decide to put it right above. My movements are slower than a turtle's, but inside I am so excited, too excited, and my heart beats hard against my ribs.

Bathroom mirrors are not good places to inspect yourself. Everything is too bright. My lips shine and so does the skin above my eyes. I try out a smile, my lips stretching up, but feel fake. Fake and phony and stupid. I don't even know if I like Paolo. I don't even know if I should be going out. My sad sister sulks in the guest bedroom. Mike pretends to read the classifieds, but is really drinking spiked Pepsi. My mother is running around cleaning and acting like everything is normal, which it isn't. My sister's bruises shine out against her skin. A strange man has made our house his personal bar.

I don't even know who I am.

"You been in there a long time," Mike yells, banging on the door.

"I'll be right out," I say.

"There are other people living in this house," he mutters from behind the wood.

My face doesn't look like his. My face doesn't look like my blue-sock-wearing father's either. My face looks stupid with lip gloss on it. It will be dark at the game, no one will notice.

"My first date," I say out loud to myself and then smack my leg. What a cornball I can be. It's humiliating. It's like that song I have to sing in *South Pacific*, about being as corny as Kansas in August.

Mike waits in the hall, leaning against the wall, his arms crossed over his chest. "Where do you think you're going?"

"What do you mean?"

His breath smells like Scotch. He looks me up and down, not the way a father would, but the way one of those nasty lecherous men in bad movies do, the kind of men who pull the teenage girl into their car and lock the doors. He notices my nice clothes and lip gloss. I think of newspaper headlines: *Merrimack Girl Slain By Mother's Live-in Lover.*

"What you all dressed up for?" he asks, hunkering down his shoulders, taking up all the space in the hall. I feel little all of a sudden, really little.

"I'm going to a game."

"You aren't going to any game." His eyebrows raise up looking for the moon.

"Yes, I am."

"You don't care about sports. You're just going to look at the boys."

"No, I'm not. I am going to watch the game."

"I know what teenage girls go to games for and it's not to watch the sport."

He scratches his nose. My cowboy boot twitches, wanting to stomp.

"So what?" My sister comes to the doorframe of the spare bedroom. She's been listening. Her bruise has changed color. It's darker. Her makeup doesn't hide it. "Big deal if she wants to look at boys."

"She can't," Mike says, turning to her. And she gets his eyes like a snake's, like the holes in a gun barrel.

I don't want him to confront Jessica, not after Brian and the hitting and everything. The last thing I want is for her to confront another idiot man, so I say, "I have a date."

"See?" Mike says, turning back to me. "A date."

"Really?" Jessica says. "No way. Your first one?"

"Uh-huh."

"Want me to help you with your makeup?" She looks me over.

"You don't wear makeup," I say.

"I used to," she says, taking my face in her hand. "Show me what you have."

I do a little cat leap and head back towards the bathroom. Mike crowds the hall. He blocks my way.

"You aren't going," Mike says and smiles. He picks at the dirt under his fingernails.

"What?" My trigger finger itches.

He stands up straight. He is a tall man, Mr. Wayne, a tall man like you and he takes up all the space in the house suddenly and says all cold and slow, "I said you are not going."

"Like hell I'm not going."

"You aren't going. And don't you use that crap language on me."

Jessica and I look at each other. I wonder where my mother is when I need her.

My voice turns frozen and hard and mean, stronger than a voice I've ever had before, and I'm not quite sure where it comes from. "You can't tell me what to do."

"Yes, I can," he says.

And like a third grader I taunt back. "No, you can't."

"I'm your father," he says, right in front of Jessica, "and you had better listen to me, girl."

"What? What are you talking—" Jessica starts to say, but I drown her out.

"That's crap," I yell and with two hands push against his stomach—because I'm so short I miss his freaking chest. He sways a little 'cause he's a drunk bastard. I run towards my room instead of the bathroom. I've caught him off guard for a second. He barrels after me. His feet sound loud, like tornado thunder. He chases me. He grabs my shirt. I keep running. It rips. His hand whacks the back of my head. Pain explodes. I plummet to the floor. He grabs my boot, yanks me back towards him. Jessica screams in the background. I don't know what she's saying. Maybe it's not words. Maybe it's just screams. That's how it is in my head: just screams.

My hands grab at the carpet in the hall. It's no good. I think about Paolo and parkour. Try to plan. I twist onto my back and kick up at him as hard as I can. I kick and yell. He takes my head and slams it into the ground. Jessica's face, twisted and yelling, is suddenly right there and she's hitting him with her fists, making words: "Leave her alone. Leave her alone."

"Get off me," he roars, and he loosens up on my ankle enough so that I can get out from under the weight of him, and it's enough, and I'm up on my feet and running.

Something growls behind me. For a second I think there's got to be a grizzly in the hall with us, but it's him. It's this foul drunk man, my mother's man.

I scramble into my bedroom. I slam the door, but not before I see his face, two wild eyes glaring at me. I push my bureau in front of the door. I've only run down the hall, but I pant and feel as if I've been running all afternoon.

Oh, I know, I should go out there and give him the what for. I should go out there and say, "Listen, fella, let me tell you a thing or two." But I don't. I don't. I leave my poor sister out there with him, wondering about what he said, facing him alone, maybe. But there's no noise now. No noise at all except the distant yammering of the TV set.

I know he's outside my door, breathing, listening the way he does. I can't hear my sister at all. I have to be brave. I push the bureau away from my door and reach for the doorknob, but I can't turn it.

"Listen, fella..." I start to say, but I can't keep it up. I shake too much, and I just keep thinking of my step-uncle, the one from California, and what he did.

Then I think of the way Mike O'Donnell looked at me. Their eyes were the same, that predator look.

I hear him walk away. One footstep. Another.

He is not my father. I refuse to let him be my father. That's it.

That's it.

That's all there is to it.

But I cannot stop shaking.

One Man Dead in Bar Fight.

One Girl Wimps Out in her Room.

Lights from a car shine into my window, and I hope that it's Paolo and his brother out there waiting to pick me up and not Brian, not Mike O'Donnell trying to trick me. Working quick, I shove my camera and sleeping stuff in my backpack. It's risky, but I open the window, pop the screen out, and jump into the dead stalks of tulips and run for the top of the driveway. Behind me, I hear Mike return to the hall outside my room, swearing and banging on the door, and behind him I can hear the higher voice of my sister yelling, yelling, yelling for him to stop.

Grizzly bears don't stop, not once they've tasted blood. They growl and rip things apart and bat you around like you've asked for more.

Dear Mr. Wayne,

You aren't supposed to cry on the first date you have with a guy who likes you, maybe. I mean maybe he likes you, but you can't be sure. How can you be sure? You can't be sure of anything, ever, not even about who your father is, or who'll protect you, or that your sister will get married and be happy and not have her husband beat her up, or that your best friend is one person and not somebody else. You can't be sure of anything, except maybe that you're not supposed to cry on your first date with a boy who is cute, cute, cute.

People pack the car. Paolo's brother drives in the front seat with another guy by the window and two girls between them.

They laugh over their shoulders when I look in with big eyes and they say, "We're using the same seat belt."

"Oh, good," I say like I'm some sort of seat-belt cop. My head pounds. My hair must be a mess. I run my hands through it. My hands shake and get caught in a tangle. I rip through it. My eyes flash up towards the house. What if he follows me? Nothing moves.

In the back seat, Sasha and two other boys and Paolo smile at me.

Paolo gets out of the car, all gentlemanly. "Hey."

"Hi," Sasha says. "You okay?"

"Sure," I say, trying to figure out where I'm going to sit and slugging on my coat, hoping no one's seen the rip in my shirt. "Just ran down the driveway."

Paolo smiles at me and says, "It's kind of squished in there. I hope you don't mind."

"No," I say, shaking my head. "Where should I sit?"

He shrugs and looks apologetic. "On my lap?"

"You're so little, Lily. You're the lightest. Do you mind?" Sasha asks. She smiles. "Little Lily. Little Lily."

"Oh," I say, mostly just to get her to stop singing my name like that. "Okay."

Paolo sits back down. I take a big breath and get on his lap, leaning forward. My bottom rests on his knees. The roof of the car meets the top of my head.

"You okay?" he shifts underneath me. His breath pulls in all sharp.

"Sure," I say. "Are you?"

"Yeah. You don't have a seat belt," he says.

"It's okay."

"It's not safe," he insists.

"Somebody's going all parental," Sasha sings.

We ignore her because sometimes she needs to be ignored.

"I could hold onto you," he says as his brother pulls a sharp right out of the driveway and laughs. All four people in the front seat turn around to look at me. I smile, but I want to roll my eyes. I wonder if anyone saw me climb out the window. God, my head hurts something fierce.

Paolo's hands grab my waist the way a boy's hands touch you when you dance with them, sort of firm, but cautious. I like the way his fingers feel and try to suck my stomach in.

"That's why there are so many of us in this car," Sasha says. "So they have an excuse to get us to sit on their laps."

"Not so," says the boy she perches on.

"You know it," she laughs and leans back pretending to smoosh him. He pretends he can't breathe.

We drive along for a while, everyone talking and laughing except for me. The lights of other cars flash into ours and illuminate everyone's faces for a moment: beautiful faces of people who know who they are, all of them hooting and singing along with the radio. Paolo talks too, but I just sit on his lap, shoulder smashed against the cold, smooth pane of the window, wondering where I'm going to go after the game, wondering if I could ask Sasha if I could sleep over at her house and if I'd have to tell her why. I imagine telling her about my mother, about Mike, and know I can't tell her any more right now. Sasha isn't of that world. I don't want to be her charity case, her mission.

Maybe I could call Nicole, but I can't because we're fighting. Outside everything looks lonely.

"Lily?" Paolo says.

"What?"

"Are you there?"

"I'm sorry. I was thinking." I smile. My back rests against his chest. "It requires a lot of effort."

That's true, because just keeping my head up seems to make it throb.

Paolo's brother yells, "Sasha asked you to sing us a song."

I jerk my head so that I can see Sasha. I glare. "A song?"

"Please," Sasha says, making puppy dog eyes. "I'm tired of the radio."

"You're kidding," I say, shifting on Paolo's lap so that I lean back more solidly into him. He's so warm. I turn my head, look into his eyes. They flash with the headlights going by, and there is no mean grizzly in there.

"No, sing for us," Paolo says, and he lets go of my waist with his hands and instead just wraps both arms around me. I'm caught, but I don't mind. I see Mike O'Donnell's face. I remember the smell of his breath. What would he think if he saw this?

"Uh, I don't know," I say.

Other people say "come on," and I go to Sasha, "You have to sing with me."

"What should we sing?" Sasha asks. No one knows. All sorts of songs are suggested, but no one knows all the lyrics to any, except for Christmas carols and *South Pacific*, but I'm so sick of those. Everything inside me shakes, trying to keep control, keep it normal and real. Paolo's arms tighten. I think he sniffs my hair. Nicole says that when guys sniff your hair it gets them all excited.

"'O Holy Night,'" I announce. "That's the hardest to sing."

We start in, and pretty soon everyone croaks it out in false opera voices, trilling every note above high C. Everyone laughs, all thrilled with themselves for being so stupid and silly and irreverent, and no one notices that I stop singing or that tears stroll down my cheeks.

But Paolo notices. He pulls me in closer and turns me sideways, so my back is to the others and I'm staring out the window. He keeps singing, really loudly and pretty darn badly, covering me, covering for me, and then he does the best thing. He puts a hand on the side of my face and keeps it there, even when a tear rolls down and hits his thumb. He doesn't move.

I have always wondered what it's like to be on an honest-to-God date. I have seen it from the outside, watched people feed each other McDonald's French fries, put their hands in the back pockets of each other's jeans, huddle up under a blanket to watch a game.

Now that's me.

We huddle under a big Princeton blanket that Sasha

brought with her. It's got a tiger on it because that's Princeton's mascot. Her mother went there, I guess.

My mother didn't go anywhere, not even secretarial school. I can't imagine not going to college, just working at Sully's or something.

I snuggle in between Sasha and Paolo. He puts his arm around me and keeps shooting me protective looks mixed with smiles. I can smell Sasha's bubble gum. She keeps popping it. She's given me a couple of aspirin and a hairbrush and I don't feel so bad anymore.

"You okay?" she asked me when I popped the aspirin in the bathroom. She handed me her comb.

"Yeah," I shrugged. "My mother has a rotten boyfriend."

She nodded. "My mother had a boyfriend who was a nurse. He stole OxyContin from the hospital and got fired."

My mouth dropped open and I stared at perfect Sasha Sandeman. "Really?"

"Yeah."

So with my head better and Sasha human, I lean close to Paolo who smells good, like Old Spice, the same way my stepdad used to smell. I lean against him and close my eyes.

Life can be good, Mr. Wayne. In little snippets, it can be good.

Sasha even tells a John Wayne joke about this little old lady who goes to the store and wants to buy the cheapest toilet paper possible. She jumps up as she tells it, all ham, all stand-up comic.

"So the guy tells her, 'I've got three brands: Charmin,

Angel Soft, and the least expensive is a no-name.' The lady takes that and comes back the next day, stomps up to the clerk and says, 'Young man, I've got a name for your no-name toilet paper.' 'What's that?' he asks. 'John Wayne,' she says, ''cause it's rough, it's tough, and it don't take no shit.'" Sasha smiles and bows as I laugh. Sorry, but it's a good joke and laughing is like swallowing hot chocolate on a cold day. I forget about things for a second.

I'm still laughing when Sasha mutters, "Oh God."

Her eyes go all big and she looks at me. Life can also be bad.

"What."

She moves her head to point.

Nicole teeters to our right, standing in front of the bandstand, leaning against the fence that keeps people from falling down into the field, or jumping onto the field if there's a bad call.

"What is she wearing?" Sasha says, not in a mean way really, more in the stunned way of a mother who can't understand tongue piercings.

What Nicole's wearing is a micro skirt with bright red tights, even though it's freezing out. She also has on those heels that make you look like you're a runway model or a hooker, those super-high kind. She looks absolutely ridiculous. Her legs remind me of the tiny bones of a bird.

The worst part, the absolute worst part, is that her hand is in the back pocket of Travis Poppins' super-sized jeans. She has settled. She has given up, given in, gone out with Travis because she's so afraid of being alone. My stomach buckles into itself and for a second I think that Nicole is just like my mother. I push the thought away and just stare at her hand in Travis' pocket. Nicole's evil brother is on Travis Poppins' other side.

"She knows you're here," Sasha says and then her face gets a soft look. "I just saw her looking over at you."

From the way Sasha says it, I can guess that Nicole was really closer to glaring than to looking.

I've told Sasha all about my fight with Nicole, which is probably not a good thing. Right after I did, it I felt like I was betraying Nicole a little bit. No, betraying her a lot.

"I'm going to say hi," I tell her.

Sasha gives me big eyes. "Oh, Lily."

"I have to," I say, because I feel so bad for this Nicole, this Nicole who wanted to be cool so bad and now she's given up. Maybe this is something I can fix.

Sasha looks at Stuart Silsby, who's sitting right behind us, eavesdropping and trying to get close enough to Sasha to smell her hair without being obvious. He pounds his chest with his fist two times and intones, "Be brave, little one."

"I'll be right back," I tell Paolo.

He nods and says all warm, "I'll be waiting."

It's not a long walk down the three concrete steps and over to Nicole, but it feels like I'm hiking the Appalachian Trail. My legs shake, and it seems I'm still dizzy despite all that aspirin. For a second I worry that Paolo is staring at my bottom and that it might look big. Then I get to Nicole and tap her on the shoulder.

I'll ask her to sit with us, I think. That's what I'll do.

"Hi," I say when she looks at me.

I want to tell her what a loser Travis Poppins is, with his black heavy-metal T-shirts and his mullet, but I can't. I want to ask her why she's with him, tell her I'll give her Paolo, anything. I want to ask her what she's read in *Cosmo* this week, tell her that there's a hole in my heart where our friendship used to be, that my shirt is ripped and I need her.

"Hi," she says like an ice-princess hotel heiress and then turns her head back to the game. I'm left staring at her back.

"Nicole?" I say. I poke her shoulder. "Nicole?"

She whirls around, hands on her hips. "What?"

"I don't want to fight any more."

"We aren't fighting." She stares. She chews her gum.

My body feels a little softer. "Oh, good. That's good. I hate fighting—"

"We aren't fighting because you no longer exist."

"What?"

"You don't exist," she says. She waves. "Bye-bye."

She turns back around. I crumple inside, but don't move. Everybody yells because we've scored a field goal. Nicole jumps up and down and kisses Travis' cheek and I just stand here, and stand here, and stand here, and here comes Paolo striding down the bleachers and putting his arm around me. I gulp big, and let him. I wish he would kiss me on the top of my head. He just turns me and brings me back to the bleachers.

"Bad night, huh?" he asks.

I shrug.

"I'm getting popcorn," Sasha says. "Want some?"

Paolo gives her some money. She takes off with Stuart, who is practically doing some Irish step dance down the aisle because he's so happy to be with her. Now that there's room, I edge away from Paolo a little bit.

"I saw you go out the window," he says.

My stomach falls. I swallow hard and stare ahead.

On the field, the boys move in an M pattern down the field. It must be nice to have all the plays figured out for you ahead of time, to have a coach telling you what to do.

"Did anyone else see?" I ask, finally.

He shakes his head. "Maybe my brother. He'd understand. We do it all the time."

I look at him, try to imagine him getting his big body through a window, how his shoulders could possibly make it through. "You do?"

"Yeah, my dad. He's got a temper ... you know ..." he says, and he grabs my hand. I twine my fingers into his. Mine look little compared to his, but I bet they're almost as strong.

"My mom's boyfriend ..." I start to say, but I don't finish. Paolo knows anyways. He can tell in my eyes, I think.

He squeezes my fingers. "Did he hurt you?"

"I'm fine," I say, which isn't really a lie or an answer. "Don't tell. Okay?"

Sasha comes back with popcorn. We eat some and she hugs me, because she thinks the only thing I feel bad about is Nicole. And my sister. She doesn't know I'm a bastard. She doesn't know who my potential biological father is.

"Her loss," she says.

I try to smile. Sasha starts flirting with the boys. She calls her lips bacon lips.

"They're so big," she says, but it's like background noise, like a TV is on in the other room.

"Can I put my arm back around you?" Paolo asks after a minute.

I nod. He stretches his arm along my shoulder and drops his big hand down my arm. I scoot closer and breathe in the smell of popcorn, the cold air of fall, the sweet smell of Coke. I lean my head against him and he doesn't move away.

Sometimes I think hugs are like helmets. Sometimes I wish I could walk around with someone hugging me the whole time. You could probably make a lot of money doing that, being a professional hugger.

Dear. Mr. Wayne,

I call my dad from Sasha's cell phone. She has a zillion Anytime Minutes, so it's no big deal. I tell him I'm sleeping over at his house and to ask no questions.

He says okay and I breathe out a long, cool sigh like I've been out in the war too long and I've finally gotten my papers to go home. In the distance bombs go off, but I know they aren't real. They're just trucks backfiring. I will myself to breathe in and out, real slow. I try to nestle into Paolo's side.

Paolo's brother drives me to my dad's. Since we have to go all the way to Hancock, I'm the last one he drops off. Paolo rides with me in the back seat and holds my hand.

He doesn't ask me questions either, just talks to his brother about football and soccer. His brother puts the old Volvo into what he calls turbo drive and we zip down Route 114.

I don't know if there's such a thing as turbo drive, but

I like that he calls it that. It makes me feel like we're in a comic book and about to return to our superhero alcove after ridding the world of hyperactive zombies.

As we drive, panic starts to hit me. What if Paolo starts thinking about me climbing out that window? What if he knows how crazy mixed-up my family is? I mean he already thinks my dad is gay, what if he figures out that I'm a bastard and my real dad is a tall drunk man with danger in his smile? I mean, let's face it. I'm a girl with a lot of baggage and what if he decides I'm not worth it?

I feel him slipping further and further away, sort of like at Christmas when you're really hoping for a reindeer—any reindeer, it doesn't have to be Rudolph—and you keep opening present after present and it becomes increasingly clear that you aren't going to get the reindeer, at least not this year. Santa probably won't bring it next year either, and maybe you just weren't good enough, you know? Maybe you just don't make the reindeer-cut.

Maybe I don't make the Paolo Mattias-cut.

"Walk her to the door," Paolo's brother orders him when we get to my dad's little beige ranch house.

"Oh, you don't have to do that," I say, suddenly shy and all polite.

"I *was* going to walk her to the door, jerk," Paolo says, unfolding his legs to climb out of the car.

"Yeah, right," his brother says like Paolo needs dating tips or something. "You're such the gentleman."

Paolo gives him the finger and slams the door. His brother laughs.

We walk up the path to my father's door in silence. Only chipmunks scurry in spruce trees above our head. Over them are stars.

"I'm really okay," I tell Paolo, stopping in the middle of the path.

He just looks at me. He frowns.

I start walking. He strides next to me but the path isn't big enough, so his left shoe keeps going off the concrete blocks and onto the grass. The dog next door howls. A chipmunk shrills out a warning.

Paolo howls back at the dog and I start laughing. All the strangeness is gone. He is a weird, weird boy.

"My grammy—" I say.

"Woof?"

"She'll think you're a werewolf from Moravia," I tell him. "No howling."

He barks instead, running around in a circle, and I start laughing so hard because he looks silly pretending to be a dog. He pants. He scratches like he has a flea. I laugh and laugh and bend over with this pain in my side because he's so funny and life is so weird and tonight is both the worst and the best night in my life.

He takes my shoulders in his paws. I mean, hands. In his hands.

"Don't lick me! Don't lick me!" I shriek.

Now, this has to be one of the all-time stupid Lily things to say, because here I am with this cute cute boy who is trying to make me laugh and who was maybe about to kiss me. He shakes his head at me. He makes eye contact.

"Oh," I say.

He just leans in and touches my lips with his. They're warm, not too soft, not too wet. The backs of my knees start to feel all wiggly. I put my hand on his chest. I wish I could feel his heart.

He pulls away and I start laughing. I can't stop. His face turns blank.

"What are you laughing at?"

I shake my head. He looks hurt.

"I'm sorry," I say. "It's just—it's just so good."

My dad opens the screen door right then and says, "You're supposed to walk her all the way to the door to kiss her."

Everything crashes down. The chipmunk scolds some more. I'm not sure who. Me? My dad? Paolo? I bite my lip and I'm afraid to look at Paolo. He laughs.

"I was going to kiss her there, too," he says. I absolutely die.

They act like old friends. My dad winks and shuts the door, yelling, "I'm going to my beddy-bye now."

"My father is weird," I mutter, walking towards the space in the door my father just occupied.

"Weird is good," Paolo says and he leans in and kisses my cheek. Then he bolts down the sidewalk and opens the passenger door of the Volvo. Before he gets in, he howls at the moon.

I watch them drive away. The bumper of the car reads *Mean People Suck.* Another sticker says *Free Tibet.*

There should be more variety in bumper stickers, I

think, going inside the house. I lock the door behind me. I try not to hum. I try not to jump up and down, but I can't.

I look at my dad. He looks at me. I jump up and down and my dad laughs.

"My little Lily-kins, kissing the boys at the door," he teases. "Smoochie. Smoochie."

He is not the most mature man.

"Dad!" I say and flop in the chair by the phone. "Do you think he's cute?"

"He's hunky," my dad says, jumping up to sit on the counter. Grammy hates when he does that, but she's long asleep by now. "He's a hunky hunky hunk."

He's so strange, Mr. Wayne. Can you imagine a father saying that? I shake my head at him and he turns serious.

"Does your mother know you're here?" my dad asks. He's wearing his baby blue bathrobe and navy blue slippers. He smells like Noxzema Skin Cream, which I'm not going to ask him about. His feet swing in the air.

"You promised no questions," I say.

He nods and grabs a toothpick, puts it in his mouth. It turns in circles.

"Grammy's asleep," he says.

I nod.

"Your boyfriend's cute."

"It was just a date."

"Lily's got a boyfriend. Lily's got a boyfriend," my dad sings, and he jumps off the counter and starts prancing around the kitchen like a five-year-old ballerina.

I open the fridge and grab the orange juice.

"How old *are* you?" I ask him.

"Old enough to know that my baby's got a boyfriend."

I'm afraid to look at him because I think he might be crying again. He grabs me in a big hug and I have to try hard not to drop the orange juice.

"Jessica's here," he says, pulling away.

I start pouring the juice.

"Oh."

"Brian's been hitting her," he says, all serious again. All my stuff forgotten, replaced by her bad plot line.

"I know."

"Someone should have told me."

I put down the juice and hug him then. He feels so sturdy beneath his bathrobe, but his body just shakes.

"Jessica should have come to me. Daughters should be able to come to their fathers," he says, sitting down in Grammy's wheeling chair.

"She's here now," I tell him, sitting on the floor at his feet. I wonder why she left our mom's house, if it was because of Mike and me. I wonder if she'll tell my dad what Mike said. I grab his feet and rub them. He likes that.

I can hear the clock above my dad's head ticking. When they got divorced, my mother was so angry about him taking that clock. He loved it though, loved the little cuckoo. A German friend of his gave it to him a long time ago.

"I'm here," I say.

He nods, but I'm not sure it's enough for me to be here. Maybe he already knows this isn't where I belong.

Dear Mr. Wayne,

Saturday morning and I'm at the dining room table with my grammy, who is not really talking much because she's too worried about everything. Really, you can feel the worry pouring off her as she rubs Pond's hand cream into the tops of her hands. She's vain about her hands, unlike her feet, because people can see them.

I think she's abandoned her feet, declared war on them, because she feels as if they've abandoned her. She hates that they don't work like they used to, that she can't just bound out of her chair and go off to work in the garden whenever she wants.

My head still hurts, but when I think about Paolo howling, it doesn't hurt too bad. I sip my cranberry juice, nibble at my toast, and watch her rub her hands in circles.

"Want help?" I ask and take the white jar. Her skin

feels like phyllo dough when I rub and I'm afraid to press down hard.

"You should eat more," she says. "Your father eats bacon and four eggs and potatoes in the morning."

I take her other hand and begin spreading moisture on that one. I would like to explain to her about heart attack risks and cholesterol levels, but she's a lady, the kind who calmly waves goodbye to the heroes while standing at the front door of the homestead, and I don't want to break her heart.

We stay like that for a while, me putting moisturizer on her hands, she looking out the sliding glass door onto the little deck my dad made.

"Your sister hasn't come out of the bedroom," she says.

"She sleeps late sometimes," I say, eating another corner of my toast. It's perfect toast, not too dry.

"You don't."

I shrug.

She pays no attention to me. "Grown ladies don't sleep forever. You can't get anything done. It's just not right, not when you're so young and there's so much to do."

"Grammy," I say. "You know about Brian?"

"It's giving up, sleeping all day. It's just giving up on life," she says, slapping her feet on the floor and scooting her chair towards the kitchen. "I'm poaching you some eggs."

She keeps going and yells back to me, "And you're going to eat them."

I stand up and all my bones creak. I wonder if we've

switched bodies somehow, or minds. By the time I've walked over to her she's already in the refrigerator, or at least her head, shoulders and arms are.

I put my hand on her shoulder and feel the bones of it, the blade of it pushed out through the cloth, and it reminds me of a bird's wing, a fragile bird that's fallen out of a nest and for no reason at all I ask her, "Grammy, have you ever been in love?"

She doesn't hesitate. "No."

"Not with Grampa?"

"He was not an easy man."

"Oh," I say. "Do you think Dad loved my mother?"

"Maybe," she says, breaking an egg. "Who is to know?"

I am to know. I want to know something, something solid. It seems like too much of life is like flower smells—just fragrances. They waft past your nose, you get a good sniff and then they are away, off to somewhere else. How can you hold onto that?

I want the feel of Paolo's shoulder, not the feel of Mike O'Donnell's hand ripping my shirt.

"Can I help you?" I ask her.

"Yes," she says and smiles.

One thing I do know is that in the kitchen it's possible to help another person, to break an egg, to throw away a shell, to wipe up the mess.

My mother calls me and my grandmother forces me to the phone.

"I was worried sick," my mother says, but her voice sounds like acting to me.

"Uh-huh."

I play with a pencil on the counter, start scribbling on the prescription note pad, drawing circles over and over until they lose their circle look and become knots.

She keeps lecturing, all cranky-voiced. "You're in big trouble, young lady, you just can't do that. Sneaking out a window. Then Jessica leaves in a huff. Is she there too?"

"Yep."

She's silent, and that's when I do it. That's when I saddle up. Wagons ho! One big swallow and I launch the words out.

"Mom, he tackled me. He hit my head into the floor. He's freaking scary, Mom. He's not a good man," I say and it's like there's this great big hand pressing down on my chest and it's threatening to turn my whole entire soul dark if my mom doesn't answer the right way. That horrible feeling is already spreading because I know she isn't going to answer the right way, because she didn't before, with Uncle Mark, and that was so much worse. I manage to say it again. "He hurt me."

"Come home and we'll talk about it."

I watch the seconds on the clock go by. When I was little before the divorce and my family all still lived together, my father would come home from work and the first thing he'd do was lift me onto his shoulders and we

272

would wind all the clocks. We'd fix all the minute hands on all the clocks in the house and make sure they all said the same time.

My dad used to tell me that it was important in a family to have that kind of consistency, the same truth in all the clocks' times. Maybe it wasn't the real time, he'd say, but it was family time.

I cut off my mother's sentence, which is just about how awful I am, and I ask her, "What time does it say on the kitchen clock?"

"9:42."

"And how about the clock in the living room? Can you see that one?"

"Yes, why?"

"What time does that one say?" I ask her. Grammy looks over at me, away from her poetry book.

"9:38," my mother says, sighing.

"That's the problem," I say.

There's silence on the other end for a little bit, but I can tell that she's there because I hear her breathing. She breathes heavy because she smokes too much.

"You hate me, don't you?" she asks, begging.

I don't answer. Meanness is all bottled up inside of me, I guess, and I can't answer. I think of her that time on the boat with my step-uncle. I think of her noises with Mike O'Donnell. Then I say, "I want him gone. He scares me."

Now she's silent. I wonder if she'll listen. She didn't listen about my step-uncle. On the other end of the phone, she starts to cry.

"I get lonely, Lily," she says. "I'm human, you know. I'm just human."

"He is not a good man. He. Is. Not. Good," I say. I take a big breath. I fire my gun and it feels like I'm shooting my own self in the gut, making a big black hole. "It's him or me."

She says, "That's not fair, Lily. That's not fair. You'll be leaving for college soon and where will I be? All alone without..."

But I don't hear anymore because Grammy wrenches the phone out of my hand as I howl. I howl so loud that even my mother should be able to hear it with a phone or without one. It's a long howl, like that of a cat who has been alone on the fence too many nights, a cat who can't find its way home and it's raining, raining hard.

The tension in my father's house is too much, with my sister hiding and my father trying to make everything jokey like it's a happy, sitcom-family reunion and my Grammy wringing her hands, so I beg Sasha to let me sleep over and she lets me.

"What a great idea!" she says. "We can go over our lines."

In the afternoon, I go to Sasha's house and as usual she has some really good ideas about what to do.

First, we go over our lines by repeating the lines of the person before us. Then they repeat our lines before saying theirs. This is supposed to help us with the intentions of our character and the objectives of the other character.

Sasha's mother listens to us and applauds once in a while. She's a big-hugging woman, whatever that means. She's the type of mother who understands that alone time is a good thing when you're a freshman in high school. So after a while she tells us to buzz off and go hang out in Sasha's room.

"Come here," Sasha whispers when we're in her bedroom alone. There are all kinds of cool lava lights everywhere, and beads dangle around her bed. On the walls are pictures of John Lennon. She loves John Lennon. That song about imagining there's no people is her favorite. She says it's better than the national anthem.

I think it's funny how we both like dead Johns, but how our Johns are so different. It's hard imagining you singing *Let it Be.* Or maybe it's the other Beatle who sings that. Paul?

I go to where she's sitting on the floor by her bed. "What?"

"Let's make prank calls."

I stare at her. "Why?"

"Hone our acting skills."

"Isn't that kind of mean?"

She shrugs. "We'll do nice ones."

I don't want to, but say I will.

"You do the first one," she says, holding out the phone.

"Me?"

"You need to loosen up."

"I'm loose," I say.

Sasha just laughs and dials a number. I take the phone. A nice old-lady voice answers.

"Hello," I say. "Is your refrigerator running?"

Sasha rolls her eyes.

The old lady says, "What dear?"

"Is your refrigerator running?"

"Why, yes it is ... " she says.

"Oh, um, that's good," I say. "I must have the wrong number."

I slam the phone down and Sasha laughs so hard she rolls on the floor like a dog.

"What?" I say.

She starts snarfing out her juice. It spills on her shirt, which makes me laugh too. We grab each other's shoulders, but it takes us a long time to calm down.

"Why did you laugh so hard?" I ask her. "I screwed it all up."

"Your problem, Lily," she says all serious, looking into my eyes, "is that you're too afraid."

"I'm not afraid," I say. "I'm not afraid at all."

I tell her I have a plan. And then I tell her the rest of it. I tell her about my mother's man and what he says he is, and what I think he's done.

Sasha and I decide that we'll go on a double date with Paolo and Stuart Silsby tomorrow night, since it's a long weekend and we don't have school Monday. Sasha thinks Stuart's a bit too pedestrian, but good to practice kissing on. "When I have enough practice, I'll move on to Tyler," she says.

We stand in front of her bathroom mirror, which stretches the entire length of the wall and has big light-bulbs all along the top like a mirror backstage in a theater.

Sasha's mom is good at the makeup thing. She puts gold eye shadow on the inner part of my eyelids to make my eyes look wide. Sasha puts some gloss on my lips.

"Wet and kissable!" she says and I blush.

Then she rubs it in more and starts singing a song from the play, "Some Enchanted Evening." I throw a cotton ball at her and she says in an over-big voice, "Oh, roses from my fans. Thank you dahlings."

I brush my hair and stare at myself in her mirror. I look better than usual, but it doesn't really feel like me.

"Do you think I look Irish?" I ask Sasha.

She puts her head next to mine. It's longer and her eyes are big and brown. She has little freckles on her nose.

"Do you think I look Jewish?" she asks back.

"What does Jewish look like?"

She shrugs. "Who knows? What does Irish look like?"

"I think you're beautiful," I say. "Plus, you know all those Christmas carols. You're the beautiful Jewess who croons Christmas carols, the shining star of Merrimack, Maine."

This makes Sasha laugh. "So are you dahling, so are you."

Then she puts on her serious Sasha face. "It doesn't matter who your father is or isn't. It matters who you are."

I shrug.

"Paolo likes you a lot," Sasha says. "Is he a good kisser?"

"Sasha!" Olivia sticks her head into the bathroom. "You're so nosey."

"Like you don't want to know," Sasha said.

"Inquiring minds want to know," Olivia says, holding a lipstick dangerously close to my face. "Tell us or you get the famous lipstick torture."

Her voice is like a vampire's.

"Ves, tell vus," Sasha vamps.

"No. No. I have sworn myself to secrecy," I say. "I must not tell you what the infamous Paolo Mattias kisses like, what the fantabulous Paolo Mattias kisses like... it is a secret I shall take to my grave."

They laugh and Olivia drops the lipstick back onto the counter. I sigh inside because how can you explain a kiss, how can you explain it without a million words and a poem and a painting?

A fist, that's a lot easier to explain.

Dear Mr. Wayne,

I have found some things that say Hannah Dustin felt guilty about what she did, about how she killed all those Indians, scalped them, so that she could escape slavery, go back to her family. It says she had nightmares. I hate that people fought and killed and died and had to live with what they did. I hate that people still do.

I can't imagine just having a baby, seeing that baby die, being kidnapped with another woman. At the camp of your captors you see a young man who's been stolen from another town. You live there, with the kidnappers, the women, the children. Go to a wide angle shot. See them camped out on the island.

Zoom in on your face. You, Hannah Dustin. You live there and you long for home. You live there and you learn that you will go further north, be sold into slavery. The young man knows how to scalp, and that's what you do, you scalp. Not just the men. You kill the women. You kill the children and you escape. You bring the scalps to prove what you did.

It makes my stomach sick. The colonists did so many, so many crappy things; they murdered, raped, kidnapped, stole land, spread disease, lied. People do this over and over. People do this now in our country, to other countries. People do it on a smaller scale to each other every single day.

But what you have to think about is that on the individual level, the smallest level, this is a mom. This is a mom who will do anything to get back to her home. Anything.

And you have to wonder what it is that you'd do, don't you, Mr. Wayne? You have to wonder if you could go to such great lengths, break commandments, break lives, just to get home.

Dear Mr. Wayne,

On Sunday Paolo comes over. He kisses Grammy's cheek and her face just starts glowing. She grabs onto his hand and doesn't let go.

"So, you're our little Lily's beau?" she murmurs.

I gasp. She shoots me a look, all mischief-eyed.

Paolo just smiles. "Yep."

"You treat her well, young man."

"Gram!" I cross my arms over my chest.

"I will," Paolo says and she lets his hand go. He stands up and we take off outside. My dad's backyard is lush with big Scottish pine trees he planted himself, and a rock wall and a garden. We hold hands and just stroll around until we get closer to the woods and the garden. This is a good place because spying eyes can't see us. Clouds pass over the sun and it gets a little darker. The wind moves through the trees, making the branches whisper against each other.

"You know my gram's watching," I say and sit on my dad's tractor. It's huge. I have to climb up it to get in the seat.

"She's cute."

"She's embarrassing."

"Grandmothers are supposed to be embarrassing." He starts scrutinizing the tractor. "I think I could vault this."

"Vault it?" I make a fake sports-announcer voice. "Paolo, Mr. Parkour Man, begins his preparations."

"It'll be easy, like in gymnastics."

I shake my head. "This is way bigger than a gymnastics vault."

"I know." He backs up, surveying. Then he comes back to me. Some chickadees trill in the woods. He reaches his hands up. "Hop off?"

"Say please," I tease.

"Please."

I hop down and he catches me. My nose smashes into his sweatshirt and I laugh.

"Are you hurt?"

"No, I'm good."

He squeezes my hand and lets go. "Okay. Watch."

He backs up, runs at the tractor. His body launches into the air and goes almost horizontal, I think, right where the seat is. Then he tucks in and somersaults to a perfect landing on the other side.

I gasp. "You show-off."

"It's just about figuring out where you want to go and not letting anything get in your way," he says, trotting back around.

I remember to breathe. The chickadee stops singing. "Do you think you can do that with life?"

"That's the point, I think. You take the confidence parkour gives you and bring it into everything."

I nod. A cloud that's been blocking the sun moves out of the way. "That's amazing. You'll teach me, right?"

He smiles, comes closer, pulls me against him. The soft cotton of his sweatshirt kisses against me.

My arms move around him, wrapping just above his waist. His voices comes out sweet like new corn. "I'm glad you're here with your dad now."

"I am too."

Dear Mr. Wayne,

After the movie, we go up Cadillac Mountain on Mount Desert Island and look for UFOs. I think that all the things everyone sees in the sky around here are military planes they're testing out. In Cutler there's a naval tracking station, and up in Millinocket there's an air force base. I mean, it only makes sense. Still, it's way more fun pretending.

We all get out of the car and huddle up on a granite boulder looking at the sky, waiting for aliens to come make our lives exciting, to whisk us away and make us heroes in our own adventure.

Paolo sits behind me and I lean back against his chest. The zipper pull on his sweatshirt digs into my back. I don't mind.

"We're going to go kiss each other until we can't breathe," Sasha says, standing up and taking Stuart's hand.

Stuart jumps straight up into the air, taps his feet together and yells, "Yippee!"

Then they take off.

"Watch out for alien abductors," Paolo yells after them. Then he waits an entire millisecond and puts his arms around me. It's good to rest against him, all nestled up beneath a blanket. We sit there for a while and look at the stars. I don't get scared or anything, because Paolo feels so solid, the way I imagine you would feel, Mr. Wayne.

Instead, I just nestle in and sigh and don't think about anything but the stars. I kind of turn my head so I can look up at him, and Paolo leans his head down. His face gets so close. His lips, the lips that stretch above his jaw, the soft above the solid, they open a little bit. My eyes blink shut. Our lips push against each other, long and slow. My heart beats fast and swoony. My body turns more so my hands can reach into his hair, so it's easier for my mouth to touch his. Soon, I'm kneeling in front of him and his arms around me push me closer and closer, like we're going to meld together, and I think that maybe I *should* try to explain this to Olivia and Sasha somehow.

He tastes like cinnamon gum. I must taste like mint, because Sasha kept feeding me tic tacs in the movie theater.

When we stop he says, "You sound like you're purring."

I jump away, land on my butt. "Oh God."

"No, it's good." He stands up. "It's sweet."

I hide my face in my hands. He touches the back of my head, feels the big lumps there and then he screws it all up and says, "You shouldn't move back to your mom's."

I wait and stare at things, the blanket, the sky, pebbles. In acting, we would call this a poignant silence.

"You shouldn't. Not unless that guy moves out. He could be dangerous."

"Uh-huh," I say, standing up too. My voice a flat dead thing in the night.

"And if he's your dad ... those clippings ..."

"Wait. How do you know that?"

"Sasha."

"Sasha," I choke, like a half-laugh sort of thing. "I'll have to kill her."

"She's trying to help."

"Uh-huh."

"We're all trying to help you."

"Right. Let's help Lily. She's our crusade."

"It's not like that." Paolo grabs my hand. I try not to hold it, but I'm weak and I grab on tight just like when I was jumping up onto the bike rack at school. It steadies me.

Above us a plane roars, but there are none of the airplane lights on the wings and the shadow seems more rectangular somehow, not really plane-like. It blocks out the stars as it passes. The wind of it moves my hair against my face. Without thinking, I move closer.

"Did you see that? Did you see that?" Sasha comes running out of the woods. "It was right there. Did you see it? A real UFO!"

I try to nod, but I'm too busy crying, too busy.

Stuart follows her, tripping and then righting himself. He jumps up and down, pounding his chest. "Take me!

Come back and take me! Get me out of here! I hate Merrimack! I want to go to Planet Zigna, baby! Or you could drop me off in New York! Broadway, maybe?"

Sasha notices me. Her face turns sad. She hauls me up and says, "Okay. Enough. It's time to be empowered. It's time for the plan."

The first house we go to is my sister's. Brian's truck waits there. The light is on in the living room and a football announcer's voice sneaks into the lawn.

Tiptoeing, I peek in. He's on the couch. The back of his head doesn't move. The game fills the TV screen. Budweiser bottles line up on the end table.

"Who's winning?" Paolo whispers.

"Patriots," Stuart says.

"You can see that?" Paolo asks, squinting. "How can you see that?"

"He'll hear you," I tremble. "Shhhh."

"We could take him." Stuart's breath comes out in little puffs. It's cold tonight. "Just go in and take him down."

"Violence is not the answer," Sasha says all preachy. Both the boys groan.

"It isn't!" she insists. "Give me the note."

She takes the paper from my hand, runs up to the front door, opens the screen door and takes her gum out of her mouth. She smooshes it into the door and sticks the paper on it. Then she does something unbelievable. She pounds on the door.

"Run!" she yells.

Unable to make anything work, I stand there frozen. Brian clambers off of the couch. It's like when you know the bad guy's going to shoot, but you just can't move because you're worried you aren't fast enough, worried about the ladies hunkered down and hiding in the saloon. What if a stray bullet hits them? But then, you've just got to do it, just got to take your gun out of your holster and fire, no holds barred.

"Run!" Sasha yells again. She's already back at the car, opening the door.

Stuart yanks on my arm. I take off and pass him, leaping over a pothole in the driveway. I feel like I'm flying; I soar.

"Yes!" Paolo yells in the car, punching his fist into the roof as Stuart peels out.

"I can't believe you knocked, Sasha," Stuart says. "You are psycho. Psycho!"

"She's an insane woman," Paolo says from the front seat.

Sasha giggles. I don't know whether to kill her or hug her, but I settle for a hug.

"Mad?" she asks me.

"Tell everyone what I wrote on the note."

Sasha takes a real dramatic breath and says, "It said, Real men don't hit women."

"Tell her the whole thing, Sasha," Stuart says as he turns onto the highway. He sounds like her father.

She looks at me. I look at her. I put on my seat belt.

"You added something?"

She nods and tries to do her Sasha Innocent look on me.

"Just tell me."

"Swear you won't get mad?"

"Fine."

"Swear."

"I swear I won't get mad."

"It said, 'Real men don't hit women, potty face.'"

Paolo whoops and smacks his hand on the ceiling.

Stuart swerves and gets back in the right lane. He only got his license last week. He stayed back in first grade, which is why he can drive. He probably should have stayed back in drivers' ed, too.

"'Potty face?'" I ask.

"I wasn't feeling very creative." She shrugs.

Something inside me trembles in a really happy way like I've just jumped from one high building to another.

In the car, Sasha and I cuddle up in the back seat.

"Did I really just do that?" I whisper.

She nudges me with her elbow. "You went all hero on us, girl."

I shake my head. Doubt makes my stomach spasm. "It won't make a difference."

"Of course it will."

We drive fast. Stuart shrieks around a corner. I grab her hand. Our fingers wrap together. "You really think so?"

"Yeah," she says. "I do."

✦

Next step? I write my mother a note and we drop it off. The house is all dark except for where her bedroom is.

Stuart and Paolo and Sasha and I park on the road. We run up the driveway; the gravel crunches beneath our sneakers, and I'm so scared we'll get caught or that Mike O'Donnell will come running out in his tightie-whities swinging a baseball bat around and Paolo or Sasha will get hurt. If he does, I will kill him. I will take him down, tackle him and kick him until he can't get up. I'd punch him, Mr. Wayne, but I don't have big fists. You have to remember I'm a girl and no firefighters ever trained me to fight, like they did for you when you were still little and called Marion.

I steel myself and think of how I will kick his legs out first, and then smash my palm into his nose.

This doesn't happen.

We run up all stealthy and I leave the note on the front door.

Then we run back down and squeal off in Stuart's little Mazda and go to Dairy Queen. We all deserve ice creams, we say.

The note said,

*Mom, I'm not coming home
until he is gone.*

We're slurping down our soft-serve when Sasha says, "Oh my God. What if he finds it first?"

We didn't think of that, which just goes to show we're kids and this is my life, not a movie. If it were a movie, I'd be cuter, my breasts would be smaller and our lines would be better.

I think.

Either way, though, I'm here with my hombres, partners in justice. All my secrets an open book.

Something inside my gut loosens up a little bit, like a lasso letting loose, tension easing. It feels good.

Dear Mr. Wayne,

My mother doesn't want me. She calls my dad's house and says, "You can't make me live my life the way you want."

She says, "I am the mother and you are the child."

She says, "I will get a court order to get you back. I have sole custody. Sole custody. Do you know what that means?"

I say, "Who is my father?"

There is a pause and then she whispers, "I don't know."

I say, "What do you know about this guy? He drinks. He's violent. He's a total ass, Mom. A super-big ass and what about the newspaper clippings? What about those?"

"Lay off, Lily," she says, voice colder than a cowboy in the Colorado mountains in the middle of January. "You think you know what it's like to be lonely? You think you know? You think you know how hard it is to be a woman alone? Well you don't, okay. You don't."

She hangs up the phone on me. She just hangs up.

Dear Mr. Wayne,

This is what I do, the second part of the plan. I take matters into my own hands. I do what a hero would do, a girl hero in Maine, not a man hero in an old Western.

I call the police.

I call the Merrimack police from the only pay phone I can find, which is outside of Hannaford's. Stuart and Sasha wait in the car for me. Paolo stands next to me and keeps his hand in mine.

I tell them, "There's a man at my mother's."

I tell them, "There's a man who has a photo album full of newspaper clippings about a bar fight and a man being killed."

I tell them, "He drinks. He drinks and he is not a good man."

I tell them, "His name is Mike O'Donnell from Oregon. Can you run a check on him?"

I tell them, "No, he's not my father. I'm not related to him at all."

Then, I put the pictures of my sister's bruises in a manila envelope. I write down important facts, put on the stamp and mail it to the sheriff's office.

It may not be the right thing to do, but it's the only thing I can think of.

Dear Mr. Wayne,

Today, Paolo, Sasha, Stuart and I take a bunch of the letters I've written to you and put them on my stepfather's grave. My hands tremble when I set them down and I want to grab them back, clutch them to my chest and run. The wind will take them. Maybe they'll get stuck in the barren branches of the trees. Maybe it will rain on them. I don't know. There's a large gulp in my throat, seeing them there by Daddy's grave. I'm dangerously close to losing it.

"This is harder than I thought," I tell Paolo. I look at the letters. It hurts to burn them, like putting your finger in a candle flame on purpose. But turtles have to move forward. They have to break apart their shells.

He nods. "I remember you writing that letter in the Alamo Theater. Nicole made fun of you."

"You thought it was weird," I say. A crow lands in a tree in front of us and announces its presence.

"It *is* weird."

"Not as weird as you pretending to be all into John Wayne just to get me to like you."

He throws his hands up in the air. "I like John Wayne."

"But you don't love him. You don't adore him. You don't recognize him as the greatest hero portrayer of all time."

Sasha groans and flicks the lighter. It has a smiley face peace sign on it. "If either of you had ever gone to therapy, you'd understand that Lily was merely trying to come to terms with her feelings of loss caused by her stepfather's death. She transferred those feelings onto John Wayne, the typical father figure."

I shove my hand over her mouth to shut her up. She licks it.

"Yuck." I wipe it on Paolo's sleeve. He laughs.

"This is not the appropriate tone here," Sasha says the moment her mouth is free again. She makes dramatic eyes. "I shall change the mood."

She sings some sort of mourning song. Paolo groans. Then Stuart sings too. It doesn't sound that awful really. It just sounds sad.

"This is really corny," I announce.

"Give in to the corny-ness," Stuart yells. He grabs some leaves and throws them in the air. "Give in!"

Paolo puts his arm around my shoulder and Sasha holds my hand, but I don't need them to. I'm okay all by myself. Still, it's nice to have friends, buddies to ride off into the sunset with, who know you're a little off but like you anyways, even if you're a theater geek and your dad wears tights.

I get ready to burn the letters, grab the lighter from Sasha. But before I do, the wind takes one letter, skittering it across the cemetery. My shell cracks. A piece of it falls. Sasha squeezes my hand a little tighter. A bigger gust of wind blows most of the papers away. I look into the sky, a sky that looks more like my dad's eyes than Mike O'Donnell's, and I smile.

Saddle up.

I nudge Paolo with my elbow. "Think there are any hyperactive zombies hanging out around here?"

"Don't worry," he says as a couple of crows skitter-land on an oak branch above our heads. "We can take them."

Dear Daddy,

For two weeks, I live with my dad and we get in a routine. He likes to hear about Students for Social Justice. He likes to hear me tell him all about the musical, about how Stuart Silsby and Sasha got in trouble because they were "practicing kissing" in the greenroom. I tell him how I cheated at poker during one of the downtimes between scenes and none of the guys caught me.

"You have the innocent face," he says. "You got that from me."

"Sasha says that poker is her favorite game because the kings are like cowboys and the queens are the bitches and they get to control everything."

"Lily!"

"Sasha said it."

He laughs and laughs. He hits his thigh with his fist and bends over. I smile at making him laugh like that.

My mom calls on the phone, crying. It seems the police came. There was an Oregon arrest warrant out for Mike O'Donnell. My mom says she doesn't know the charge. Yeah, right. *One Man Dead.*

"Come home, honey," she says sniffing.

I stare at the phone.

"Come home, honey. I'm lonely."

But I can't go. I can't say anything. My voice vanishes. My sister takes the phone. My sister takes charge. She helps my mother pack Mike's things, but there's no place to send them. The police took the photo albums, but they left the rest of it. My mom and Jessica haul it all out to the garage, just the two of them, with Jessica all pregnant. I feel guilty.

"No wonder he didn't stay at his sister's," Jessica says when she comes and eats dinner at Dad's. "The police had already checked for him there."

She shakes her head. She stabs a tomato slice with her fork. "I'm going to live with Mom for awhile."

She looks at me and I look away. I wonder if she knows about the photos. I wonder if she knows about me. I swallow. I cannot go back. The wagons are moving forward, Daddy. The wagons are going straight to new frontiers. I hope you aren't disappointed, but I just don't think I can go back yet.

My dad and I go to Friendly's, just the two of us, and it isn't horrible boring like I'd thought it would be. He's put a pink triangle sticker on his immaculate little car. The sticker represents gay pride, but I don't tell him I know that. He doesn't say anything either, and I realize that this isn't like the Mike O'Donnell secret. This is something that is solely his and if he wants to officially tell me someday, then he will. It's about him, not me.

Don't you think so, Daddy? Do you think that's the right thing to do?

In the parking lot, I turn and say, "Dad, I have something to tell you."

He switches off the car and holds the keys in his hand. "What, honey?"

"When I was younger, right after Daddy died, his brother touched me."

"Touched you?" He swallows but keeps staring at me, head on. His blue blue eyes don't look away from mine. Dead on.

"Inappropriately," I say in a flat, calm voice, because it was a long time ago. "It wasn't too bad, not like talk-show bad."

"I'm sorry that happened," he says and he grabs my hand in his. The keys get all jumbled up with our fingers.

"For a while," I say, my voice not so flat anymore, "I was really mad at you. I don't know. I thought you should have been there to protect me. You or Daddy."

"I'm sorry we weren't. I'm sorry we weren't there for you," he says, kissing the top of my head the way you used to.

I sniff in and pull away, wipe my nose on the back of my hand. "I'm sorry too."

He wipes at his eyes with a handkerchief. Yes, he still carries a handkerchief. I'm sure I'm the only kid in town with a possibly gay, handkerchief-using, truck-driving father who only watches public television.

"Mike O'Donnell is obviously a manipulative narcissist," I say. "I think he may have killed somebody once. I think that's what the arrest was all about."

My dad doesn't even blink. "Well, after dinner maybe we should look into that. Find out what that warrant was exactly for. Okay?"

"Okay."

He opens his door, and before he gets out of the car he says, "Does your mother know?"

I'm not sure if he means about Mike O'Donnell or my uncle or what, but either way the answer is the same.

"Yep."

He sighs and shakes his head. We walk up the sidewalk to Friendly's. There's a metal bike rack by the front door.

"Check this out," I tell my dad.

"What?"

Instead of answering, I cat-leap up to the top of the rack, walk across it, totally showing off. It wobbles a little bit and my dad rushes over. "Lily!"

He grabs my hands. I hop down with my fingers wrapped around his. "Pretty cool, huh?"

"Amazing. Is that the parkour thing?"

I nod.

"Think you could teach this old dog?" he asks, opening the door to Friendly's. He holds it for me.

"Maybe," I say and give him a really fat wink. He laughs.

The waitress gives us a booth. Once we're all settled on the dark green vinyl I tell him my Hannah Dustin theories. I tell him that I think she liked it with the Indians, but got scared about going to Canada. She didn't know what would happen and Canada just seemed impossibly far away.

"I think she regretted killing them," I say. "Even though they killed her baby."

"I can't imagine killing anyone," my father says. "I'm pro-gun control, you know."

"And pro-choice," I say because I know his political litany by heart, having heard it every election year just like we always do. It sounds a lot like Sasha's. "Pro-environment. Pro-the middle class. Pro-equal rights. Pro-blue socks. Pro-union. Pro-ankle bracelets."

He holds up his hands, laughing. "You've got me. You've got me."

"You know, in my Hannah Dustin report?" I eat a French fry, smoosh it around in the ketchup. "The father, Hannah Dustin's husband, he left her in the house."

"Wasn't he protecting the children?"

"That's what they say, but how do we know it's the truth? That he wasn't just running away?" I ask.

"That's always hard to know." He gulps his iced tea. I watch his Adam's apple slide like Jessica's does.

All of a sudden, halfway through the food, I push aside my French fries, just inhale real deep. And since it's the day for saying things, just laying it all out there like John Wayne does, like the way you always used to, I say, "What if you aren't my real father?"

"What if I'm not what?" he says and then gestures with his fork for me to pass the salt.

"My real father."

He holds the plastic saltshaker in his hand in mid-air above his plate. He doesn't even tip it. "Where did you get that idea from?"

Slowly, he comes back to life and starts shaking the salt over his New England Country Thanksgiving Dinner, which is sliced turkey and Stove Top stuffing, I think.

"Mike O'Donnell."

"That man's a drunk, Lily. Plain and simple. We've seen that man's a lying drunk."

He looks at me and I try to keep my face all blank and innocent like I don't know anything in the world.

"I wouldn't trust a thing he says." He's not angry and I don't want to be, but I have to know. I just have to, and I'm afraid he'll turn mean like men sometimes do and kick me out of his house because I'm not his real daughter, and I'll have nowhere to go.

But I need to know, because it's just like Mr. John Wayne used to say: *When you come slam bang up against trouble, it never looks half as bad if you face up to it.*

So, slowly, I say, "Are you sure?"

He gazes up at me and I just stare at him because maybe this is the last time I'll ever see him in my whole life.

"How could you not be mine?"

All the breath I've been holding inside of me rushes out and flows across the table. It whirls around the restaurant and out the door, free.

He eats the rest of his meal, even the cranberry sauce, but we don't order sundaes, which are the best part of Friendly's. I don't know if you remember this about him, Daddy, but my dad will come here just for the sundaes. He's such an ice-cream-aholic. The way you were addicted to cashews.

In his eyes is the glimmer of doubt, and I think of how this wasn't really my secret to tell, was it? When secrets are so strange and full of deepness we forget who they belong to.

We go out to the parking lot and get in his tiny beige car, and he says, "For years I've thought you were mine. That means you are. There was never any question."

"Uh-huh," I say and everything inside me breaks, because I miss you, Daddy, and I miss my father being my father and everything being simple. So I do a very un–John Wayne thing and start crying. I'm so ashamed, I put my face in my hands.

"I think he's lying," my father says. He rubs my back in little circles.

"Why?"

He takes his hand away and puts the car in reverse to get out of the parking space. "That I don't know. But you are my daughter, end of discussion."

"End of discussion?" I ask, looking up and trying not to laugh at him suddenly being all parental. He notices.

"What?" He lifts his hands off the wheel, waving them

around. "Isn't that a good-father thing to say? I'm trying to be a good father."

I grab his hand, hold it and say, "You are."

He blinks. "What?"

"You are a good father," I say.

And then it's his turn to cry.

Acknowledgements

Dear Mom, Dad, Debbie, and Bruce, You are NOTH-ING like the family members in this book. You are actually a million times better. Thank you.

Dear Doug Jones, You are always being a hero in ways large and small. You have literally saved lives.

Dear sweet Emily, You are the best kid ever. Thank you for being so brave and so cuddly and for always speaking out for others all the time, even when it's hard.

Dear Rob Eaton and Shane Lowell, Both of you guys have rescued me when I needed rescuing. Thank you. I know you don't think you are, but you are absolutely heroes.

Dear editors, Andrew Karre and Sandy Sullivan, You truly are heroes in the word world. Thank you for doing so much to make stories into books.

Dear Entire Flux Crew and especially Brian Farrey, Thank you for being so darn brilliant, and for working so hard to get this book out there. You make me proud to be a Fluxor.

Dear agent gurus, Edward Necarsulmer and Cate Martin, You guys are superheroes. I've said it before. I'll keep saying it. Thank you for saving me from many free-falls.

Dear Tim Wynne-Jones, Sharon Darrow, Louise Hawes, and Ellen Howard, You all inspire and give every day. That's what being a hero is about. Thank you for helping me with this book.

Dear Jackie Ganguly, Jennifer Osborn, Meloyde Shore, and Laura Hamor, Thank you all for being woman heroes. To Mary McGuire, Dottie Vachon, Doris Bunker Rzasa, Gayle Cambridge, and Alice Dow, Thank you for being awesome friends and for being mother-crusaders. And to the Whirligigs of Vermont College, the Schmoozers, the LJers and the PWs, You give me so much. I can never thank you enough. I love you.

Dear Will Rice, Bethany Reynolds, Phil Bailey, Dexter Bellows, Heather Martin-Zboray, Evelyn Foster, Kate Simmons, Hannah Pingree, Sean Faircloth, Howard Dene, Starr Gilmartin, Cliff Vaux, Don Radovich, and the rest of my campaign crew, Putting your faith in someone else is not only heroic, it is beyond brave. Thank you for all you do to make the world a better place. You all prove that politics isn't just about power. It's also about people, compassion, and caring.

Dear people who know how Lily feels, Thank you for surviving and thriving. You are all the biggest heroes of all. Thank you for being such great people. The world is better because of you.

Dear John Wayne, Thank you, too. The entire time I wrote this book I imagined you giving me that look … *Wagons forward!*

© DOUG JONES

About the Author

Carrie Jones likes Skinny Cow fudgicles and potatoes. She does not know how to spell fudgicles. This has not prevented her from writing books. She lives with her cute family in Maine. She has a large, skinny white dog and a fat cat. Both like fudgicles. Only the cat likes potatoes. This may be a reason for the kitty's weight problem (Shh . . . don't tell). Carrie has always liked cowboy hats but has never owned one. This is a very wrong thing. She graduated from Vermont College's MFA program for writing. Along with several column, editorial, sports writing, and photography awards from the Maine Press Association, Carrie has also been awarded the Martin Dibner Fellowship and two Maine Literary Awards—the most recent for her YA debut, *Tips on Having a Gay (ex) Boyfriend*.

OTHER BOOKS BY CARRIE JONES

Tips on Having a Gay (ex) Boyfriend
Love (and other uses for duct tape)